But He's My One Regret

A COZY ROMANTIC COMEDY

ANNAH CONWELL

Cover design by Alt 19 Creative

To those who wear a badge and those that love them: thank you for your service.

So, even in a different life, you still would've been mine, we would've been timeless.

-Timeless (Taylor's Version), Taylor Swift

Contents

Content Warnings

This is a closed door romance, which means there are no explicit scenes. There is, however, heavier make out scenes.

And while this is a romcom, it does deal with some heavy topics. There are discussion of grief, parental death, homicide investigations, life of a homicide detective, mentions of PTSD, minor mentions of violence that happens off page.

Chapter One

Dahlia Chamberlain

What does it say about me as a therapist that I have anxiety about my first day at my new job?

"It says you're human," I tell my reflection in the visor mirror. I'm a verbal processor. And since I don't have anyone to process *with*, my reflection has to do.

I reapply my strawberry lipgloss and flip the visor up before taking a deep, cleansing breath. In through my nose, out through my mouth. I repeat that action a few times while staring at the looming concrete building I'm parked in front of.

The Sandy Springs Police Department is no small building. It's home to the police force that serves this suburban community outside of Atlanta. And while it's not in the heart of the city itself, it still helps a large amount of people. It's a little intimidating knowing that I'll be working here, even if I know I'm qualified.

After one more shaky deep breath, I get out of my peach Jeep and straighten my sunshine-yellow sweater. I've always been a *big* fan of color, so I was happy to hear that the precinct didn't have many rules on what I wore. I think it's probably because I'm their first-ever therapist, but I don't care about the reason if it means I get to wear my favorite outfits to work.

I'm a lot more comfortable in my cuffed jeans and sweater than I would be in a pencil skirt, that's for sure. And I think I'd feel like I was suffocating if I had to wear a work blouse. Or really anything you can find at Ann Taylor. No offense to Ann, but I need a little more *life* in my closet.

My white platform sneakers squeak on the tiled floor of the entrance. It's even colder than the October weather outside, and I'm thankful I went with pants this morning when choosing my outfit. My eyes scan the lobby. It's not the most pleasant place, being devoid of color and creativity. The walls are shades of grey and beige, concrete seems to be the main building material, and sadness the theme of the space.

To my right, people mill about, some rush, others just lazily make their way around the various clumps of desks. There's a buzz of constant conversation that reminds me of working in a coffee shop, except it's missing jazz music and the sweet smell of espresso. Instead, everything is tense and heavy, the air carrying a metallic tang that makes me think of dried blood.

The receptionist hasn't looked up since I walked in. I walk over to where he sits at the desk behind a pane of plexiglass, playing Candy Crush on his tablet. I tilt my head to the side as I wait to be noticed. Recognition never comes.

"You should switch the red candy over," I say, tapping a seafoam-green fingernail against the glass. The man jumps, rattling his desk and making the ice in his drink clink.

"I didn't see you there, I'm sorry," he says, locking his tablet and straightening his back. "How can I help you?"

I give him a wide smile to show I'm not bothered by his being preoccupied.

"I'm the department's new therapist. I have a meeting with Chief Wells," I tell him.

"Oh." He blinks. "Yes, someone said you'd be coming by today. Okay, just sign in here on the visitor form and I will give you a badge, then you can head down this hallway to the right and follow the signs to his office."

I jot down my name with the pen chained to the counter, then take the sticker that will severely ruin the vibe of my outfit and stick it on my shirt near my shoulder.

"Thank you!" I chirp and saunter off down the hallway, leaving him to his game.

Chief Wells' name catches my eye a ways down the hall. I knock on his door, waiting only just a moment before I hear a gruff, "Enter."

"Good morning," I say in my most upbeat voice when I walk in.

Chief Wells sits behind a pristine and organized desk. Awards line a shelf to his right, but besides that, his office is devoid of any personality. The man behind the desk, however, has plenty of personality. By which I mean he's wearing a frown so intense I'm concerned this is his default expression.

"You must be the shrink," Chief Wells grouses and I fight to keep my smile from falling. I was under the impression that the Chief wanted me here, but it seems like HR fibbed a little during our interview based on the lack of enthusiasm in his voice.

"I'm the new department psychologist, Dahlia Chamberlain," I correct him in a placating tone.

"The shrink," he repeats in a deadpan tone. Okay, he definitely isn't a fan of therapists. Message received. "I tried to avoid having you come here, but the governor is on some *mental health* kick right now and mandated it."

I straighten my spine and meet his hardened stare. His brown eyes are framed by bushy gray brows. I'm no stranger to the older generation's contempt for my career choice though.

"I'm sorry you don't like the idea of me being here, but I intend on doing good for this precinct. I think you'll see that my work is valuable. In your line of work, it's important to implement self-care and therapy is a great way to do that."

"We don't need any of your woo-woo self-love crap," he says and crosses his arms over his chest. "You're only here because of blasted politicians sticking their noses where they don't belong."

He gives me a look that says if lightning struck me right now he wouldn't even blink, much less feel a glimmer of negative emotion. There's a chance he'd even smile, though he doesn't seem like a man who smiles much.

I get the feeling that he appreciates blunt honesty, so I don't put my words through my therapist filter.

"Regardless of why, I'm here now. You can't get rid of me and I care too much about helping the people of this department to be scared off. So I would appreciate it if you could show me around the precinct and then to my office." I cross my own arms.

He raises one fluffy brow and sniffs.

"Fine, follow me."

"Thank you," I say with a saccharine smile and follow him out of his office.

We walk through the building in silence. The only time Chief Wells speaks is to briskly say what a room is. Soon we arrive at a door and the block letters reading *homicide* on it are plain and unexciting compared to what's contained behind them. Overtime, gruesome crime scenes, and hours upon hours trying to find the next lead. It all combines to be a heavy weight on the shoulders of each detective, one I hope to lessen.

"I will introduce you to each division briefly. Then you can go to your office and everyone can get back to what's important."

I nod in response–since he seems like the type to appreciate non-verbal communication–and he opens the door. We enter into the covert chaos of shuffling papers and clacking keyboards. It may not look like much, but there's an undercurrent of tension that is thick in the air.

Chief Wells claps his hands hard two times. All of the detectives drop whatever they're doing and look toward us. I spot a man, likely the Captain, in his windowed office with someone across from him. He must have heard the clapping too, as both he and the man stand. Chief Wells walks to the middle of the room and I start to follow him.

The other man turns and my steps falter. Our eyes lock and his hazel irises are time machines. They transport me back to salty air, warm skin, and sweet kisses. Memories I've tried for years to suppress come flooding back, stealing the breath out of my lungs.

Levi. Levi is here. How is this possible? I drink him in, losing track of time and space. Who cares what the Chief is thinking or doing when Levi is standing here in the flesh? His hair is in that style where it's cut tight on the sides with just a little length up top. The perfect length to run your fingers through–I know from experience. He's clean-shaven though, which is different. When I met him he had this delicious stubble that scraped my skin and left me raw in the best way after we kissed.

The time and distance between us didn't lessen my attraction to him, that's for sure. He's still the same magnetic man from before, even if there are a few details that are different. Like the badge clipped to the waist of his dress pants. That makes my heart drop to my stomach. *No*. Levi can't be a detective. I glance at his badge again, hoping that I was mistaken, but no, there it is shining bright under the fluorescents.

An ache swells up and consumes my previous elation at seeing him. I can't think of a potential patient in a romantic way. I'm not even supposed to be overly friendly with my patients. There are strict boundaries to uphold.

I bite the inside of my cheek hard. The last time I saw him was the night before we were supposed to reveal our last names and exchange phone numbers after our week of adventures. But then I ran away, leaving just a note on his beach condo door.

Why? Why am I seeing him now, *here*, after all these years? Whenever I dreamt of seeing him again I pictured us running into each other in a bookstore on a rainy day. The dream always ended in a wonderful kiss. Once again I recall the feverish kisses we shared years ago. Each memory is a beautiful bubble of happiness that our current circumstance bursts.

"Everyone, this is Dahlia Chamberlain," Chief Wells bellows, drawing my attention away from Levi. "She is the new department therapist. If you need to see her, you'll find her contact information in your emails." He makes it sound like seeing me would be as pleasant as going into surgery without anesthesia.

"It's nice to meet you all," I say, my voice coming out shaky at first. I steel myself, then continue. "If you need anything at all or have any questions, feel free to reach out. My door is always open." I punctuate my sentence with a smile.

"Okay, back to work."

Everyone turns back to what they were doing, except Levi. His eyes are locked on me, making it hard to draw in a full breath. He recognizes me, I know he does. What I don't know is what it means.

It can't mean anything, I scold myself. He's a potential patient. If he comes to see me, I'll have to listen to whatever he's willing to share, which could include deep trauma and pain. I can't cross this line. My heart is beating out of my chest. I want to say something, but not even a greeting will fall from my lips.

Just when I think he might say something, I'm forced to turn away from him and follow Chief Wells out of the room, all the while feeling Levi's gaze on my back.

Chapter Two

Levi Carter

Dahlia, *my Dahlia* is here. Not only is she here in Atlanta, but she's working in my precinct. I stand frozen in place, staring at the door she just walked out of. I can't believe she's here. She looked as surprised as I feel right now. Her blue eyes wide in shock.

Someone bumps into my shoulder, shaking me out of my trance.

"I know she was hot, but that doesn't mean you can stand in the middle of the bullpen daydreaming about her," Rhodes says with a laugh as he walks toward our shared desk clump. Chase Rhodes is a notoriously shameless flirt. He reminds me of my brother Grayson, except Grayson doesn't have to try to be smooth and Rhodes tries a little *too* hard.

Jealousy flashes hot and quick like a road flare in my chest. Logically I know I have no claim over her, but my emotions seem to think otherwise.

"I was just thinking about a case," I lie and sit down at my desk. "You shouldn't talk about her like that, it's unprofessional." My voice is taut and he raises a brow.

"Do you know her?"

"No," I say because I don't need Rhodes in my business. And also because I really don't know Dahlia, at least not anymore.

It's been five years. I had no idea she was a therapist. We didn't talk about work. I wanted to get away from mine, and she told me if I didn't want to talk about mine she wouldn't talk about hers. During the week we spent together, our subjects ranged from what we wanted out of life to our favorite color. We talked about everything and nothing all at once. But every answer she gave could be different now.

Does she still not have a favorite color because she loves them all? Does she still want to get married on a balcony overlooking the Adriatic Sea? Is she married, engaged, or dating? That last question makes my bile rise in my throat. If she came back to me after all these years and was taken it would be a gut punch.

It's probably foolish to hang my hopes on a woman who ran away five years ago, but I've spent these years replaying that week over and over in my head. I know she didn't leave because she didn't care for me, but because she wasn't sure how much I cared for her. We were both too scared to change our lives for a person we'd only known for a few days.

"I have a feeling you're lying to me, but we've worked together long enough for me to know you're never going to tell me." Rhodes' words make a smile crack through the hard exterior I was putting on.

"You're correct," I say with a laugh. I'm not gruff like my brother Adrian, but I do keep my private life private. Compartmentalizing my life has helped me cope with the intensity of this job. The less work mixes with home the better.

"I'm sure dating a therapist is a pain anyway. She probably dissects everything you say and definitely doesn't do casual."

"Please stop talking, I'm trying to work."

Rhodes laughs, but stops. He knows we don't have time to waste. There's not a lot of downtime as a homicide detective. Every second counts.

I open the file on my desk. We just got a new case this week–a shooting in a strip mall parking lot–and I had to visit the scene this morning. Now I need to compare the physical evidence with the video footage we gathered and the autopsies of the two recovered bodies. I can already see the evidence piling up against a guy we've been watching for a while now but have been unable to nail down.

My mind keeps pulling me out of work though. I find myself wondering where Dahlia's office is, if she's settling in, or if she went home and isn't starting until next Monday. There's this feeling deep inside of me, like something tugging me toward her. It's unsettling. I always thought if I saw Dahlia again it would be on a beach somewhere–not that I get time off anymore, but still. This place isn't where she belongs. It's the one place I've been able to block out the memory of *her*. I know it's pathetic or borderline obsessive to still be thinking about a woman after having only spent a week together years ago, but there's something about her that's been impossible to forget. She nestled down into my veins–into my very DNA.

She also changed the way I look at life. After my mom died, I felt like I was on autopilot for years. She showed me what *living* looked like. It's been hard to hold onto that reminder lately, since becoming a homicide detective and dealing with atrocities and death every day, but I still cherish those memories with her.

When I have time again, I'll find her. As much as I've missed her, this case is too important. Lives are on the line. So I force myself to focus on the evidence in front of me. Dahlia works here now, she'll be here every day. I'm bound to see her around. And if I don't, I'll book an appointment with her, even if I don't need therapy. I'll do anything to see her again.

I'm not one to stick around after my shift, but I'm hoping I'll run into Dahlia. It's unlikely I'll find anything but an empty office though, at almost eight at night. But maybe fate will smile upon me twice today.

In the email about the department acquiring a therapist, they noted where her office would be located. Light spills out of the room that is supposed to be hers when I turn down the hall. Every step I take fills my body with frantic energy. My heart is pounding in my chest when I stop in her doorway. I've gotten used to dealing with intense situations for my job, but the thought of talking to Dahlia again is throwing me off balance.

Dahlia's door is open and her back is to me. She's arranging a bookshelf, humming a lilting melody that sends chills through me. Through her window I can see dark out already and the warm light pouring from the fixture above fights the darkness. Shadows dance against the wall, multiplying her beautiful curves as she moves. I could watch her all day, but I'd rather talk to her.

"Dahlia," I say and she freezes, her hand on a picture frame. I can't make out the photo from this far away. Is it of her husband? Does she have kids already? I tear my eyes away, looking toward the floor.

"Levi," she breathes out.

I've missed her voice, it's not the same in my dreams. I look up and I'm met with wide blue eyes. Her eyes always mesmerized me, how they changed from green to blue depending on what color she wore. Sometimes I swore her mood affected the color as well. When I told her that, she laughed and said that irises weren't mood rings. Then she kissed me, and when she pulled back her eyes were the most beautiful crystal blue.

I wish they were that tropical color now, instead they're a stormy indigo. Pain flashes across her expression. My heart sinks. She must have moved on and–sensing the *pathetic* oozing off of me–doesn't want to hurt me.

"I'm sorry I didn't say anything earlier," I tell her and she waves off my apology.

"It's okay, seeing you was..."

"Shocking? Disconcerting?" I fill in and she gives me a small smile.

"A surprise," she finishes and I chuckle.

"Sure, let's go with that. It's good to see you. You look ... good." Understatement of the year.

I lean against the doorframe and her eyes track the movement before roving over me. Satisfaction rolls through me seeing her take me in.

"You do too," she replies and crosses her arms, except it looks more like she's hugging herself. Her pale-yellow sweater bunches with the movement. I want to draw her into my arms and kiss away the furrow of her brow.

Silence sits between us like a stranger who has come in to observe us. I don't know how to begin what I want to say.

"So you're a therapist," I say and she nods.

"And you're a detective."

"Yeah."

She bites her lip and the small action must press the off button on my filter.

"Are you single?"

Her eyes get wide and she blinks a few times. I'm about to apologize when she speaks up.

"I am." I expect her to ask me the same, but she doesn't.

"Good," I say and she raises a brow, making me let out a nervous laugh. "I just meant, I missed you." I hesitate, but decide to take the plunge. "What would you say to picking up where we left off?"

Her expression becomes pained again. I push off the door and cross the office to be closer to her, desperately needing to close up this space between us.

"We can start over. I know things between us were–" I run a hand through my hair, my blood heating at the memory of that week together. "Intense. But I know it's been a long time. I just want to get to know you."

"Levi, I can't." She looks up at me. "I can't date a detective as the precinct therapist. It's unethical."

"I'm not your patient, we're basically coworkers."

She shakes her head, giving me a sad smile. "I'm going to have to see you at least once a year for your mandated psych eval. And then if something happens and you need someone to talk to, that someone is me."

I can feel the weight of losing her again settling in my stomach like a rock. "So that's it? There's no chance for us?"

"I'm sorry," she says, taking a step back to put distance between us. "But it's been five years. We had just a week together. I'm a different person now, and I'm sure you are too."

Yeah, I am, because of *her*.

"I'd like to get to know who you are now."

"I just can't. This job is too important to me to risk it."

Voices float down the hall, sounding like they're getting closer.

"You should go," she says, looking nervous. I'm sure me being in her office afterhours doesn't look good.

"Okay, I'll go. But I don't think this is it for us."

"It has to be, Levi." Her tone is pleading. But something in her gaze is telling me she doesn't mean it. Her eyes flick to the door when the footsteps and voices sound closer and louder.

"Let me know if you need any more help moving boxes," I lie in a loud voice and gratitude fills her eyes.

"Thank you, I appreciate your help." She looks down, twisting a silver sea turtle ring on her right ring finger.

Even though it pains me, I turn and leave the office, passing some administrative workers on my way down the hall.

I don't plan on just accepting our circumstances. I haven't spent the past five years in constant regret to just give up when the woman of my dreams appears in my life again. I'll figure out a way for us to be together. Somehow, someway.

Flashback

Levi Carter

Summer, Five Years Ago

I slide off my sunglasses and blink as my eyes adjust after leaving the Florida afternoon sun to step inside the seafood restaurant. I'm the first one here, which is unsurprising. My brother Grayson says that vacation plans are *flexible*, meaning he can be late and get away with it. And since our other brother Adrian, Grayson's twin, isn't here to force him to be on time, he's likely napping by the pool and won't be here for another half hour. I wouldn't be surprised if he showed up in his swim trunks.

Since he warned me before we booked this vacation that this was the case, I can't complain too much. I ask the host for a seat at the bar and then head that way. My shoulders relax when I snag a seat that faces an exit–a habit brought on by my job–and I smile as I order a beer from the bartender.

I'll be at Rosemary Beach for this entire week, which is a welcome and rare reprieve from work. I have it on good authority that I'll be transferred into the homicide division soon and my vacation time is likely to become nonexistent. Grayson has to fly out in the middle of this week, but he wanted to crash at the condo I'm renting until then. He's an Air Marshal, so he's always taking advantage of minimal amounts of time off too.

I drum my fingers on the bar top, waiting for my beer. My brows furrow in concern when I see a beautiful girl across the bar leaning away from a man probably three times her age. He lays a wrinkled hand over hers and she pulls away, only for him to do it again. Before I can think too much about it, I walk over to them.

"Is everything all right over here?" I ask and the old man turns to glare at me.

"Yes, we're having a conversation, aren't we sweetheart?"

The woman's eyes are wide, discomfort, and disgust written all over her face. But when her gaze lands on mine, something on her face changes. "Babe!" she shouts, making a few heads turn our way. "So happy you finally made it."

She grabs my hand and I stare at her in surprise. I could have gotten the guy to leave without pretending to be her boyfriend, but now that I'm looking into her coastal blue eyes ... I'm fine to commit to my new role.

"I'm sorry it took me so long, beautiful," I say and move so that my arm is around her shoulders. She leans into me and a luscious mixture of coconut and suntan lotion washes over my senses.

"Larry, this is my boyfriend, Jake."

"Nice to meet you, Larry," I say and hold out my hand. He does not accept it.

Larry narrows his eyes at us, grumbles something about two-timing hussies, and then hops off his barstool before stalking out of the restaurant. The stranger tucked beneath my arm starts to giggle, making me look down at her with a smile.

"Thanks for playing along, and for coming to check on me. He was a creep." She shudders.

I–hesitantly–remove my arm from around her but decide to take the spot Larry was occupying.

"No problem," I say and hold out my hand. "I'm Levi."

She slides her hand into mine. Her skin is soft and warm and golden from the sun.

"Dahlia. And darn, I was hoping you'd say Jake."

"Why?" I chuckle. "Do you have a thing for guys named Jake?"

When her lips turn up in a mischievous grin and those bright blue eyes sparkle I decide right here and now I'd let her call me anything, including Jake, if it meant she'd look at me like this. Her hand slips from mine and I immediately want to hold it again.

"No, but it would have been cool if I was right." She shrugs and takes a sip of her drink with a cocktail umbrella in it. "Though if I was, I'd have to assume we were soulmates. I don't believe in coincidences."

"Soulmates, huh? I'd say me getting here at just the right time is more of an indicator for soulmates than guessing my name correctly."

She leans in and tension crackles like a beach lightning storm between us. "Are you looking for a soulmate, Levi?"

"Aren't we all?"

Her smile grows and she sits back once more. "I like you," she says and though it sounds elementary it feels eternal. "Want to buy me a drink?"

I want to buy her a diamond ring, a house in the suburbs, or maybe even an SUV, because something about her has me believing in love at first sight.

Chapter Three

Dahlia Chamberlain

"I'm home!" I call out as I walk into my apartment. "Sorry I'm late, I got caught up decorating my office."

I kick off my sneakers and set them on the rack by the door, trading them out for the lavender slides I wear as house shoes. The smell of Italian spices lingers in the air and I follow it to the kitchen.

"I was bored so I made bolognese," my little sister, Jasmine, says from where she's sprawled in our living room. Her feet–clad in fuzzy socks–are propped on the arm of the couch while her laptop rests on her stomach.

"Only you would make from-scratch Italian cuisine when you're bored." I laugh as I walk into the kitchen. Our apartment is an open concept–well, it's not so much that as it's just *small* so the builders didn't make walls a priority.

We don't need much space though since it's just the two of us. Three years ago, my parents died in a freak boating accident while vacationing in the Florida Keys. So that left me the sole guardian of my teenage sister. Our twelve-year age gap helped me secure custody without too much hassle. It probably helped that I'm a therapist, too.

So, at twenty-six I started taking care of a fourteen-year-old, and now she's seventeen. Soon she'll be off to college, or probably culinary school. But for now, it's just us taking on the world. That's another reason I can't risk losing this job. I have to support her and myself.

I pull the lid off a pot of fragrant sauce and take out a spoon to try it.

"Oh my gosh, this is *amazing*, Jaz. Seriously, you should bottle this and sell it somewhere."

I start to make a bowl, laying down a bed of pasta first before spooning a healthy amount of the sauce. Eating a full bowl of pasta at nine o'clock at night probably isn't healthy, but I've had a long day and can't bring myself to care. I need some carb-filled comfort food.

"Thanks, it could use some tweaking though."

Jasmine is a perfectionist when it comes to her cooking. Her bedroom might look like a laundromat exploded, but if the garnish doesn't sit just right on a dish she's panicking. I have a feeling she's going to be working in some Michelin-star restaurant one day running her kitchen with an iron fist.

"It's perfect, but I'm sure whatever you add next time will only make it better." I plop down on the couch beside her head. She scrunches her nose when my movement jostles her.

"How was school?" I ask around a mouthful of pasta. She pauses her scrolling through Pinterest and glances up at me.

"It was school."

I give her a look that says that's not a good enough answer for me and she sighs.

"*Fine*. I got an A on a pop quiz in history. Mr. Dalton yelled at a bunch of boys for vaping in class which was funny. His vein pops on his neck when he's mad. And we learned a new routine for the pep rally during cheer practice today."

"That sounds like a good day, thank you for sharing." She rolls her eyes. "Did you get all your homework done before you went into chef mode?"

"Yes, it's all done and I even finished my English paper a day early."

"Look at you go, I'm impressed."

"Does that mean you'll let me stay out with my friends after the game on Friday?" she asks in a too-sweet voice.

"It means I'll consider it. It would help if you cleaned your wreck of a room."

"If I clean it, then can I go?"

"Clean it and we'll talk."

"But what if I clean it and you say no?"

"Then you'll have a clean room to rest your pouty self in."

"*Ughhhh*."

She shuts her laptop and sits up with a huff. I glance over at her mess of dark curls that reminds me so much of Mom's. It hasn't been easy shifting from the cool older sister who took her out on the town whenever I visited to being a guardian. For the first year, she spent most of the time in her room blasting music and ignoring me. When she wasn't doing that she was yelling how I'm not her mother.

After we got over that hump though, things got better. She realized that I have to say no sometimes and I can't be just a big sister anymore. We ended up crying together as I told her I didn't want this either, that I hated this change just as much as her. Now she begrudgingly respects my decisions with a smidgen of teenage angst that isn't fun but is much more manageable.

"I want names of all the people you're going to be with, a clean room, and *at least* a B on your math test tomorrow. Then you can go." She squeals and bounces in her seat. "*But* you have to be home by eleven, and if I see you anywhere remotely shady when I check your location I'm coming to get you in my most embarrassing pair of pajamas."

"Thank you, thank you, thank you!" She throws her arms around my neck in a hug then hops up and rushes off in the direction of her room. "I'm going to work on my laundry then go to bed. Love you!"

"Don't stay up too late!" I call out after her. "I love you too."

I sit back and let my breath out in one long *whoosh*. With Jasmine being out of sight, the events of today come creeping back into my mind.

Levi. Levi is a detective at the department I'm assigned to. What are the chances? I set my half-eaten pasta to the side and close my eyes. Images of him leaning in my office doorway come flooding back. Him saying he wants to pick up right where we left off. Heat creeps up my neck when I recall exactly where we *left off*. I'm convinced if Levi wrote a book about how to kiss a woman, he'd become an overnight bestselling author and women everywhere would thank him for his wisdom.

I resist the urge to groan out loud. I shouldn't even reminisce about the man. There's no chance we can be anything but therapist and patient so long as we both work there. If I was being totally ethical I'd probably disclose our prior relationship. But there's no use bringing it up now. It was a bit of harmless flirting and kissing five years ago, nothing to ruin a career over. I can be professional about it.

Levi seemed to not care about my concerns though. To know he feels so passionately makes this all the more difficult. It would have been so much easier if he'd moved on. I would have cried for a few days since I've been dreaming of him for five years, but then I could have wiped my tears away and kept going. Now, I know he's been missing me. All this time I assumed I was the only one who felt this way. I was sure he'd moved on or forgotten about me or both.

I pull out my phone and open up the text thread I share with my best friend Isabella, who also lives in the apartment next door.

Dahlia: I saw Levi today...

A minute later there's a knock at my door, making me laugh. I should have known she wouldn't just respond with a text.

I open the door to see Isabella with her newborn son, Fletcher, bundled against her chest. Isabella and her husband Marcus welcomed us with open arms when we moved here two years ago after selling our parents' house back in Alabama. Isabella and I have been best friends ever since, and I even helped throw her baby shower.

"Tell me everything," she says as she walks in.

"Shouldn't you be sleeping?" I ask her and she rolls her eyes.

"I don't even know what that is anymore. Fletcher won't sleep unless he's being held and I can't sleep in a chair. Marcus stayed up with him last night. So it's either reread my favorite Sloane Rose book or listen to you tell me about the only man you've ever loved."

"I'm honored that you chose me over Sloane," I say as we settle into the couch. I hand her a blanket to put over her legs.

"This is Levi we're talking about. Your story is as romantic, if not more, than a book. Plus, I can't talk to the characters." She pauses. "Okay, they can't talk back to me. I totally talk to them."

I laugh at her. I introduced her to my favorite author shortly after I moved in. Obsessively reading romance novels makes up at least half of my personality, so it didn't take long for the subject of books to come up in conversation. Now she's just as obsessed and had Marcus build her floor-to-ceiling bookshelves in their bedroom to house her new addiction.

"I think our story is more of a tragedy than a happily ever after," I say and then begin to recap the entire day.

"I love a man who goes after what he wants," she says with a happy sigh once I've finished my story.

"Did you not hear the *forbidden* part? I could get fired."

"Maybe he'll quit his job just to date you."

"That sounds healthy," I deadpan.

"It doesn't have to be healthy if it's romantic."

"I think you need more sleep."

She laughs at me but stops when Fletcher starts to whine. She bounces and shushes him until he calms down.

"Dahlia, you left the man behind because you were afraid of how in love you were with him. Now he's here, showing you he felt the same. In all seriousness, I think it's sweet he wants you after all this time. You deserve love."

"While I appreciate the sentiment, there's just no way this can work. I need to keep my distance. Maintain a professional boundary."

"That's so boring. I should have stuck to my book."

I roll my eyes at her as she tries to stifle more giggles.

"I'm being realistic, Isa."

"And I'm being *optimistic*. It's much more fun."

I had hoped Isabella would have strengthened my resistance against Levi. She knows how important this job is to me. But with no help from her, it's a lot easier to dream about a life where I can have it all; Levi and my career.

"We haven't even brought up Jasmine," I say in an effort to add more reasons to stay away from him.

"What about her?"

"I'm her guardian. Levi might not be willing to take that on."

"Considering she's well on her way to moving out, I don't think it would be an issue." She softly pats Fletcher's back and shoots me a look. "You've used Jazzy as an excuse to not date for the past two years, D. It's not a real reason anymore."

I twist the sea turtle ring on my finger, the one from the vacation I met Levi on. It's usually a soothing mechanism, but tonight it just serves to keep my mind on him.

"I know." I sigh. "But I really can't be with Levi. As much as I'd like to."

"Well, then you should put yourself out there again. Because working near a man hot enough to stick in your brain for five years is going to be rough if you don't at least try to move on."

My stomach sours at the thought of dating. I haven't been on a date in over three years.

"I'll think about it." Whenever I'm not too busy thinking about Levi's hazel eyes boring into mine, that is.

"Try to sound more excited," she teases.

I know Isabella means well, and I'm sure her advice of getting back out there is sound. But the thought of dating someone else when Levi is ready and wanting to be with me feels all kinds of wrong. I need to do something though, or else I'm going to be miserable trying to ignore him. Though I get the feeling that no matter what, I'm bound to feel terrible attempting to distance myself.

Levi has lived in my head for the past five years, there's no way he leaves it without a fight.

Chapter Four

Levi Carter

I push the bar up off my chest with a hard grunt and rerack the weight at the top. Sweat drips down my temples so I sit up and wipe my face with the bottom of my T-shirt. Benchpress is always pretty brutal, but the burn is a great wake-up on early mornings like this one. Especially after I spent all night tossing and turning, thinking about Dahlia.

My mind tortured me with memories of us together and then flashed to what she said in her office. Even pushing myself to the limit this morning hasn't gotten her out of my head completely.

My phone goes off so I pick it up off the ground where it's lying near my water bottle. I usually don't touch my personal phone at work, but since I'm not officially on the clock yet and just working out in the precinct's gym, I make an exception.

MJ: Maddie says good morning to her favorite uncles.

My sister's text to our sibling group chat is accompanied by a photo of my twelve-year-old niece sporting bedhead and sticking her tongue out. She has a dance recital tonight, one that I'm praying I'll be able to make. During the week of recitals or competitions, she always tries to get out of school claiming she's too tired. Unfortunately for her, her new mom is a teacher and doesn't let her get off that easy.

My sister adopted Maddie as her own when she married Maddie's uncle/adoptive dad last year. And even though Maddie's blonde hair and light eyes look nothing like my sister's dark hair and hazel eyes, there's no mistaking the maternal kind of love MJ has for her.

Grayson: Tell Mad Dog I'm ready for her to beat all of the other dancers tonight!

I chuckle at my youngest brother Grayson's enthusiasm. Last year we all went to one of Maddie's dance competitions and Grayson made us shirts that said *Mad Dog's Crew*, as well as a shirt for Maddie deeming her *Mad Dog*. The stage name turned into a fond nickname we all use now. That little girl has us wrapped around her finger, as the many TikTok videos she's conned us into starring in will attest to.

Adrian: It's a recital, not a competition, so she doesn't need to beat anyone.

Grayson: She can still be better than everyone else.

I shake my head at Adrian and Grayson's back and forth. As identical twins, they look exactly the same, but their personalities couldn't be more different. Grayson is outgoing and playful while Adrian is reserved and gruff. Yet somehow, Adrian is the one engaged to be married.

Maverick: I'm bringing her favorite chocolate peanut butter bars tonight. Does anyone want anything else from the bakery?

Grayson: One of everything.

Adrian: You do not need that much sugar. Mav, don't listen to him.

Maverick: I know better than to give him that much.

Grayson: I'm a grown man capable of monitoring my sugar intake!

Adrian: You're a man-child in need of constant supervision.

MJ: It's way too early to be dealing with all of you. Levi, are you going to make it tonight?

The smile on my face falls and I sigh. The thing about being a detective is that your hours are rarely predictable. I plan on being done in time, but if something comes up I could get stuck here, especially on a weeknight. Right now I'm focusing all my energy on proving myself to my Captain too, so I work longer hours and try to fit in family time when I can.

This is just a season though, or at least that's what I keep telling myself. I love my work and what I do is important, but it also takes up a lot of my time. It's easy to put on a front for my family, but this life has started to take a toll on me. I'm hoping that if I put in the work now I can move up the hierarchy and have more control over my hours.

Levi: I'm going to try my best to be there. Save me a peanut butter bar!

Grayson: You better come. We haven't seen you in two weeks, man.

I lock my phone with a sinking feeling in my gut. I feel like I see my family enough, especially considering we're all grown and living on our own. But I'm starting to think their little comments and quips in the past about me working too much are more than just messing with me. Maybe I really am an absent brother and uncle.

My legs burn when I push to stand. Yesterday was leg day and I pushed hard then as well. I walk to the showers, my mind feeling like a tumultuous sea, but a polluted one with all kinds of muck and debris in it. It was hard enough dealing with the everyday stress of being a detective and trying to have a semblance of a personal life. Now I have Dahlia to worry about too.

Is it impossible for me to have it all? Can I have a job, see my family, and get my dream girl? When I think about it, it does seem ambitious considering all of the detectives I know seem to have terrible home lives. The divorce rate in my division is astounding, and if a detective is still married they seem to be in a constant state of making up for lost time with their spouse and family.

The hot water burns my back and neck, but I make no move to turn it down. This morning I'm trying everything to distract myself from the heavy weight that's been pressing on my shoulders. When you're good at what you do–which I am–you feel a responsibility to solve the most difficult cases. The more cases I can solve, the less crime there is on the street. That's why I transferred to the homicide unit. But now I'm neck deep in politics, dealing with attorneys and trying to make my superiors look good.

Most days I can push through. I remind myself of why I do what I do and sleep it off. But after yesterday with Dahlia, it's harder to shake the tightness in my chest. It's beyond just seeing her again, it's about realizing I'm thirty-four and don't have my own family yet.

Not many women want to commit to a man with a career that keeps him away from home so much. It's understandable, but it doesn't make the bitter pill any easier to swallow.

I towel off and get dressed in the thick post-shower steam. Now is not the time for whatever these feelings are. I need to get to work and I need to face Dahlia as well. Though I'm sure she won't come in until later. It's way too early to be here since she's just a therapist and not a detective or officer. Hopefully by the time she shows up the tight band around my chest will have dissipated.

I throw my clothes in my locker and then barrel out the door–and straight into Dahlia. Something clatters to the floor nearby. She lets out a little squeak and I wrap my hands around her arms to steady her. Her skin is warm and soft under my hands, begging for me to trail my fingers across it.

"Sorry, I didn't see you there," I say in a low voice. Her head tips back, those sapphire eyes meeting mine.

"It's okay, I shouldn't have been standing by the door."

"Are you all right?"

She nods and I can't help it–my eyes drop to her lips. It's just for a split second, but the desire that courses through me from having her this close is *strong*. Her teeth sink into her bottom lip, only drawing me in further. It's as if the past few years have built up my desire for Dahlia instead of dulling it.

"Good," I rasp out.

My thumb traces a circle on her upper arm and it breaks whatever moment we were sharing. She quickly steps back, pulling her arms from my grasp and putting distance between us.

"I should get back to my office. I was trying to get a feel for the layout so if I needed to find someone in the future, I could." She twists the silver ring on her finger as her gaze bounces around the room, avoiding meeting mine. Her face is visibly flushed, too.

My mouth quirks up in a half-grin. I have an effect on her the same as she does me. I can work with that.

"You know, I could give you a tour if you want. That way you don't get lost."

She's already shaking her head no before I even finish speaking. "No, that's okay!" She takes a step back, bumping into the corner of a desk and wincing. "I'm totally fine on my own," she says, rubbing her hip.

She's as colorful as ever today with her pink wide-leg jeans and pastel-striped t-shirt. Her hair is shorter than when we first met–it hits at her shoulders now–but just as wild and wavy. The whole combination suits her perfectly and makes me smile even as she's backing away from me. I remember hearing something drop so I glance down to find a royal blue notebook covered in daisies and a pen beside it.

"You dropped this," I say and bend down to pick it up before walking it to her.

She takes the notebook from me, then the pen, her fingertips brushing mine. Tingles shoot up my arm at the contact, making me long for the days when I could touch her whenever I wanted because she wanted it too.

"Thanks," she murmurs.

"You're welcome."

Our eyes catch for a second, but then she's turning on her heel and speeding out of the room as if the whole place is on fire. I let out a sigh and walk down the hall to my desk, dropping into my chair.

I have a feeling convincing her to take a chance on us isn't going to be easy.

Chapter Five

Dahlia Chamberlain

Levi's touch lingers on my skin well after I've made it to my office and sat down to get to work. Seeing him around is not going to be easy. I need to focus on my work and being professional. Not that I have any work to focus on, though.

I have no patients. Not a single one. I didn't expect to get many, but *none*? It's hard to not feel discouraged looking at my appointment system and seeing no new requests. In January I'll see everyone for their yearly mandated evaluations, but it's only mid-October. That's three months of sitting here in my office looking and feeling useless if this trend keeps up. What if the department cuts my hours? They might think it's not necessary for me to be full time.

I knew that people would be hesitant. Therapy is new to them; it probably seems foreign and scary. But I know it will help the people here. I've seen studies on departments with therapists and how much better the unit performs in comparison to those without. I just don't know how to convince them of that.

I rest my chin on my hand with a sigh. My eyes catch on the framed photo on the corner of my desk. It's the last photo that was taken as a complete family before my parents died. We were celebrating Thanksgiving. My mom is wearing the same sweater as me because she wanted to feel young and hip. Jasmine and I made fun of her for saying hip while we snuck her homemade apple hand pies out of the kitchen in our apron pockets before dinner. Dad kept our secret because we brought him a pie too.

Everything was perfect back then. My dad was a therapist too. Whenever I was struggling with anything in college or even after, I'd call him and he'd walk me through it. By the end of the call I'd feel like I found the answer myself rather than him just giving it to me.

"I wish you were here now, Dad," I whisper to the frame, tears burning my eyes. "You'd know how to get them to see how important this is."

I squeeze my eyes shut and take a few slow, deep breaths. Grief has been a rocky road for me. Even as a therapist who knows all the right things to tell myself, I still struggle with coping with the loss. Three years isn't that long ago, and the wound still feels raw on days like today. Days when I wish I could call my parents, or go and visit and listen to them argue over whether or not it was a good idea to use pesticides in their home garden.

"Dr. Chamberlain?" a female voice inquires and I jump, my eyes springing open. A woman wearing a beautiful maroon sweater and a nervous smile stands in my doorway.

"Yes, how can I help you?" I stand up and adjust the top of my high-waisted pink pants. Thankfully, my tears subsided before they could ruin my makeup.

"My name's Kennedy. I'm married to one of the detectives in the gang and narcotics division. He mentioned that you just joined the department, and I was wondering if you see family of the unit as well."

"Yes!" I say with a little too much enthusiasm judging by the way her eyes widen. "Yes, I do."

"Okay, that's great. I've been wanting to see someone, but I didn't know how to find the right person. When Seth mentioned you I was relieved to hear that you would be in the department."

"I'm so glad you came by." I give her a warm smile before pulling out a packet of patient paperwork. "You can have a seat and fill this out, or take it home with you and bring it back whenever it's finished."

"I can do it now. I brought lunch by for Seth, but he couldn't sit and chat, so I've got time." There's a hint of disappointment in her voice that makes me feel sorry for her. She takes a seat in front of my desk and I set the paperwork and a pen down in front of her.

"I'm sure it must be hard finding time to spend together while he works in a demanding division."

She sighs. "It really is. We just got married last year. I feel like we skipped the honeymoon phase." She lets out a half-laugh as she fills out the first page. "The hardest part has been knowing how dangerous his job is. When he works late I have to wonder if he's doing paperwork or if he's hurt and they just haven't called me yet. I haven't slept much lately."

I give her a sympathetic smile. "Being married to a detective is difficult, but we can work on some ways to help you cope and maybe even get you sleeping normally again."

She looks up at me, relief flooding her expression. "That would be *wonderful*. I bet the other spouses would love to hear that you'll see them too. Could I post your information in our Facebook group? I wouldn't have heard about you if Seth hadn't mentioned it. And you know some of the other detectives won't say a word to their spouse." She shakes her head, but she's smiling.

I bite the inside of my cheek to keep from asking why they all don't already know about me. I was told that everyone–including family–would be notified of my presence here. Something tells me a certain chief prevented that from happening.

"I would really appreciate that," I say. "They can fill out the paperwork online or come into my office any time I'm not with a patient."

"Great!" She finishes up the paperwork before sliding it over to me.

"Okay, I'll get you set up in my system and then we can get you on the books."

"Thank you so much, Dr. Chamberlain." Kennedy stands and smiles. "I'm so glad the department hired you."

After exchanging goodbyes, she leaves and my heart fills with warmth. Maybe it'll take some time for the men and women who work here to book an appointment with me, but helping their families is important work too. And who knows? Maybe they'll see their husband or wife going to therapy and it'll inspire them to want to go too.

I log into my computer with renewed purpose, sparing a glance at the photo of my family. The smile that stretches my lips is full and genuine. I think my dad would be proud of where I am now. I just have to keep going. No distractions. Which means ... *no Levi*.

I made it through the rest of the day without seeing Levi. My mind and heart have been warring about his not showing up. My mind says it's good he didn't come, but my heart wants to see him again. Actually, my heart really wants me to *kiss* him again. Or maybe that's my hormones. Either way, I need to be smart and listen to my brain.

I also got two more patients in my system, both spouses of detectives in the gangs and narcotics unit, so that was another win for today. One that I will celebrate with a hot chai latte from one of my favorite cafes, The Sweet Bean, and a reread of my favorite Sloane Rose book: *Captivated*. It's an angsty romance where the main female character is forced to marry her grumpy boss in order to keep custody of her younger brother. I never get tired of reading it; it's my comfort read.

Not sure what it says about me that my comfort read usually makes me cry, but I'm not going to dissect that. There are some parts of my brain I don't let the therapist side of me touch.

My laptop bag bounces against the side of my thigh as I walk down the hall toward the lobby of the precinct. It's been a long day, but soon I'll be cuddled up on the couch, my only worry in the world being checking Jasmine's location to make sure I don't have to ground her for the rest of her high school career after tonight's football game.

When I see Levi standing in the lobby talking on the phone, my step falters just like it did yesterday when I saw him. I'm convinced I could know his exact location at all times and still not be prepared to see him. He's so gorgeous it hurts. His dress shirt is fitted, showing off his defined arms. The arms I remember wrapping around me under the balmy heat of a beach sunset.

His gaze lifts and locks on me as if he felt my presence as soon as I stepped into the area. The grin he shoots my way makes my knees embarrassingly weak. Why can't I be stronger? I think if I hadn't already fallen in love with him years ago, this would be easier. But deep down I know I would have fallen for his hazel eyes and sexy smirk just as fast as I did back then.

I grip the strap of my bag tight, letting the fabric bite into my skin in an attempt to jerk myself out of the dumbstruck haze I'm trapped in. My sneakers squeak against the tile as I book it toward the door. He's on the phone, so maybe I can get around him without any issues.

A strong arm blocks the door before I can push through it.

"Yes, Grayson, I have my shirt. I'll miss the opener, but I'll be there for the rest of the performance," he says into the phone.

I glare at him and try to go to the other door, but he's faster and blocks it too, all the while smirking at me.

"No, I don't have time to pick up flowers. I'll buy her hot cocoa after the show to make up for it."

My brows furrow. Flowers? Hot cocoa? Is he going on a date after this?

"Okay, I have to go. I'll see you soon, save me an aisle seat." He hangs up and smiles down at me. "I was just about to stop by your office."

Butterflies swirl in my stomach at his words, but I stamp them out with logic and reason. The only other person in the lobby right now is the Candy Crush addict, but it's still a risk for us to be seen fraternizing. Someone might see us and ask questions.

"Will you let me leave? If someone sees you acting this way they'll be suspicious."

He opens the door for me and I huff as I walk through it.

"I made sure no one who'd notice was around before I did anything. How was your first day?"

"It was fine. Don't you have a date to get to?" I speed walk to my Jeep, but he keeps up with me without missing a beat.

"A date?" he questions, looking confused. "*Oh*, you heard my phone call. I'm not going on a date, I'm going to my niece's dance recital."

"Oh okay, that makes sense."

Realization lights his eyes. "Wait a minute, were you *jealous*?" he asks, grinning like the Cheshire cat.

"No! Absolutely not." I roll my eyes at him. "I just wanted to be sure you didn't turn into a two-timing hussy while we were apart." The reference to our first encounter slips out without me meaning for it to. Something about being with Levi always dissolved my filter, and I guess that's still the case.

He laughs. "I did not."

I unlock my Jeep when we get close to it, then stop and look up at him. "Well, good. I'm glad you're not some playboy type."

"I've only got eyes for you, Doll. Been that way since the first day we met. Why look at anyone else if they can't even compare?"

My heart skips in my chest and my face heats. Levi always had a way with words. I remember telling him he was too smooth, and he said it was only around me. His use of the nickname I haven't heard since the day we parted ways only adds to the melt-factor of his words. He's making this too hard. It's not fair.

"Levi, you can't say things like that–"

His phone rings, so he pulls it out to silence it. "I have to go, I'm already so late. Try to think about me too much this weekend."

"Don't you mean try not to think about you?"

He grins as he backs away. "Nah, I meant what I said." He winks before turning and jogging away, leaving me a blushing mess of a woman.

How on earth am I supposed to resist him?

Flashback

Dahlia Chamberlain

Summer, Five years ago

I sign my name on the dotted line and smile at Levi across the table. He looks up, his hazel eyes crinkling at the edges. I watch his eyes drop down to my exposed waiver, so I snatch it back up.

"Nuh-uh!" I chide him as he grins. "We agreed no last names. Which means no peeking," I say as I press the waiver to my gauzy white beach coverup.

"I'm beginning to regret our deal."

"The mystery is a part of the fun. You said you'd spend this week my way."

"Yes, but *your way* seems to include risking my life with a woman whose last name I don't even know."

"We're not risking our lives, we're parasailing. People do it all the time."

I push up from the picnic table and slide on my gift shop sunglasses Levi bought after mine fell off on our jet ski ride yesterday. This is our second day spent together, and at the end of this week, we'll part ways. I have to get back to work and finish my doctorate in psychology. Levi hasn't brought up what he does, but he did say he doesn't get a lot of time off.

So, I suggested we live this week to the fullest. He seems like the type to live by a strict routine which has made me want to shake him up. I told him at the end of the week I'd tell him my last name if he played along the whole time. He reluctantly agreed.

"I'm afraid of asking if you'd jump off a bridge just because your friends were doing it."

I laugh. "I'd probably be the one who came up with the idea to jump."

"Of course." He gets up from the table and grabs his paperwork.

Jet Skis didn't take too much convincing, but he put up a fight when I suggested parasailing. It's quite clear he prefers to be in control. My taking over is probably pushing all sorts of his buttons, and now someone else is going to be driving the boat while he's suspended in the air.

"We don't have to if you really don't want to," I say as we walk back toward the counter to hand over our waivers. I want to push him, but now I'm worried I went a little too far with parasailing on only the second day of our adventures.

"Oh, *now* you give me an out after you spent all morning convincing me that the *view will be worth it* and it's *incredibly safe*."

"It will be!" I grab his hand and squeeze it. "Do you trust me?"

It's a ridiculous question to ask. He's known me for barely forty-eight hours. But I meet his eyes and wait for his answer anyway. He holds my gaze for a moment.

"Yes."

That one syllable makes my heart leap for joy. A grin takes over my face. "Good, then let's fly."

After we pay for our tickets, we board the boat and shrug on our lifejackets. Levi buckles mine for me and our close proximity has butterflies swarming in my stomach. I take in the beautiful emerald water as the boat takes us further and further out. Levi's hand in mine is warm and strong. He feels steady even as we're about to do something he doesn't love the idea of.

The workers help us get set up in the seats of the parasail. Once we're buckled in, I reach across and snag Levi's hand again. At this point, I'm taking any and every excuse to touch him. Thankfully, I don't think he minds.

I'm looking at our joined hands when suddenly, we're flying backward. I squeal as we soar higher and higher over the water. My face is going to hurt from how much I'm smiling at the end of this. The view is everything I'd hoped it would be. Miles and miles of stunning crystal waters, a sky with fluffy white clouds, and a glimpse of the shore in the distance.

"Isn't the view incredible?" I yell over the sound of the wind and waves.

"Yeah, it is."

I look over and my breath catches in my throat. Instead of looking at the gorgeous view around us, Levi is staring right at me, looking at me the way people look at a shooting star. Like I'm rare and beautiful and fleeting. I've never felt so special before.

I squeeze his hand and he squeezes mine back. We don't say another word, which I'm grateful for. I'm afraid I'll say something that will make him run in the other direction before the week is up. It shouldn't be possible for me to feel so strongly for someone who's basically a stranger, but my hopelessly romantic heart rarely dwells in the realm of possible.

Chapter Six

Levi Carter

Finding time to talk to Dahlia has been difficult. In my line of work, some days it feels as though I barely have time to take a full breath, much less have a personal life. Today is one of those days. I spent *five hours* interrogating a suspect this morning.

Interrogation is an odd thing. It's like going on a date with someone you don't like. You're trying to talk to them, but the last thing you want to do is be sitting across the table from them. And they feel the same way about you. Sometimes that means they confess just to leave the table, but sometimes it means they shut down and make it difficult on you.

Today's suspect chose to make my life miserable. Round and round we went until finally he broke and confessed to taking the lives of three people in a drive-by shooting. It was exhausting, and now I'm expected to just keep going with the rest of my workday like I didn't just spend hours doing mental gymnastics.

I escaped to my truck for a few minutes of silence and privacy while I eat a quick lunch. My eyelids are heavy with exhaustion and my body is numb. I'd give anything for a nap, but there's no time. If I stay in here too much longer someone will come looking for me. I tip back an energy drink and chug a quarter of it, the sickly-sweet liquid burning my throat. I don't even like these things, but coffee isn't strong enough.

These are the days I wish I had someone to lean on. Someone I could text and they would understand me. If I texted my family, they'd worry about me more than they already do. It would just add more emotional weight. And talking to other detectives is no use, we're all too jaded and numb.

I spot Dahlia walking past my truck, a paper cup in her hand. She must have gone to get an afternoon coffee. I roll down my passenger-side window.

"Hey, Doll!" I yell out and she stops, turning toward me.

She stomps over, her waves whipping around her in the October wind. "You can't yell that nickname across the parking lot, Levi," she scolds. "Are you trying to get one or both of us fired?"

Her cheeks are flushed and her blue eyes are flashing. I can't help but grin down at her.

"Has anyone ever told you that you look beautiful when you're angry?"

She tips her head back toward the sky like she's asking God for strength to not throw her drink at me. "I've told you, you have to stop saying stuff like that." She sighs and then eyes me, her gaze falling to the energy drink in my hand. "What are you doing in your truck anyway?"

"Had a brutal interrogation this morning, needed a minute to myself."

Her expression softens and she surprises me by opening up my passenger door and hopping into my truck, placing her coffee cup in the cup holder like it's the most normal thing in the world.

"Do you want to talk about it?" she asks as she tucks a leg under herself and adjusts the sleeves of the oversized burnt orange sweater she's wearing.

I did. I do. And Dahlia is probably the perfect person to talk about all of this with, but I can see what she's trying to do here. I don't want to be her patient, I want to be just *hers*.

"Are you asking as Dahlia or Dr. Chamberlain?"

She looks down at her hands in her lap.

"Levi." The way she whispers my name is a blow that my tired brain can't handle. "I've tried to tell you I can't do this. I can be your therapist. I can listen and try to help you, because that's what I'm here for. But I can't be anything more."

"What about friends? Is that against the rules?"

"It's a bit more of a grey area," she admits, toying with the lid of her to-go cup. "But it's definitely frowned upon. I need to have boundaries if you're my patient."

"But if I'm not your patient, then can we be friends?"

"Technically, yes, but in January I'll have to do your psych evaluation and I don't want things to be murky. It's too important."

"You and I both know that evaluation is a bunch of questions detectives answer just the right way so that they don't get chained to a desk. Our relationship won't affect that."

She looks up and meets my eyes. I watch as she wars with herself. She bites her lip and I force myself not to directly focus on her mouth. If I can get at least one of her walls down, then maybe the rest will crumble.

"Okay, we can be friends. But that's it, Levi. Really."

Pure elation shoots through my veins and I feel like I'm floating. A smile breaks out across my face. I'm about to respond when my phone starts to ring, making me groan instead. I glance down and silence it, seeing it's just Rhodes and knowing he's going to ask where I am.

"My moment of peace is officially over."

"I'm sorry, hopefully you can rest tonight. They should give you more time to rest after interrogations. I know those are mentally taxing."

I take another swig of my energy drink and shrug. "It's all part of the job."

"I know, I'm saying it shouldn't be. You shouldn't have to chug an energy drink to make it through the day."

I give her a reassuring smile. "I'm fine, Doll. It's sweet of you to worry though." I turn off my truck and open the door. "Thanks for the talk, it helped."

"We didn't actually talk about anything," she says as she gets out of the truck.

"I know, but just being around you helps," I tell her as we walk toward the building.

"If you say so." Her cheeks are pink and I can tell she's fighting a smile.

It takes too much willpower to not grab her hand or throw my arm around her. I have to hold back though and bide my time. There's got to be a way for us to be together in spite of this rule. I also have a feeling the rule isn't the only thing keeping Dahlia from taking a chance on me. But I don't want to push her too far by asking. I could lose her.

And I can't cope with the thought of losing Dahlia again. Last time she left without saying goodbye, but I don't blame her. I've had five years to dissect everything that happened that week. She wanted me to commit to something more than a week and I was so stuck in what I thought was important at the time that I couldn't give that to her. So she left a note on my condo door and disappeared.

It's not a coincidence that she's here again. Something in my gut tells me we need each other. I just have to hope that I'm right.

"Who's ready to get beat at pool?" I ask when my foot steps off the last stair into Grayson's basement.

As the youngest brother and a guy who's still single, you'd think he'd live in a typical bachelor pad. But no, he lives in a two-story craftsman in the suburbs. The only thing resembling a bachelor pad is his basement man cave. He's counting on his future wife loving the house and wanting to live here. I told him his wife might want to choose their home, so he then informed me that Jim bought Pam a house in *The Office* and it worked for them. There's no convincing him to change his mind once he's made it up.

"I'm not losing to you this time," Maverick says from his spot on the leather couch nearby. "Drew just got a pool table and I've been playing him lately. You're going down."

Drew is Maverick's best friend from childhood. We all hung out together, but they played football together so they were closer than the rest of us.

"You can practice all you want, I'm still going to take all your money." I throw myself down on the opposite end of the couch.

"You almost snapped a pool stick last time, Mav," Grayson says while grabbing a Coke from his mini fridge. "I seriously considered getting rid of the table. But then I realized that a little animosity between brothers is good for the soul."

I laugh at him, then laugh even harder when Adrian comes out of the bathroom and says, "You told me you're keeping it because you want them to get in a fight so you can film it and become TikTok famous."

"Same thing." Grayson waves off his twin and propels himself onto his giant beanbag chair.

"You're going to have to get famous a different way because I'm never going to be dumb enough to get into a fight with Mav," I say.

The man's knuckles are scarred from years of boxing. I know I could hold my own, but he's the quiet grizzly bear type you don't want to mess with. People think because he owns a bakery and spends his days around sugary confections that he's soft. But he's far from it. If I made a list of which of my brothers I'd fight first, he'd be at the bottom.

"Also, I wouldn't fight Levi over a game," Mav says.

"Y'all are boring. Where's the drama to keep me on the edge of my seat?" Grayson asks with a dramatic sigh.

"Don't you get enough of that watching your reality TV shows?" I ask him.

"It's different than seeing it in real life. Now that I'm an executive, I sort of miss the days of tackling people and dealing with people trying to kill me."

Grayson used to be an Air Marshal, but he retired the same time Adrian did from the CIA. They started a private security business together so that they could be home in Atlanta and have more time for family. All three of us used to be busy, which helped keep the spotlight off me, but now that's changed. Now I'm the only one who is missing family functions for a job since they joined Maverick in the slowed down lifestyle of business owners. Not that they don't work hard, they just get to choose their hours.

So when he says he misses having a dangerous job, it's hard for me to hold in a biting comment about how he can say that now because he's in his cushy corner office. But I know if I sound even remotely bitter about my job he'll tell me to quit and join them at Carter Security. Since I'm not ready to leave my job, I keep my mouth shut.

That same reasoning is why I showed up tonight even though I'm dog-tired. If I told them I couldn't hang out, they'd start to worry. Or really, Grayson would start to worry and then talk everyone else into worrying. I can't handle that on top of work stress and trying to win over Dahlia. So even though my body is aching and all I want to do is go home, lay in bed, and blankly stare at my ceiling until I fall asleep ... I'm here with my brothers having a 'guys night'.

"Levi, you good?" Grayson asks and I blink a few times before pasting on a smile. I must have zoned out.

"Yeah, man, I'm good. Let's play some pool."

Thankfully, he doesn't question me further and we all get up to start a game. I just have to stick around long enough to not look suspicious, then I can get home and catch a few hours of sleep, if I don't fall asleep leaning on my cue first.

Chapter Seven

Dahlia Chamberlain

I look up from my desk when I hear a soft knock. Standing in my doorway is Audrey Wells, Chief Wells' wife. Thus far, I have no department staff in my system, but I do have quite a lot of spouses. Audrey came in last week to hand me her patient paperwork in person and gift me a potted succulent as a 'welcome to the unit' gift.

She's a kind woman with deep smile lines and bright green eyes. I felt at ease around her, and I was happy to hear that she wanted to start seeing me on a regular basis. I'm excited to be able to help her, and an added bonus is that if she spends time with me then maybe she can get her husband to have a more positive outlook on therapy and my role in the unit.

"Audrey, so nice to see you," I say with a warm smile. "Have a seat wherever you'd like."

She smiles and takes a seat on the edge of the couch catty corner to my desk. I move from my desk to a chair that's closer to her.

"I'm glad you had time for me today. Most days I keep my grand-children, and this was the only day this week I could get someone else to watch them."

"Of course, I always try to work around my patient's schedule."

I also don't have enough patients to fill up each day, so it wasn't hard to get her on the calendar.

She takes a deep breath and wrings her hands, her wedding bands glinting in the light.

"Why don't you start off by telling me why you decided to come see me?" I ask, giving her a reassuring smile.

"Well, I've been married to Charles for almost forty years now and he's been in the force for all of them. And when I saw the post in the precinct's spouse Facebook group it dawned on me that I've never talked to a professional ... ever."

I wait, able to tell by the look on her face that she's still forming her thoughts. Sometimes what people need most is to be able to speak freely, without someone trying to lead them in a certain direction.

"Sure I talk to some of the wives that I'm close with, but they're in the same boat as me. They worry about their husbands and they miss them too. All I get from them is feeling like they understand me, but they can't exactly help me. So, I thought why not see if you can?"

"And what do you think you need help with?"

Oftentimes what a person answers isn't what they really need, but it's a good place to start digging around.

"I think–" she cuts herself off and looks down at her lap. I give her a moment before I speak up.

"You're safe here, Audrey. Whatever you need to say or do, you can."

She inhales a shaky breath. "I resent Charles," she blurts. After her admission, she sinks back into the couch, her previous decorum abandoned. "I don't want to feel this way, but I do. The other night I was in bed, staring at my ceiling while he snored beside me and it just hit me that I've sacrificed so much."

I nod and hum as she continues to speak, telling me how she feels guilty for all the times she wishes he would quit because she knows his job is vital to the community. She lays out scenario after scenario of times she felt like she came second. The stories and information are endless, I can't write fast enough in my notebook. It's like drinking from a firehose.

When our time comes to an end, Audrey is practically panting.

"I don't think I've ever said any of that out loud," she breathes out as I stand to place my notebook on my desk. Her eyes are wide and her hand shakes when she pats her carefully done curls.

"That's how a lot of people are when they first come in. Over the next few days you might feel a little raw. You essentially opened up your chest to do heart surgery. So make sure to practice some self care. Bubble baths, taking a walk on your own, a hobby. And I think it would be beneficial for you to try journaling in the days until our next session. You need to release this pent-up emotion."

She nods and pushes up to her feet. "I can do all of that. I can't remember the last time I took a bubble bath, it sounds nice."

I smile at her and lead her to the door. "Well you can tell the Chief it's doctor prescribed."

He already thinks my job is ridiculous, might as well embrace it and have him think all I do is tell people to take bubble baths.

I open my door and none other than Chief Wells is standing on the other side of it, his fluffy brows drawn together.

"I told him I'd be seeing you," Audrey explains before wrapping me up in a floral-scented hug. "Thank you so much. I already feel better."

"You're welcome. Send me an email if you need anything before our next appointment."

"Will do." She smiles then grabs the Chief's hand. "Come on honey, you can walk me to my car."

He eyes me for a moment, then turns his attention to his wife and walks her down the hall hand in hand. Watching them go makes an odd feeling settle into my stomach. Audrey isn't the first spouse to have these issues. Are all detectives and officers doomed to have strained relationships?

I can't help but think of Levi as I turn and go back into my office. I'm trained to know how to handle these stressors, but even I can't imagine what it would be like to constantly worry for my husband's safety plus dealing with long hours and the normal stress of day to day life.

Thankfully, we're just friends. So I can rest easy knowing that isn't my fate. And maybe one day I'll be counseling *his* wife. Unfortunately, that thought just makes me feel even sicker.

The remainder of the week goes by without much fanfare. Levi pops his head in my door on occasion to say hello or that I look beautiful. I tell him not to say the latter but end up smiling once he closes the door and leaves.

I've heard from a few spouses that there's a pretty big case in the homicide division, so that's probably why my interactions with Levi have been so short. My slots have slowly been filling with spouses, but I also had my first on-staff patient fill out paperwork. They work in the gangs and narcotics unit and decided to come in after their spouse told them about me. I'm hoping this is evidence of a ripple effect and not just a fluke.

"Hey, Dahlia, you got a minute?" I look up at the sound of Levi's voice and see him along with another detective standing in my doorway.

"Yeah, what's up?" I ask, my curiosity piquing.

"So, Rhodes" —he gestures to the guy next to him— "was talking to a buddy of his that works in the Birmingham PD and they mentioned how their staff psychologist helped them with interrogations. Is that something you're trained in?"

"Yes, it is. I don't have much experience interrogating in my career so far, but I do know a lot about body language and emotional cues."

"Perfect," Levi says and lifts a laptop he had tucked under his arm. "Do you have time to review an interrogation tape? We're interviewing a witness to a shooting and he won't budge even though we know he knows who did it."

"I can try," I say and gesture to my desk. He sets the laptop down and gets the footage pulled up.

The video starts and I watch as Rhodes interrogates a large, buff man named Vince. Rhodes is a great interrogator, but Vince seems unbreakable. Oftentimes, witnesses to these kinds of shootings want to take care of things themselves. Levi's right, Vince knows who did it, but he wants to be the one to enact justice. The problem is, there's a good chance more people will be killed in the process. It's an endless cycle, unless the unit can put a stop to it.

I can feel the two detectives' eyes on me as I pause the tape, rewinding to watch certain parts. The interrogation is around an hour long, but I don't have to watch the whole thing to find a chink in Vince's armor.

"He's prideful," I say and Rhodes snorts.

"No offense, gorgeous, but that's easy to see."

I look up, prepared to tell him not to call me that when I catch Levi glaring at him.

"Her name is Dr. Chamberlain. Be professional," Levi growls and Rhodes' easy grin fades.

"Sorry," Rhodes mumbles and I nod before continuing.

"As I was saying, he's got a big ego. He takes pride in the fact that he's strong enough to not break, and it's clear he takes pride in his family and community as well. Appeal to that pride, show him that giving you the name of the shooter will make him a hero. Don't talk to him man to man, because he thinks you're lesser than him. Talk to him like a boss who you'll do the dirty work for so he doesn't have to."

Rhodes nods as he thinks over what I'm saying and Levi shoots me a proud grin that makes my stomach swoop.

"All right, I'll try it out. Can't hurt. Thanks," Rhodes says and tips his head before leaving the office. It's clear he's on a mission to get this case closed.

Levi closes his laptop and tucks it back under his arm. "Thanks for all your help, Doll."

"Weren't you just telling Rhodes that he needs to be professional?" I ask in a teasing voice.

"Yeah, but that doesn't apply to me."

"And why is that?" I ask, preparing for him to throw me some cheesy line.

"Because we're friends." My heart sinks when he doesn't say what I thought he would. Which is dumb, because I don't want him to say those things. No matter how fluttery and wonderful they make me feel.

"Speaking of being friends," he says as he walks to the door. "You should come watch the Thrashers game with me and my family this weekend."

My eyes get big. His *family*?

"I don't know if that's a good idea..." I trail off. It feels like a line I shouldn't cross.

"Come on, friends hang out, right? It's not like we'll be alone either, so you can still keep up your boundaries."

I sigh and sit back in my chair, giving him a once over. After our time talking in his truck a few days ago I've been worried about him. Maybe this would help him relax and I could indulge my curiosity about his family. Besides, how much trouble could he cause in front of his whole family? It's not like he'd pull me in and kiss me ... at least, I don't *think* he would.

"I'll think about it," I say instead of giving a straightforward answer.

"I'll email you the address and my phone number," he says with a smile. "See you later, Doll."

"See you."

He leaves and the quiet of my office increases the volume of my thoughts. I went from not even wanting to talk to Levi in a way that wasn't professional to now potentially going to meet his family. This doesn't bode well for the future.

Deep down I know we can't be together though. There's too many things standing in the way. Maybe we were brought back together just to be friends. I could use a friend, and I'm sure Levi could too.

The only problem is, I don't know many friendships that began with the people *making out*. That tension is still there, hiding right below the surface like an alligator in a river. If I'm not careful, the tension could snap and consume me whole.

Chapter Eight

Dahlia Chamberlain

I should not have cyberstalked Levi's family. My intentions were harmless, truly harmless. All I wanted to do was see what I was getting into this evening when I went to his sister, MJ's house. After I decided to go, he sent me the address and told me it was for her house, so of course I googled MJ Carter. And what came up? Oh, nothing. Just the fact that her name is now MJ Holt—as in the head coach of the Thrashers Sebastian Holt's WIFE.

Photos of their intimate destination wedding were showcased on ESPN in a press release congratulating the happy couple. This led me to their social media accounts where I found just how popular they both are, not to mention their daughter Maddie who's incredibly TikTok famous.

At first I enjoyed seeing the funny videos of Levi dancing with his niece on her account. That was until I saw the millions of views on each video. Suddenly, I felt on the verge of throwing up. There's no way I can be on their level. I should text Levi and tell him I can't go.

My phone rings and Isabella's name pops up on the screen.

I answer it and immediately blurt out, "Levi's family is super rich and famous."

"*Okayyy,*" Isabella draws out the word. "And?"

"And I can't meet them tonight because they'll see that there's nothing fancy or rich about me and–" I cut myself off, realizing she called me. "Wait, what were you calling about?"

"I was going to ask if you could watch Fletcher tomorrow morning so that Marcus and I could go to brunch after church. But I'm going to need you to back up because you're meeting his family? What happened to keeping things professional?"

I groan and flop backwards onto my bed, which is covered in a pile of clothes I was trying to choose an outfit from. "We decided to be friends and he somehow convinced me to go to his sister's house to watch the game tonight. But it doesn't even matter because I'm going to text him and tell him I can't make it. I don't even own any Thrashers gear. How can I meet the coach's wife and not wear a jersey?"

"Wait, his sister is MJ Holt? I follow her on Instagram! She only posts like once a month but everything she does is so aesthetically pleasing. I'd spend our life savings on a piece of art from her if she ever started selling her work."

If I wasn't so distressed, I might laugh at her theatrics. "*Isaaa,* what am I going to do? MJ is a masterpiece and I'm the dirty rag you wipe your paintbrushes on."

"Oh, don't you even start with that mopey woe-is-me bit. Your closet has clothes from every color of the rainbow. Find something in Thrashers colors and *make it work*."

"Don't quote Tim Gunn after being mean to me."

"I'm not being mean, I'm telling you it's dumb to call yourself a paint rag when you're beautiful and fashionable and *usually* confident."

"*Fine*," I grumble. "I will put together an outfit." I pause and stare at the spinning blades of my ceiling fan. "What if they don't like me?"

"Then they have terrible taste and you should steal something expensive on your way out the door to get back at them."

I laugh as I sit up, looking across the room at my open closet. An oversized baby-blue button up catches my eye, and I tilt my head to the side, imagining it half tucked into a pair of straight leg jeans.

"With my tan belt," I mumble.

"What?"

"Oh! Sorry Isa, forgot we were still talking."

"I feel so loved."

I roll my eyes and walk across the room to snag the shirt and look for the right jeans. Georgia Thrashers colors are baby blue, white and brown. So this should look like a classy way of dressing in team colors.

"The amount of times you've forgotten to text me back is atrocious. If either of us were sensitive about that sort of thing we wouldn't be friends."

She laughs, making me smile. "True, true. Okay, so now that your fashion crisis has been averted, can you take care of Fletcher?"

"Yes, of course. You and Marcus deserve some alone time."

"Thanks D, you're the best!"

"That's why I'm your *best*ie."

The line is silent for a moment. "Never make that joke again."

We burst into laughter and it takes a minute for us to stave off our giggles in order to say goodbye. At least if this all goes terribly, I'm not totally alone. Isa will always be by my side.

"Dahlia Chamberlain," I tell the guard manning the gate. "I'm friends with Levi Carter."

The guard takes my driver's license into his station for a moment, then comes back. "You're cleared, have a nice day."

"Thanks, you too," I say with a smile then drive through the gate.

I'm not sure I've ever been to a house that had security. Prickles of sweat form on my back as my nerves set in.

"You can do this, Dahlia. You talk to strangers about their deepest fears and traumas for a living. A party at a mansion is easy," I say to myself as I roll down the winding driveway.

The house is stunning. It's essentially a glass castle, shining and glittering in the setting sun. The house is surrounded by trees dipped in autumnal shades of orange, yellow, and brown. I search for Levi's truck as I'm pulling up, but I don't see it. Maybe he rode with one of his brothers or maybe he has a second vehicle.

I park my Jeep near an identical white one whose dash is covered in ducks. My mood lifts at the sight of a fellow Jeep person in this sea of sports cars and luxury SUVs. I pull a duck out of my console and hop out to go place it on their windshield as a gift. One of my favorite parts of owning a Jeep has been the trading ducks back and forth. It's so whimsical and fun.

My hands are sweating even though the autumn air is brisk. I wipe my palms on my jeans before knocking on the front door.

"Come in!" a collection of voices yells out.

I didn't text Levi, but now I'm wishing I would have so that I didn't have to walk in alone. It just felt too much like a girlfriend thing to have him come out to walk me inside.

The doorknob is cool against my palm as I twist it. The door opens to reveal a forest of plants. It smells like a greenhouse, fresh and warm and wild. I walk through the foyer mouth agape. This place is a dream. I could spend hours staring at the art on the walls and guessing what each plant was.

All of this makes me long for a house with plenty of windows and a yard instead of the closed-in apartment I live in now. It's so beautiful and full of life.

The further I get into the house, the louder it gets. There are way more people than I expected in the open concept living area. And through the wall of windows I see even more people outside around a firepit.

"You must be Dahlia," a low, but still feminine voice says and I turn to find a woman with long dark hair smiling at me from where she's standing near the kitchen in their open concept home.

Well, smiling is a stretch, but it's not a scowl so I'll take it as a welcome. When I fully face her I realize she's MJ, the owner of this magical fairytale castle of a house.

"Yes, I am, and you must be MJ. It's so nice to meet you, your home is unbelievably beautiful."

Her smile grows by a centimeter and she lets her gaze sweep the room. "Thank you, I'm happy with how it turned out. You should have seen how bare it was before I moved in."

"I can't imagine it any other way, it feels like the house was made to be like this."

"It does, doesn't it?" She seems lost in thought for a moment, and I get the impression she's a woman not just comfortable in silence but fond of it. It's a wonder why she invited so many people to her house. "Levi just called, and he's going to be late. He had to work some on a case, but he said he'll get here as soon as he can and to tell you he's sorry."

"Oh, thank you for telling me." I clear my throat, nerves creeping up fast.

Perfect. I'm in a house full of strangers and the only man I know is working late. I'm reminded of all the spouses who have sat across from me ranting about how their loved ones are always missing out on things because of their job.

"Don't worry, I gave the phone over to our brother Grayson who gave him an earful about how rude it was to leave you hanging like this."

I smile at her words. I'd heard Grayson's name before when Levi and I first met. Levi and Grayson were on vacation together, but Levi started hanging out with me and, according to him, Grayson has never struggled to find company.

"I'll have to thank Grayson at some point then."

"Oh he's already zeroed in on you. I think he's resisted coming over as long as he can, which is never long enough."

She looks around me and I turn just in time to see a tall, dark-haired man with a giant grin bounding toward us from the living area.

"I hear we have a doctor in our midst."

"Well, it's just a doctorate in psychology, not exactly med school." I don't usually downplay my degree, but I don't want anyone thinking I'm something I'm not.

"Still a doctor. You sat through way more school than I ever could."

"You were great in school, you just didn't know how to *sit still*," MJ says in a pointed voice and Grayson waves her words away.

"Anyway, I'm pleased to make your acquaintance, Dr. Chamberlain." He bows slightly and I can't help but giggle. I mean when a handsome man bows to you it's hard *not* to.

"The pleasure is all mine," I say and humor him with a brief curtsy. His eyes light up like it's Christmas morning.

"Oh, please don't encourage him," MJ groans, making me laugh.

"I had to show my gratitude for him scolding Levi on my behalf."

Grayson sighs at this, giving me an apologetic look. "All of my siblings are not well versed in the social and emotional areas of life. I try to teach them, but they're all a bunch of stubborn mules."

"Hey, I'm married," MJ cuts in, "that's plenty social."

"Spending your days hiding away in your mansion is not social, MJ," Grayson says, sounding exasperated.

"I'm throwing a party!" She gestures around at all of the guests.

"Only because I convinced you to when you decided to stay home instead of flying with Bash to the game."

"I'm going to check on the food," MJ huffs and leaves.

"See? What'd I tell ya? Stubborn mules." He shakes his head and I laugh. "Okay, you ready for the low down on this party, doctor?"

"Bring it," I say, matching his energy.

He gestures to a man who looks identical to him except for their haircuts and clothing. "That's my twin, Adrian. He prefers silence to talking any day of the week."

Adrian's arm is around a petite blonde who looks as though she stepped right out of a Pinterest board. She took the subtle route with her team spirit as well, dressing in a pleated baby blue skirt and an oversized white sweater. Adrian's smiling down at her and chatting amicably.

"He seems sociable enough."

"Oh, that's because he's with Juliette. She's his fiancée and the sun he revolves around." Grayson says all this in a tone that shows just how happy he is for his brother.

I watch Adrian and Juliette for a moment longer. Every time he looks at her–which is often–his entire countenance changes. He hangs on her every word and when she smiles it's as if his entire life is made better by the simple expression. The clear love shared between them makes my chest ache.

"And that's Maverick, he's on the quiet side too, but he's got a big heart and makes a mean chocolate chip cookie."

I follow with my eyes to where he's pointing and see a broad man with a healthy amount of scruff on his face and his muscled arms crossed, leaning against a wall. His expression is dark and he looks as though he's ready to hit someone.

"Is he okay?"

"Yeah, he's fine, he just got some bad news about a friend." Grayson is purposefully vague.

"And what about you? What's your deal?" I turn the tables on him, but he grins as if he doesn't mind one bit.

"I'm the entertainment," he says with a wink.

I'm about to respond when his eyes lock on something–or rather, someone–behind me and he smirks.

"Looks like your man decided to finally show up."

My man?

Chapter Nine

Levi Carter

This is awful. After convincing Dahlia to be friends and then come to this party, I got caught up at work and I'm late. It was out of my control, but no one will see it that way. They rarely do.

"I know, I'm late and I'm terrible," I say in lieu of a greeting as I walk toward Grayson and Dahlia.

Dahlia turns around and my heart picks up speed. She looks so beautiful it makes my arms ache with the need to draw her to me. After a day like today I wish more than anything that I could. But she's probably upset with me and rightfully so.

"It's okay," she says, surprising me. Her expression is soft, and there's a small smile on her pink lips.

"You're not mad?"

She shrugs. "Grayson kept me company, so it wasn't too bad."

I look at my smirking little brother. He knows better than to flirt with Dahlia after I explained who she was on the phone, but that doesn't mean he didn't cause trouble of another kind. Mischief runs through his veins.

"Don't give me that look," he says, as if reading my thoughts. "Me and the doctor here just had a nice chat."

"Whatever he told you about me was a lie," I tell Dahlia and she laughs.

"We didn't talk about you," she says.

"See? No harm done, we didn't even talk about you."

"I'm too tired to deal with your games," I say and immediately regret my slip up.

Grayson's brow furrows in concern and I know he's going to tell me I should leave my job. This is how it always goes. If Maverick complains about being tired, no one asks *him* to shut down his bakery and stop waking up at five in the morning to bake bread. But as soon as *I* have the slightest amount of stress I'm offered a new job and told to quit mine.

"Why don't I introduce you to some people?" I ask Dahlia before he can say anything.

"Uh, sure," she says, eyeing me.

I place my hand on her lower back and lead her away from my brother. I can feel the watchful gazes of my family on us, so I purposefully lead her outside through the back door where Maddie is hanging out by the fire with her friends. They're all talking and laughing, looking at something on Maddie's phone.

"I really am sorry about showing up late," I tell her and she shrugs.

"It's not in your control," she says and my shoulders relax. I didn't realize how much tension was built up in them.

The smokey scent from the crackling bonfire curls around us as we walk through a smattering of yellow-and-orange leaves. I'm about to thank her for being so understanding when Maddie looks over at us and grins. It's not long before she's hopping up out of her chair and bounding over to us.

"Uncle Levi, who's this?" Maddie asks in a not-so-innocent voice.

"This is Dahlia, she's a friend from work. Dahlia, this is my niece Maddie."

"It's nice to meet you," Dahlia says.

"A *friend*. You've never brought any *friends* over to our house before," Maddie comments, mischief dancing in her blue eyes.

"There's a first time for everything. Why don't you get back to your friends? We were just going to walk around the property."

"Fine, but I want to talk to you later," Maddie says to Dahlia.

Dahlia laughs a little. "Okay, that sounds good."

Maddie heads back over to her friends. Dahlia and I head past the fire toward the edge of MJ and Sebastian's property. I tuck my hands into my Thrashers hoodie pocket to keep them warm in the chill of the evening.

"Before Maddie walked up I was going to say thanks for being so understanding about me being late."

"It's my job, remember?" Her tone is light, but the notion hits me like a punch.

Of course she understands, she's *paid* to. If she wasn't, she'd probably react the way everyone does. They all want detectives to keep the murderers off the street, but none of them want to be related to one or start a family with one. That thought reeks of bitterness, but it rings true all too often.

I look down at Dahlia and she meets my eyes, a question in her gaze.

"Are you okay? It's really not a big deal that you were a few minutes late. Your family gave you enough grief for it so I don't have to." Her smile makes some of the rain clouds in my mind float away.

Maybe I'm overthinking all of this. I'm so used to people trying to pull me away from my career. What if her being a police therapist is the reason we'd work? She'd understand when I have to work late because she knows the hazards of the job. There wouldn't be any judgment because she gets it. I wonder–not for the first time in my career–what it would be like to feel truly understood.

"I'm all right." I grin down at her. "You're cute when you're worried, Doll."

She rolls her eyes. "I thought you said I'm cute when I'm mad?"

We're further away from the party now, the remaining rays of sunlight fading from the sky as night begins to take over. It feels peaceful out here and I'm grateful for the reprieve.

"Pretty sure I said beautiful, but you're always cute."

"Just what every woman wants to hear, that she's *cute*."

I snag her hand and tug her closer to me, leaning down to whisper in her ear. "Would you prefer I tell you how unbelievably sexy you look tonight and how I can't bear to look away from you? Or maybe how every time I look into those pretty blue eyes of yours I lose all sense of time and space?" I brush my lips over the shell of her ear, smirking when she shivers. "Is that more what you were looking for, Doll?"

"I-I wasn't fishing for compliments," she stutters out. I run my thumb over the back of her hand.

"You'll never have to with me."

She looks up at me, her eyes a deep indigo in the low light. "Is this how you talk to all your friends?" she asks and I shake my head.

"I've only ever been this way with you, Doll. I told you that."

Leaves crunch as she takes a step back, pulling her hand from mine. "Levi, I think my coming tonight was a bad idea."

My heart sinks. I pushed her too far with the compliments, but I couldn't help myself. It's so easy to get lost in her.

"I'm sorry I took things too far," I tell her. "But don't write off tonight. Let me take you back inside and we can get some food and you can meet my brother Adrian's fiancée. I think you two would get along."

She shakes her head, taking another step. It feels colder than before without the warmth of her close by. "I think it's best that I leave. Tell MJ and Grayson it was nice talking to them. I'll see you around work, okay?"

"Dahlia, please." I reach out for her, but she shakes her head.

"No, Levi. I'm sorry, but we can't keep going like this. I could get fired and even if I wouldn't, we just can't pretend that picking up where we left off is an option. Too much has changed in the last five years."

I know a lot can happen in five years, but she acts like we're entirely different people. I search her expression, those eyes that give away her mood, but I come back with nothing.

"What's changed, Dahlia? What's so different that we wouldn't work?"

"It doesn't matter. I'm not giving up my career and neither are you. That's the end of the story. Now, please, don't make a scene. I just want to go home."

I nod, resigned. The last thing I want to do is make things worse than they already are. "Okay, I'll tell everyone you had to leave. Drive safe."

"It's better this way," she reassures me before walking away.

My heart feels battered and bruised as I watch her walk around the side of the house, not moving until she's disappeared from sight.

It's too cold to stand out here any longer though, so I make my way back inside and face my too-observant family. Grayson's eyebrows raise when he spots me without Dahlia. I pray that he doesn't bring it up or make it into a big deal.

All of my family is incredibly observant and they don't miss anything, even the smallest detail or change. So the fact that Dahlia just left isn't going to slide by unnoticed, even in a party as large as this one.

In an effort to avoid confrontation, I join the group that MJ's talking to. She used to live with three other women who were her best friends and roommates. They're all still close and they try to see each other often. One of those women, Grace Parker, is talking to MJ, a hand resting on her pregnant belly. Her husband–famous country star Wyatt Parker–stands next to her, his arm slung around her shoulders.

The first time I got to meet Wyatt I was a little starstruck since I enjoy his music, but over time I got used to his presence. He's really just a small-town guy who happens to be a great singer.

"That's odd, I don't know anyone with a peach Jeep," MJ says when I step beside her. My stomach drops. So much for avoiding confrontation. "Levi, does Dahlia drive a Jeep?" she asks, turning the attention of the small group to me.

"She does, why?" I ask, afraid that someone is going to say they saw her leaving early and I'll have to make up an excuse.

"I went out to my car to get some heartburn medication and saw her adorable Jeep. She even placed a duck on my windshield. I gave her one back as well before coming inside, but I wanted to thank her in person," Grace answers for MJ in a sweet voice.

"She actually had to leave, but I'll let her know you said that."

MJ pulls me aside, telling Grace and Wyatt she'll be right back. "What happened? Did Grayson say something to scare her off?"

I sigh. "No, I did."

"Oh." She gives me a sympathetic look. "Well, I–"

"I'm heading home," Maverick says, butting into our conversation. "The party is great, but I've got a long day tomorrow at the shop."

"All right, be safe," MJ says and lets him pull her into his side for a hug. She's not much of a hugger, but she makes a few exceptions for us as her brothers. "Thanks for bringing dessert."

Mav nods and then stalks off looking like there are storm clouds circling his head.

"What's up with him?" I ask, hooking a thumb over my shoulder.

"Evie eloped with that dumb male model."

I scrunch my brows together. "So what? I mean, that's not the best decision on her part, but what does that have to do with Mav?"

"You know how he is, he's protective over the people he cares about. The both of you try to take care of everyone."

"I can call him later to check on him," I say and she gives me a look. "What?"

"You need to take care of *yourself*."

"I am," I say, but she looks like she doesn't believe me.

"As much as you try to be strong around everyone, I can see right through you. More easily, I can see the giant bags under your eyes."

"Thanks, sis, great pep talk."

She shoves my shoulder. "I'm just saying, you need balance. Stop worrying about other people for a minute and do something for you."

"I'll try," I reply.

Hopefully that will get her to stop looking at me like our mom used to before she passed away–like she can read your thoughts. My heart squeezes at the thought of Mom. What would she think of this whole situation with Dahlia? Would she tell me to fight for her or walk away? I know she'd be on MJ's side about taking care of myself. Living off of energy drinks and beef jerky would have earned me a scolding for sure.

"I think I'll head home too," I say, not sure if I missed anything MJ said while I was thinking.

"Okay, call if you need anything, even if it's just to talk."

I hug my well-meaning sister then leave, somehow managing to just wave to my brothers and not be interrogated. Maybe they could sense the dejection coming off me in waves. Whatever the reason, I'm grateful for it. Because my energy is waning and I'm ready to crawl into bed.

Not that sleep will bring me much relief from my problems, because it's more than likely that I'll end up dreaming about Dahlia. At least in my dreams we're together.

Chapter Ten

Dahlia Chamberlain

"Jaz, come on we're going to be late," I call out from by our apartment door where I'm searching for my favorite cranberry lip stain.

I always carry whatever lip product I'm wearing with me in my bag, then leave it in there. So my purse becomes a lipstick landfill and I'm constantly rifling through it before we leave. Every so often I put all of them back in my makeup bag, but it doesn't take long for them to find their way to my purse again.

"I can't find my belt bag!"

"Your *fanny pack* is hanging by the door," I say right as I pull out my lip stain.

I'm swiping it on when my sister breezes by me, snagging the little black bag off one of the purse hooks. My sister is similar to me in some ways, but different in many, many others. For instance, her idea of a coffee and shopping outfit is a matching workout set and a belt bag (fanny pack). Mine is a chunky knit, mustard sweater layered under coffee-colored overalls and a thrifted leather crossbody.

"I've told you a million times this is a *belt bag*," she huffs and slings it over her head so the bag rests across her chest. Her sage green leggings and matching long sleeve crop top are cute, but a little too athletic for my taste. Though it makes sense for her since she's a cheerleader and gym addict.

"It's so cute when your generation makes up words for things that have existed for much longer than you've been alive."

She rolls her eyes. "You're thirty not eighty. And don't act like your generation didn't change the meaning of a bunch of words like *slay*." She gags, because I'm pretty sure people don't say slay anymore. Isa and I still do, but Isa also says *fetch* unironically in spite of Regina George saying it's never going to happen. So, I'm not sure that we can be described as people who have kept up with the times.

"Just get your shoes on," I say and turn to the mirror by the door to assess my reflection. The bold lip color pulls together my autumnal look perfectly. The weather has finally cooled down enough in Georgia to truly enjoy fall, so I'm pulling out all the stops for this girls' day.

I babysat Fletcher this morning so Isa and Marcus could go to brunch, and after that Jasmine suggested we go shopping because she needs supplies for her spirit week outfits. I immediately said yes, because I saw on Instagram that Sloane Rose signed some copies of her latest release and stocked them in a local bookstore that's near the stores Jaz wants to go to.

Do I already own a copy of the book? Yes. Am I still going to buy this copy because it's *signed*? Also yes. No one can judge me because it's *my* hard-earned money I'm spending.

Our front door opens as I'm sliding my bag onto my shoulder. Isa steps through the doorway wearing her signature mom jeans and flannel. When Isa found out about our plans, she convinced Marcus to watch Fletcher so she could tag along. I left the door unlocked since I knew she was coming. It would probably make sense for her to have a key at this point, but I'm a little scared what she would do with a key. I could definitely see her coming in the middle of the night and waking me up if Fletcher is keeping her up.

"This is the best day of my life." She pauses. "Okay, my wedding day and the birth of my child are up there. But this is definitely third."

I laugh and shake my head at her. One of the many reasons we're best friends is her tendency to be dramatic.

"You don't *understand*," she says emphatically. "This morning I had brunch alone with my husband for the first time since Fletcher was born. Then I got to snuggle my sweet baby and have a post-brunch nap. Now I'm going out on my own for a girls' day. I could cry."

"We don't have time for tears, we need to get to The Secret Door before everyone buys up all the copies of Sloane's book," I tell her and Isa's eyes widen.

"You're right, let's go."

"I don't understand y'all," Jasmine says as we walk out the door. "You already own multiple copies of each of her books."

"It's *signed*," Isa and I say at the same time, then laugh.

"Whatever you have to say to justify yourselves," Jasmine says.

We get down to the parking garage and climb in my Jeep. There's a new duck on my dash, one with an adorable cowboy hat. I wish

I could have met the person who gave it to me at MJ's party. I also wish it didn't remind me of that moment with Levi.

A part of me regrets running away yesterday. I wanted so badly to kiss him right then. Goosebumps cascade down my arms as I think of his whispered words, his lips against my ear. But it would be foolish to think that we could be together, even if our circumstances were different.

"Can I put on my fall playlist?" Jasmine asks, breaking my reverie.

"Sure, I love that one."

Sweater Weather by The Neighborhood starts blaring through the speakers and Isa and Jaz immediately start singing along at top volume. My mind slips away once more into memories of love and laughter.

The girl Levi met that summer ... she was wild and carefree. She wasn't afraid of anything. Now, well, I'm much more cautious than before, that's for sure. If Levi is telling the truth about missing me, then he misses the *old* me. The one who made him dance on tables and ride questionable rollercoasters. I haven't done anything adventurous since my parents died and I took over being Jasmine's guardian.

Five years ago, even four years ago, if I would have seen Levi again like this I'd probably have jumped at the chance to be together. Even without being in love with him the way that I was. I would have snuck around the precinct and made out in supply closets. It would have been dangerous and exciting, everything I lived for back then.

Jasmine leans forward from the backseat and turns up a Taylor Swift song even louder, belting it out. I glance at her in my rear view mirror, smiling at the giant grin she's wearing. Seeing her smile after everything we've been through makes my throat feel tight. I focus back on the road again, blinking away tears.

She's the reason I can't take risks anymore. I have to be steady for her, a rock for her to lean on and a soft place to land. So no more thrill-seeking or living in the moment. My evenings will be spent at home, making sure she's safe and taken care of.

I park in front of The Secret Door, a popular bookstore that features a shelf where, if you pull a certain book, it leads into a room where people can read and drink coffee from the adjoining cafe.

"Okay, since we're going here first we need a time limit so we're not here until my stores close," Jasmine says as we hop out of my Jeep.

The sounds of the city mingle with the brisk autumn wind. I tug the sleeves of my sweater down over my palms with a smile. There's something so enchanting about the changing of seasons. It's as if the air is filled with magic and possibilities. It never fails to make me smile.

"We just have to grab the signed copies and then we'll leave," I tell Jasmine as she pulls on the door to the shop. A bell jingles signaling our entry.

"I know better than to think I can bring the two of you into a bookstore and just get what you came for."

Isa laughs and loops her arm through mine. "Give us thirty minutes, then come drag us out."

"We'll get coffee on the way out," I add.

"Okay! I'm going to look around, I've got my phone if you need me."

Jasmine walks off in the direction of the self-help books. I don't know why anyone would want to read books about becoming a better person when they could read about people falling in love, but to each their own.

"Now, let's secure the goods," Isa says and we march toward the romance section in sync.

The smell of paper and espresso surrounds me like a warm blanket.

"I could live here," I say on a sigh.

"Me too, girl," Isa replies.

We turn the corner and I'm grateful Isa is holding onto my arm or else when I trip over my own feet I would have faceplanted too.

Standing in the romantic fantasy section with an armful of books is none other than MJ Holt. Her long black hair is wavy down her back, reminiscent of a mermaid. She's wearing a wine-colored floral maxi skirt paired with a cream sweater. If someone told me she got paid by *Free People* to wear their clothes, I'd believe them. Her boho look is effortlessly chic and confirms once again I'll never be as cool as her.

"Dahlia, what a coincidence," she says when she spots me.

I give her a small smile.

"Hey, MJ, yeah I didn't expect to see you here." Or else I wouldn't have come. Because seeing the host of the party you ditched the night before is not ideal.

"My best friend, Grace, loves this store. She introduced me to romantic fantasies and now I swear I should pay rent because I practically live here."

This makes me give her a genuine smile. She doesn't seem upset by me running off last night. Plus, I don't have to make awkward small talk. I can always have a conversation with a fellow reader.

"Yeah, me and my best friend Isabella love it here too," I say, gesturing to Isa beside me. "What books are you getting?"

She starts to go through them, showing us one by one what's in her large stack. I'm ogling a beautiful fae romance cover when a pair of large hands lifts away the entire stack. I follow the movement to find Sebastian Holt grinning down at me. I'm not a huge Thrashers fan, but you'd have to be living under a rock not to know who he is as a Georgia resident.

"Sebastian, she was looking at those," MJ scolds him, not intimidated in the slightest by his large stature.

"I told you I was going to carry your books, beautiful wife of mine."

"Well you weren't here to hold them, so I had to make do. Plus, I'm perfectly capable of carrying them." She crosses her arms and his grin widens.

"I was getting your matcha latte," he says and tips his head toward where two paper cups are sitting on a shelf. "But please, keep scowling, you know how I love it when you get all fired up."

Her olive skin flames red and I feel heat creep up my neck too. Isa and I share a look, both of us pressing our lips together to stifle giggles.

"We're in public, behave yourself." She swats his chest. He looks the furthest thing from admonished.

"I just can't help myself when I see those pretty eyes of yours flashing."

MJ raises her hand as if she's going to hit him again, but he catches her wrist with his free hand. He bends down and whispers something in her ear and I didn't think it was possible, but her cheeks get even pinker. She jerks out of his grasp, clearly holding back a smile as she pushes him away.

"Go find Maddie and check out, I'll meet you at the car."

"As you wish, my beautiful siren enchantress," he says with a grin. His attention turns to us and I pray I don't look as melted as I feel. "Ladies." He tips his head in acknowledgement before sauntering out of the aisle.

The man is pure charisma, he practically oozes charm. I'm afraid of what it would be like for him and Grayson to be in a room together. Every woman in the vicinity would be in danger of becoming a puddle.

"Sorry about him, he doesn't understand boundaries," MJ says with an eyeroll, but she's glowing with the kind of love that makes my heart hurt.

The way her and Sebastian look at each other ... it's that all-consuming, I-can't-breathe-without-you kind of love. He looked at her like he'd crawl through fire on his hands and knees to get to her every morning if it meant he spent the rest of the day by her side. It was almost difficult to look at them because of how bright their love burned.

"You two are adorable," Isa says, because I'm still struck speechless.

"I don't know about adorable." MJ laughs. "But thank you. I should probably get going though before he finds a way to embarrass me even more. It was good to see you Dahlia, and nice to meet you Isabella."

She grabs the two lattes off the shelf nearby.

"It was good to see you, too," I say.

"Hopefully it won't be the last time," she says with a meaningful look before disappearing around the corner and leaving us alone.

I stare at the spot she vacated for a moment, processing her words and everything that just happened.

"She seems like she'd make a nice sister-in-law," Isa comments and I whip my head in her direction.

"*What*?"

"I'm just saying. She seems nice and likes books."

"What does that have to do with us *becoming family*?"

"They're good qualities to have," Isa mumbles and turns her attention to a nearby shelf. She pulls two books off of it.

"You're my best friend, you're supposed to be on my side. I need support to stay away from Levi."

"I am on your side," she says, handing me one of the signed copies, there's only three left in total, one now because of us. I don't have time to celebrate finding them because she continues. "But I also know how you felt about him. So it makes my job as best friend harder. I'm meant to be a voice of reason, not just someone who tells you what you want to hear."

"I think losing my job is reason enough to stay away."

"You're probably right," Isa sighs.

"*Probably*? I am right. It would be a terrible idea."

"Or a really romantic one."

"Isa," I warn.

"Fine, I'll drop it. I just want you to have the beautiful romance you deserve."

"The only romance I want right now is in the pages of a book," I lie, because the truth can't be acknowledged.

I can't say out loud how much I want what MJ and Sebastian have, what Isa and Marcus have. No, that deep longing has to stay locked away. I have to focus on being responsible. And falling in love, in my experience, is far from responsible.

Chapter Eleven

Levi Carter

My hand grips the pebbled leather of the football as I draw my arm back to throw it to Grayson. Savory-scented smoke drifts on the evening air, making my stomach growl. Grayson invited me over for dinner and once he started grilling he suggested we throw the football back and forth in the backyard while we're waiting on the food.

I thought about just going home and watching SportsCenter until I fell asleep, but I know Grayson hates being alone. He plays it off a lot, but I think there's something deeper there. So, I gave up a night of being lazy to make sure he's okay. It's not like he couldn't get a date in five minutes–or less–if he wanted, but as the oldest brother I always feel like I need to step up when I'm able.

"So how are things with the doctor?" Grayson says once his capacity for silence has run out. If I had to bet, I'd say he's been holding on to that question since I walked in the door.

He throws the ball and it spirals in the air before I catch it.

I raise a brow. "I'm surprised you made it this long without asking about her."

"I was hoping to lull you into a false sense of security."

I shake my head and throw the ball back. "Didn't work."

"Are you going to answer anyway?"

"I *should* keep you in the dark since you were trying to manipulate me into talking."

Leaves crunch under my feet as I shuffle back when Grayson overthrows the ball a little. I reach high to snatch it out of the air.

"Should?"

I throw the ball hard at his smirking face, but he catches it easily, the ball making a *thump* when it hits his palms.

"But I'm not going to, because as annoying as you are, you give good relationship advice. At least, you did to MJ and Adrian."

"I do try to be helpful. You're all terrible at expressing your emotions."

"Thank you," I droll. "I appreciate the encouragement."

"I'm just telling the truth. Now, tell me what's going on. Besides the fact that you're hopelessly in love with her."

He throws the ball at me and I scramble to catch it, almost dropping it at the sound of the word *love*. It makes no sense and yet perfect sense to still be in love with Dahlia. I denied the feelings I had for her during that week, then spent the past five years realizing just how painfully deep they went.

When I told my family who Dahlia was, I told them I met her a few years ago and we crossed paths again. No one knows the full story. So the fact that my feelings are that transparent even without Grayson knowing everything is a little concerning.

"Do you remember five years ago when we rented that condo in Rosemary Beach?" I ask him as I regain my composure and toss the ball back.

"Yeah, that was the last vacation you went on before you chained yourself to the precinct like some sort of protester to a tree."

I shoot him a look, but he is–as usual–unaffected. "Do you remember the night we were supposed to meet up at the restaurant and I bailed on you saying you were taking too long?"

He cringes at the memory. "Not my finest moment. But in all fairness that cabana bed was so comfortable and it was overcast that day which was the perfect recipe for a nap."

"I bailed because I met her," I say and understanding dawns on his face.

"I wondered why you didn't want to hang out as much before I left but I figured it's because I wanted to do different things."

A smile stretches my lips as memories of that week come in like the tide. Grayson invited me to do quite a few of the things Dahlia and I ended up doing instead. When Grayson suggested parasailing, I told him absolutely not, but when Dahlia did ... well, it was hard to say no to her beautiful, hopeful eyes.

"I met her that night and we spent the rest of the vacation together. We agreed to not tell each other our last names or phone numbers until the end of the trip. Dahlia said the mystery made everything more exciting."

"I knew there was a reason I liked this girl," Grayson says with a smile of his own. "She sounds like she knows how to have a good time."

Grayson doesn't throw the ball back this time, instead he walks over toward his patio where his grill is. I follow him, continuing our conversation.

"She does. It was probably the best week of my life." He raises his brows at my words. "I should have told her how I felt, but I didn't. We were supposed to meet up and exchange information before we went back home, but instead she left a note on my door saying it was fun and maybe she'd see me again someday."

"Ouch." He opens up the grill and grabs a pair of tongs, moving around the chicken and vegetables. "You weren't mad at her?"

"No, it made sense. We were both too scared. But now she's back here and it feels like..." I search for the word.

"Fate?" Grayson supplies before beginning to put the cooked chicken and vegetables on a platter.

"Is it weird if I say yes?"

He shrugs and closes the grill with one hand, turning off the flame. "Not if you end up getting married. Then it's a great story to tell your grandkids."

I let out a laugh as I follow him inside. I'm still not over the fact that he bought a family home as a bachelor. Maybe that's why he doesn't like to be alone. Living in a big house like this with no one else would probably get pretty lonely. It was made to be filled with kids.

"So let's say I think it's fate. I don't know if she agrees, or if she does, she's trying to convince herself she doesn't. And when I flirted with her at MJ's house, she ran away."

"But you work together now, right?"

I sigh. "Yes, she said it's not ethical for us to date because she's the precinct therapist."

He gets quiet as he pulls plates out of the cupboard. "Maybe she wants to know you're in this for the long haul before she risks her job," he says after a beat of silence.

"I don't think it's even a real risk since I'm not her patient."

"Either way, she probably wants to feel safe with you before taking what *she* sees as a risk."

"So how do I show her that I want a future with her, not just a fling?" It's obvious that just flirting and teasing only get me so far before she pulls back. "Should I do some sort of grand gesture?"

"I'm always a fan of those, but I think if you go big too soon you'll scare her off again." His brow furrows as he works to come up with an idea. "Maybe do small things that show her you care."

My mind starts spinning with ideas. Grayson sets a plate in front of me and we eat at his breakfast bar in silence, the smokey aroma of the grilled chicken and vegetables scenting the air. I go through everything I know about Dahlia and what I've learned recently as well, trying to come up with things that would show her how I feel without being too much.

"I think I've at least got a plan now, so thanks for that," I tell him as I'm finishing my plate.

"Anytime."

"I don't know how you aren't married yet, man. Don't let it go to your head, but you are better at all this romance junk than the rest of us."

Something sad crosses his expression as he stands to take his now-empty plate to the sink. "Just haven't found the one yet, I guess. It's not for lack of trying though." He infuses humor into his voice and by the time he turns back to me his expression has morphed back into the lighthearted Grayson I'm used to. But I saw how he looked before he turned around and how his shoulders sagged in defeat. This must actually bother him.

"You'll find her," I say, attempting to encourage him. "If Adrian convinced Juliette to marry him, there's bound to be someone out there for you."

"I'm not worried about it," he says, but after seeing his reaction earlier I know it must be a lie.

I know what it feels like to get older and wonder how long it'll take to find someone to settle down with. He's thirty and our parents had been married for ten years by this age. It's hard not to wonder why it's different for us. I'm sure seeing his twin–the one who would rather spend every night at home alone than go out and meet people–get engaged wasn't easy either.

Suddenly, I realize how selfish I've been asking him for advice in an area that probably hurts him to talk about, even if he doesn't admit it.

"Want to play 2K for a little while?" he asks and even though I should say no to video games because I have an early morning, I agree anyway.

All of us siblings have always said Grayson is the best at expressing his emotions, but now I'm wondering if maybe he's just better at concealing the ones he doesn't want us to see. I resist the urge to sigh as I flop down next to him on the leather sofa in his man cave while he powers up the basketball game.

Now I have to worry about winning over Dahlia, making sure Maverick is okay with this whole Evie being married ordeal, *and* checking on Grayson more since I've spent most of our lives thinking he was just happy go lucky all the time. On top of all of that, I have to be present and focused at my job. I can see now how most of the detectives I work with give up and don't bother having a family. It's exhausting. I feel like I'm strapped to a treadmill, running and running with no end in sight.

Even though it's difficult, I'm not going to give up like others have. I love my family too much. I might have to live off of energy drinks for the rest of my life, but I can't fail them. My mom's words come to mind, stealing my breath and making my tired eyes burn with tears.

"Take care of them, sweetheart. You've always been my strong one. Don't give up after I'm gone."

If I close my eyes, I can still see her weak smile in that hospital bed. Still feel her hand in mine, barely gripping it as she told me she loved me.

"Did you forget how to play?" Grayson laughs, dragging me out of the painful memory. "You're doing terrible."

Coming back to the present, I see Grayson maneuvering his man to score yet another basket.

"I haven't played in a while," I say, trying to ignore the tightness in my chest. "I'll beat you next time."

"Doubtful," he says as he scores again.

I try once more to focus on the game, managing to score a few points. Getting lost in the past isn't going to help me. I just have to keep pushing. For my mom, for my family, and now for Dahlia too.

Flashback

Levi Carter

Summer, Five Years Ago

A salty breeze blows, making Dahlia shiver and curl up closer to me. She traces circles on my chest with her fingertips, and between that action and the sound of waves crashing against the shore, I'm in danger of falling asleep.

"This is perfect," Dahlia murmurs and I smile.

We bought a blow-up pool the size of a bed, filled it with pillows and blankets, and set it up on the beach to watch the sunset. The sun is long gone, and the stars have come out for the night, winking at us from above. Neither of us have said a word about moving. I've never been big on camping, but I'd stay here forever if it meant she was by my side.

"It really is." I sigh contentedly. "The stars and moon are so bright tonight."

She shifts to her back so she can look up at the sky. "Stargazing always makes me think of my grandmother. She knew all of the constellations by heart and had a telescope in her backyard. We'd spend hours out there together. She passed away when I was in high school, but I still think of her on clear nights like this."

"I'm that way about sunflowers, my whole family is. My mom loved them." Emotion lodges in my throat. I rarely talk about my mom with anyone other than my siblings.

"She passed away?" Dahlia's voice is quiet, almost overtaken by the sound of the waves.

"Yeah, she had cancer."

"I'm so sorry, I can't imagine losing my mom. That must be hard." Dahlia curls against me, but I can tell it's more for my sake than hers.

"It wasn't easy at first, but it's been a few years now."

"That doesn't mean it's any easier. Grief isn't linear. It's okay if it hurts more now than it did when she passed."

I squeeze my eyes shut and attempt to take a few deep breaths. Since Mom passed, I've felt like I'm supposed to *get better* or *get over it*. I can be sad on anniversaries or birthdays, but anything outside of that is excessive. I've never thought that I was allowed to still be hurting this much.

"Sometimes it feels like I shouldn't be so sad, that I should be stronger, you know?" I can't believe I'm saying all of this out loud. I'm not sure I've ever voiced these thoughts.

"Strength isn't defined by a lack of emotions. Sometimes the strongest thing you can do is cry or scream in anger. People think it's tough to conceal emotions, when in reality it takes a lot more strength to express them than hide them."

Dahlia's words sink beneath my skin, providing relief to the aching muscles that have carried so much for so long. I don't know how much of this philosophy I'll be able to take home with me. But maybe if I can convince Dahlia to stay with me, I'll have her around to remind me of these things when life gets hard.

I pull her closer to me.

Chapter Twelve

Dahlia Chamberlain

"Good morning!" I say to Bob, the Candy Crush loving receptionist manning the precinct lobby. "What level are you on today?"

I've been trying to connect with various people in the department in hopes that being likable will open people up to the idea of me working here. Most people haven't been outright hostile–except Chief Wells–but they're still unsure of me. So, I'm doing my best to make an impression on each person I come across.

For Bob, it was pretty easy to find a talking point. I check in each day on his status in his favorite game and he beams at me every time.

"I'm still stuck on level 6,432," he huffs.

When Bob first told me the level he was on, I choked on my morning pumpkin spice latte. I had to play it off that it just went down the wrong way. Now, I simply smile and nod. I'm concerned about the amount of time he must spend playing it, but unless he books me as his therapist, I plan on keeping it as a casual talking point for now.

"I'm sure you'll beat it soon," I say and he gives me an enthusiastic smile.

"I'll let you know when I do."

"I'm looking forward to celebrating your win," I say with a smile of my own before I head toward the Chief's office.

We have a meeting this morning, though I'm not sure what it could be about considering the man thinks my job is a joke. His email just said he wanted to see me when I came in this morning. No elaboration and he didn't even sign the email with a thank you, just the department default email signature stating his position as the Chief of Police.

My brown boots click against the tile floor as I strut down the hall. A little confidence hack I adopted years ago is to walk like I'm on a runway whenever I'm headed toward a place where I'll need an extra self-esteem boost. My olive-green wide leg pants and burgundy sweater might not be Fashion Week worthy, but a girl can pretend.

I arrive at his office door and take a steadying breath before opening it.

"You're late," Chief Wells says as soon as I step through his doorway.

"You said to come in when I arrived at work," I point out. "It's not possible for me to be late to a meeting with no set start time."

He grumbles something under his breath, shifting papers around. I sit down in a chair and cross my legs, taking a sip of my latte.

"How can I help you today, Chief?" I ask, getting straight to the point instead of attempting small talk. He likely wouldn't respond if I tried anyway.

"I want to know what you and my wife have been discussing."

I almost drop my to-go cup when his words register in my brain. I must have heard him wrong. "Excuse me?"

"My wife has had a few appointments with you and I would like to know what takes place during them."

"Chief, you understand the nature of my job. Everything your wife tells me is confidential."

"I'm her husband," he says, sounding aghast at the thought of something being kept from him.

"And?" I can't help the attitude that leaks out. He's been nothing but rude to me since I started here and now he's demanding I break confidentiality? It's insulting.

He sighs. "Can you at least tell me what goes on during a typical appointment?"

"You're welcome to book one with me and find out." I give him a sweet smile. He does not return it.

"It's not professional to be so–so sassy in the workplace," he sputters and I have to hold in a laugh.

"It's not professional to attempt to breach patient privacy." He opens his mouth. "No matter the relationship to said patient." He shuts it.

"Fine, I want an appointment."

My eyes widen so much I'm afraid they're going to jump out of my head. "*What*?"

"Put me on your calendar. I want to see what this nonsense is all about. Audrey has been raving about how amazing you are, but I don't believe it. I think you're pulling some sort of brainwashing voodoo on her and I won't have it."

This time my laugh slips out. "*Brainwashing voodoo*? That's a new one. People have said a lot about therapy, but I haven't been compared to a witch before." I say, reigning in my amusement. "All right, I'll book you an appointment, but you have to fill out the patient paperwork first like everyone else."

"Fine." He waves a hand in the air. "I'll go through the whole process, that way I can prove that you're manipulating your patients."

I shouldn't goad him, but since he said I'm manipulating ... "You're not worried you'll fall victim to my brainwashing?"

He scoffs. "I've got a mind like a steel trap." His phone starts to ring. "I need to take this, but I will see you soon." His words sound more like a threat than a goodbye.

"I'm looking forward to it," I reply then get up and leave his office.

My steps are more like trudging through a battlefield post-war than strutting down a runway now. I should be excited to have the Chief in my office, but I just know he's going to be antagonistic the entire time. Fighting with him will take up a lot of my energy and likely leave me drained. I'll have to try to book him in the afternoons so that I can leave for the day after his appointment.

I pull my keys out of my messenger bag and go to unlock my office door before realizing it's already open. A frown turns my lips down. I'm pretty sure I locked the door before I left. Maybe the cleaning staff came in. I'm still not sure of their schedule yet.

I walk in and immediately freeze. Sitting on top of my desk is a large vase of dahlias in a beautiful arrangement of fall colors. It might be cliche or cringy to love the flower I was named after, but I think they're beautiful and they really are my favorite. So seeing them here makes my heart warm.

I cross the room and pluck the card poking out of the top.

I hope these brighten your day the way you do mine.

Yours,

Not-Jake

I laugh at the reference to our first encounter all those years ago. Not only is this gesture unbelievably sweet, but he knew better than to sign it with his name or initials in case someone came in and saw the card. I'm sure he was careful about the delivery too—at least, I hope so.

I bend down and breathe in the scent of the sweet blooms before pulling my phone out. I have Levi's number from the email he sent about MJ's party. Before I send him a text though, I pause. Is it good to thank him? Shouldn't I be telling him to stop?

I open my camera app and snap a photo of the bouquet. I send the photo in a text to Isa.

Dahlia: Levi sent me these. What do I do?

Her response is immediate.

Isa: Those are gorgeous!!! Kiss him.

Dahlia: ISA, NO. We've been over this.

Isa: Okay, fine. You should at least thank him.

I sigh. I can manage a thank you. It would be rude not to thank him.

Isa: Maybe flirt with him a little.

Dahlia: ISABELLA MARIE TERRANCE.

Isa: Alright, alright, chill with the full name calling. I'll stop! For now.

Dahlia: Thank you.

Isa: Tell me what he says!!!

I shake my head and open up a text thread with Levi.

Dahlia: Thank you for the flowers. I think I'm going to change your name in my phone to Not-Jake. It has a nice ring to it.

I set my phone face down and slide it away from me as if it might detonate. Then I log onto my computer and open my email to start work for the day. I'm mid-email when my phone buzzes. I almost knock over the gorgeous vase diving for it.

Levi: You're welcome. And you can call me whatever you want, Doll.

I bite my lip as a blush heats my face.

Dahlia: Whatever I want, huh?

Levi: Name it and I'll be it.

The double meaning of his words isn't lost on me. Neither is the blatant flirting he's doing right now.

Dahlia: That's a lot of power, detective.

Levi: It's a good thing I trust you.

I spin my sea turtle ring, thinking of what to say next. It's bold of him to say he trusts me. He barely *knows* me. It must be just a line. I decide to test him.

Dahlia: What if I decided to name you Stranger?

I send the message playing on his 'name it' line. Bubbles pop up indicating he's typing, then disappear again. My heart races in anticipation. I haven't felt this on edge in years.

Levi: I'd pretend for you, because we both know we'll never be strangers. A stranger doesn't know you like I do.

My face grows hotter at his words. The layers of meaning in them have me blushing like a schoolgirl.

Dahlia: What makes you think you know me after all these years? What if I've changed?

Levi: I know you better than you think, but I'll never stop wanting to know more. Call me friend instead of stranger, let me get to know you better.

I glance at the flowers on my desk, then back at my phone. Maybe it wouldn't be so bad to be friends. I just have to keep up my boundaries better than I did at the party.

Dahlia: Okay, *friend*. You can ask me one question per day to get to know me.

Levi: What's your coffee order?

His question is immediate, making me smile. I'm glad he didn't try to argue or push me to give him more than this.

Dahlia: Since it's fall, a pumpkin spice latte. Or a chai latte with extra cinnamon on top. What's your favorite dessert?

Levi: Anything from my brother Maverick's bakery.

Dahlia: I'll have to try something from there sometime.

Levi: You'll be ruined for all other desserts.

I laugh at his exaggeration.

Levi: I've got to focus on work now. Have a great day, beautiful.

Dahlia: You too.

I sit back in my office chair with a happy sigh. Maybe all of this stressing about Levi was for nothing. We can be friends. I won't have to worry about losing my job and I'll have someone in the department on my side about things.

This will be good.

Right?

Text Messages

Tuesday

Levi: Good morning, Doll.

Dahlia: Good morning :)

Levi: Would you rather read a book or watch the movie adaptation?

Dahlia: Book!!! I'd rather read a book over watching a movie in general.

Levi: What's your favorite book?

Dahlia: Uh-uh. As tempting as that question is, you only get one per day. What's YOUR favorite book?

Levi: Will you hate me if I say I'm not a big reader? Reading case files and documents all day makes reading the last thing I want to do when I have time off.

Dahlia: I don't think I could ever hate you.

Dahlia: But I am offended on behalf of all the books in the world.

Wednesday

Dahlia: Thanks for my coffee, I'm going to need it today!

Levi: Anything to make you smile.

Dahlia: Are you going to ask me what my favorite book is?

Levi: How mad would you be if I asked you a different question?

...

Levi: Okay, okay, don't ghost me, I'll ask you. What's your favorite book?

Dahlia: It's impossible to choose!

Levi: You're kidding. I wasted my question on something you knew you couldn't answer? Cruel woman.

Dahlia: It really is impossible to choose, BUT if I had to, I'd say anything written by Sloane Rose. She's my favorite author.

Levi: Noted.

Thursday:

Levi: Good morning, beautiful.

Dahlia: It is morning, but the 'good' part is debatable.

Levi: Uh-oh. What happened?

Dahlia: You sure you want to use your question by asking?

Levi: I care about how you're doing more than the question I was going to ask.

Dahlia: Chief Wells booked an appointment with me for tomorrow morning. I'm not looking forward to being under investigation. He thinks I'm manipulating my patients.

Levi: I'm sorry, Doll. You'll prove him wrong though. I've heard from countless people in the department that you're amazing at what you do.

Dahlia: Thanks <3

Dahlia: Hey, Levi?

Levi: Yeah?

Dahlia: What question were you going to ask me?

Levi: Is your favorite color still all the colors because you can't choose?

Dahlia: Yes! I can't believe you remembered that.

Levi: How could I forget anything about you?

Chapter Thirteen

Dahlia Chamberlain

"This appointment is going to be a waste if you don't talk to me," I tell the Chief and he sniffs, shifting on the couch like it's covered in sandpaper rather than suede. Half of our one hour session is over, and we've gotten absolutely nowhere.

"Why should I talk to you about my personal life? You don't know me."

I meet his steely gaze. "That's exactly why you should tell me. I'm an unbiased third party." I pause. "Well, for the sake of transparency I have a touch of bias considering how ornery you've been."

He looks slightly abashed by my statement, but I could be mistaken. It's likely that I am, because I can't imagine anything I say could make him feel remorseful. Another minute passes, and then, *finally*, he speaks. "So Audrey comes in here and ... talks? That's it? She could do that with me." There's a touch of defensiveness in his tone and I hone in on that.

"Do you wish Audrey would talk to you instead of me?"

"I'm her husband, so it makes sense for her to talk about personal matters with me."

"Do you talk to her?"

He rubs the scruff on his chin, looking thoughtful. "We talk about our kids and grandkids, sometimes I talk about work, but I don't like to because I know it would worry her."

"You could talk to me about work." He gives me a look, but I just shrug. "You don't have to, but you can. Most people talk to therapists about things that are too difficult to bring up to their loved ones."

I glance at my watch, our time is almost up and this is the closest we've gotten to a real session. He spent the first part of the appointment interrogating me about my credentials, office set up, the books on my shelf, talking about anything and everything but himself.

"Our session is almost over," I tell him and set my notebook on the end table next to me. "But if you want, you can come back next week and try this for real."

He's silent for a moment and I'm glad I trained for situations like this. The quiet is uncomfortable, but I sit in it.

"I'll come back, but only so I can understand what Audrey is doing." He stands up in an abrupt manner. "I will book once I look at my schedule."

I smooth my expression so he doesn't see the shock on my face. "Sounds like a plan."

He nods and leaves the room without another word. I trudge around my desk and slump into my chair. I pull out my phone, wanting to share this moment with Levi. This whole week I've gotten to text him daily and talk to him in person almost daily too.

He's busy–as all detectives are–but he makes time to come and see me even if it's only for a minute.

Dahlia: I survived my meeting with the Chief. I deserve an award.

I don't share more than that for the sake of patient confidentiality. It's not like any of it would surprise Levi anyway, he works for the man.

Levi: I don't have any awards on hand, but we should celebrate! A bunch of detectives are going to a nearby pub tonight, you should come too.

I twist my ring while I think. It could be crossing a boundary to go out with them.

Dahlia: I don't know if that's the best idea...

Levi: You'll get in good with a lot of detectives, might make them warm up to you.

I sigh. He's right, but he's also clearly trying to coax me into coming. The problem is, after talking with him the past few days ... I'm less inclined to care. Levi has this pull to him that I can't seem to escape, at least not entirely.

Dahlia: Okay, I'll come. BUT you have to promise to behave.

I can't have him flirting around all of the other detectives. It could get us in trouble.

Levi: Don't worry about me, Doll.

Dahlia: That's not a promise!

Levi: See you at eight.

He sends me the directions to the pub and doesn't say another word. I should tell him I'm not going. But there's a part of me–a part that's been hidden under layers of grief the past three years–that wants to see what will happen when I show up. A little thrill goes through me as I wonder what he might do or say.

I can't afford to chase thrills anymore, but what harm could one night at a pub do?

"Where are you going?" Jasmine asks from the couch when I walk out of my room. "Are you going on a date?" she squeals and sits up.

"I'm going out with a group of detectives from work. What do you think?" I ask as I spin in a circle.

I haven't gone out in the past three years, so it took forever to find an outfit that felt right. I settled on a black, long-sleeve bodysuit with distressed high waisted jeans and black strappy heels. My taste is usually a lot more colorful, but you can't go wrong with black when you're going out at night.

"Where are you meeting them?" she asks, assessing me.

"A pub, it looks pretty relaxed in the photos."

"What purse are you bringing?"

"My red one."

"Good." She sounds relieved. "You needed a pop of color. I think you look hot."

I laugh and shake my head. "Thanks, but I don't know about *hot*."

"I wouldn't lie," she says and then smirks at me. "I bet the guy you're trying to impress will agree with me."

My mouth pops open in shock. "I'm not trying to impress a guy."

She gives me a look that says she doesn't believe me. "Whatever you say."

I choose to ignore her teasing. "I don't know how long I'll be gone, so if you need anything or run into any problems, Isa said you can go hang out with her."

"Okay, thanks."

I grab my red bag from the hook by the door and put my wallet and keys in it. Then I dab on some cherry lip stain. "I'm out of here," I call out. "Be good, I love you!"

"I love you too. Have fun, try to sneak a photo of the guy you have a crush on!" she yells back.

"There's no guy," I laugh and walk out the door.

But my entire drive to the bar I'm thinking of Levi. I can't focus on the playlist I chose to boost my confidence. All I can think of is what he'll do or say when I get there.

My stomach is in knots as I park by the brick building that is Killian's Pub. Based on the photos and the origin story on the website's homepage, this is a hotspot for Sandy Springs PD. It's meant to be a place where the department can relax and unwind after difficult days and weeks.

So I shouldn't be surprised when I walk in and there's a sea of detectives taking up the crowded bar. Between all of the talking and the live band in the corner, I can barely hear myself think. Suddenly, this feels like a very bad idea. I used to come to places like this with friends in college all the time. But lately a *wild night* has been going to get cookies at two in the morning with Jasmine, whispering and giggling like we were sneaking out from our parents' house.

Great. Now I'm thinking about my parents while trying to face a daunting situation. I am in desperate need of a familiar face. My eyes search the room for Levi, and I find him by the bar–he's staring right at me, locked in as if the world around him doesn't exist. His hazel eyes are dark, and he seems frozen in place amidst the surrounding raucous laughter.

I resist the urge to flee and walk over to him, feigning a confidence I don't feel. When I get to the group he's a part of, he pushes a few of the guys back and snags my hand, drawing me in. They don't seem to notice, merely resuming their conversation about the last Thrashers game.

It's much too loud for a private conversation in here, so Levi bends down to my ear.

"Are you trying to undo me, Doll?" he asks, his breath against my neck, making me shiver.

I blush and pull away, making a show of looking him over. He's wearing his usual work clothes, but he's unbuttoned the top three buttons of his dress shirt and rolled up the sleeves, exposing muscular forearms. The desire to trace the veins on his arms overcomes me and I spin my ring to resist it. Can you get drunk from just being around alcohol? Because these thoughts are far from sober.

I push up onto my tiptoes so my mouth is close to his ear. He tilts his head down, his strong jaw on display. If I turned my head ever so slightly, my lips would brush the stubble on his jawline.

"I should ask you the same question, Detective." One look at the man and I'm already flirting just as bad as he does. I need to rein it in.

He pulls back, running a hand across his jaw, wearing the kind of smile that feels like it's just for me. A dangerous glint sparks in his dark eyes and my stomach swoops. The music stops, the band announcing they're taking a short break. Conversations from those around us start to sound less like white noise and my pulse kicks up at the realization that it's not just me and Levi in this pub. I need to be more careful.

"What's your drink?" he asks, signaling the bartender.

I look at the people surrounding us. There are definitely more guys than girls here, all of them scattered about the pub in various groupings. But I do spot a few women, most tucked under the arm of a guy.

"Water." I have to keep my wits about me. I'm not even risking a sugar high from soda around this man.

He raises his eyebrows but asks the bartender for water anyway.

The bartender places a chilled bottle of water in front of me and I thank him. My feet are already starting to hurt standing in these death trap heels, and I have to shift my weight back and forth to find relief. Even in my wild days, I preferred flats over heels. Boots I can manage, but these things are *not* made for long term wear.

"Are your feet hurting?" Levi asks and before I can answer, strong hands grip my waist and lift me up onto a barstool.

I gasp and my eyes meet his. The way he's looking at me steals my breath and every thought from my brain. His hands stay on my waist, his touch like fire on my skin. My pulse flutters and the air around us feels thick with tension. His eyes dip to my lips as his tongue darts out to wet his own. An ache swells like the tide within me. I realize just how desperately I want to kiss him.

"Carter!" a man shouts and Levi's hands jerk away from my waist.

A hand claps down on his shoulder and I recognize the man beside him as Detective Colt. He's one of the few that's come in to see me, and when his eyes land on me, he smiles. I'm grateful for that reaction, because some patients tense up seeing their therapist outside of the office.

"What's up, Colt?" Levi asks, his voice a little strained. I look down at my lap, a blush heating my face. Did anyone see us? It's not like we kissed, but that was ... intense.

"Rhodes was telling me about an arrest y'all made a couple weeks ago, but I don't believe his story. He tends to call a minnow a bass."

I let out a laugh at his fishing analogy.

"I'll come over there in a minute, but if it's the convenience store arrest, he might not be exaggerating too much."

"All right man, I told him I'd buy his next beer if his story checked out, so hopefully he went overboard."

Levi chuckles at him and tells him once more he'll be over to their table soon. A moment later a finger brushes under my chin, tilting my head up. Colt is gone, but I know we're surrounded by others who might recognize me. If he keeps touching me, I might make a mistake that can't be undone.

"You okay, Doll?"

He frowns when I shake my head.

"You're dangerous, Levi Carter."

His concern morphs into a playful smirk. "A little danger can be a good thing."

I roll my eyes at him. "It's cute that you think you're only a little dangerous. Losing my job is no small thing."

"It's cute that you think I won't walk through fire for you. What we have? It's worth the work, worth the risk. It may take time, but I'll show you we can have it all."

His name gets yelled across the pub and he sighs. "I have to go before they come back over here. Don't leave without saying goodbye, please."

He looks like he wants to kiss me, but he settles for squeezing my hand before walking over to his friends. I'm left sitting dumbstruck by the bar.

How am I supposed to respond to *that*?

Chapter Fourteen

Levi Carter

Inviting Dahlia tonight might have been a bad idea. I can't focus on any conversation I'm in, because I'm constantly searching the pub for her. My plan was to stay glued to her side all night, but after I got pulled away it's been hard to get back to her without making it obvious that she's who I'm headed for.

Not that being around her is a good idea either. She's always irresistible, but tonight it's like she turned that dial up. Every time I looked at her cherry lips I wondered if the color would rub off on my skin if I kissed her. My imagination ran with that thought. I've gone through quite a few ice waters trying to cool down, to no avail.

Even now, as our eyes catch across the bar–something that's happened countless times tonight–my blood runs hot. She gives me a shy smile and turns her gaze back to the woman she's been talking to.

"Are you all right man? You've been out of it tonight," Rhodes says from beside me. I paste on an easygoing smile.

"I'm good, just a rough work week, you know how it is."

I force myself to tune in to the conversation. It's pure agony listening to them talk about sports and work when Dahlia is in the same room. All I want is to be next to her. I'd be home tonight if she wouldn't have said yes to coming.

The next time I allow myself to look for her, she's no longer with the woman, but she's not alone. My hand tightens on my glass as she smiles at a man in a golf polo. I've never had anything against golfers or their clothing choices until now. I don't recognize him from the unit, so he must be a civilian. He puts his hand over hers on the bar and I notice her expression tightens as she slides it away. I'm hit with a sudden bout of déjà vu, only this time instead of a mostly harmless old man flirting with her, it's a retired frat boy with a smile that makes my skin crawl.

"I'll be right back," I say and slip away. I've tried to keep my distance for Dahlia's sake tonight. I know she's worried about people getting suspicious. But I can't watch this jerk cross her personal boundary and do nothing.

I'm pushing through the crowd when I see her get up from the bar and rush out the back door. The guy gets up to go after her and I give up on not making a scene and become more forceful in going after her.

He's about to walk out the door when I grab him by the back of his collar.

"What the–" He whips around, jerking out of my grasp.

"You can head back to the bar," I tell him and he scrunches his face up in confusion.

"What? No, I'm going outside." He tries to push past me, but I shove him back.

"No, I think you're heading back to the bar. The woman you were bothering is a part of the Sandy Springs PD, so I suggest you change course before everyone in here finds out you hurt one of their own."

"I didn't hurt her! I was just getting to know her and then she ran off crying. I swear all I did was ask about her family, bro." He puts his hands up in surrender and takes a step back. "I wanted to ask what I did wrong, but you can go. This is too much drama for me anyway."

"Okay, well I'm her friend so I'll check on her."

"Whatever man, just don't shoot me."

I roll my eyes and turn around. What on earth gave him the impression I was going to *shoot* him? I don't even have a gun on me.

Brisk fall wind bites at my face when I open up the back door. I hear crying and find Dahlia sitting on the concrete, back to the wall, her head in her hands. The door falls shut behind me and her head snaps up.

"Levi," she says, her voice coated in relief.

"Hey, Doll, what's wrong?" I sit down and wrap an arm around her. "Did that guy say something to you?"

He seemed like he was telling the truth, but I'd believe Dahlia over him any day.

"No," she whispers, tucking her head into my chest. "He was nice, actually. I-I thought I could talk to him."

My stomach tightens, but I don't say a word. As much as I wish it, I have no claim to Dahlia. I can't get mad at her for liking someone else.

"I just wanted to feel normal again. Flirt with someone and just be a woman at a bar. I mean, he's no *you*, but still. He was cute enough."

I smile a little and kiss the top of her head. She tenses but leans into me. "So what happened? And what do you mean *feel normal* again?"

"I've been keeping a secret," she says and my brows furrow together.

"A secret?"

She clutches my dress shirt tight without realizing it. "My parents died three years ago." Her voice is weak and broken, pain lacing every word. "I took my little sister in after their death, and I feel like I'm not myself anymore. I'm not the girl you met, that's for sure. I don't go on adventures or dance on tables or talk to guys at bars. I-I feel so broken."

My head falls back against the wall as my heart hurts for her. I knew there was something more happening beneath the surface. "I hate that you had to go through that, Dahlia," I speak my thoughts aloud. "But you should know, I've been spending these weeks trying to be with *you*, not the version of you I knew five years ago. And you taught me that grief can change us. But it doesn't mean we're broken. You're beautiful and strong."

Her tears soak my shirt and she shivers under my arm. I need to get her someplace warm, but I don't want to interrupt her if she needs to process this some more.

"How can I be anything but broken? He asked me if I was close with my family and I felt like I couldn't breathe. I'm a *wreck*, Levi. All I have is my job and my sister."

"You have me," I say with conviction. "Even if you never want anything more than friendship with me, I meant what I said before. You name it, I'll be it. If you want a devoted boyfriend, I'm there. If you want a best friend, so be it. If you want a freaking doormat, I'll lay down right now so you can walk over me. All I want is to be near you, Doll."

I shift so that I'm facing her and cradle her face in my hands. Her cheeks are wet with tears and cold from the wind.

"I know the pain of losing a parent, but I can't imagine losing two. The fact that you're still standing is a miracle. You're not broken, you're healing. Just like I was when we found each other in Rosemary. You let me lean on you then, and I'm happy to return the favor now. But don't talk bad about yourself, because you're worth more than that."

I swipe away her tears as they fall.

"I don't deserve this kindness," she whispers.

"You deserve all of this and more, Doll."

"I don't know what to say," she whispers and I kiss her forehead.

"Then don't say a thing. Just let me take you home. You shouldn't drive like this. I can get one of my brothers to help me get your car back."

She nods in agreement, and I push to my feet before helping her up. I place my hand on her lower back and lead her to my truck. After helping her into it, I rush around the front of the truck to start it and turn on the heater.

We ride in silence after she gives me her address. Eventually she dozes off, staying asleep until we arrive at her apartment building and I park in the garage.

"Let me walk you to your door," I say and she shakes her head as she grabs her bag.

"I'm fine from here."

"Please, give me the peace of mind of walking you through this poorly lit garage. I won't walk inside, I just want to make sure you're safe."

She sighs, but there's a small smile on her lips. "Fine, you can walk me up."

While I'm always wanting more time with Dahlia, I really am concerned about her walking alone in this garage. The building seems nice enough, but there needs to be more lighting. I notice a camera in a corner up high, but that won't do anyone any good if the lighting is so terrible.

We make it to her door and she unlocks it, but pauses before opening it.

"Thank you, Levi." She reaches up and wraps her arms around my neck in a coconut-scented hug. When she pulls back, she pauses, staring into my eyes. Hers are rimmed in red, and there's so many emotions swimming in their blue depths I don't know which to address first. Desire is sparking there, and while it's all too tempting to taste the lips I've been dreaming of for so long, I step back and hold her hands instead. The first time we kiss again won't be like this. I don't want any reason for her to regret it.

"I'll always be here for you, Doll. Get some rest, okay? I'll bring your car back in the morning and all you'll have to do is come get the keys from me."

She squeezes my hands, tears in her eyes again. "I'll have to get you a thank you gift."

"All I want is you safe and sound." I pull her in a hug and kiss the crown of her head.

"See you in the morning."

She hands me her car keys and then walks into her apartment. I wait until I hear the lock click before heading back to my truck. This is not how I expected tonight to go, but maybe all of this will show Dahlia I'm in this for the long haul. Even if it doesn't change her mind about us, I wouldn't change a thing. I care for her too much to be selfish in thinking she owes me anything.

I sigh and press send on a message to my sibling group chat.

Levi: I need a favor. Can someone help me pick up a friend's car and bring it back to them? There was an emergency last night, so I took them home.

Replies come in almost immediately.

MJ: I'm sorry, we're at the stadium all day today! Sebastian said he can send a driver to come get you, though.

Grayson: Such a rich person thing to say, sis. Have you forgotten your roots already?

Adrian: Why are you texting before 7 AM on a Saturday?

Grayson: It's not like you haven't been awake for two hours already.

Adrian: That doesn't mean I want to talk to anyone this early.

I sigh and start to type out a message, but more start to come in before I can formulate a reply.

MJ: We were trying to be helpful! What's the point of having money if you can't use it to help family?

Maverick: I'm at the bakery, my staff got sick so I can't leave.

Grayson: I can help if you admit that the friend is Dahlia.

I'm tempted to take MJ's offer, but it feels frivolous if Grayson is offering to help for free.

Levi: The friend is Dahlia. I would appreciate it if y'all didn't make a big deal out of this though.

Adrian: I was going to say I could help, but Jules also wanted to know if it was Dahlia so we waited.

Awesome. Even my soon-to-be sister-in-law is nosey.

Levi: Tell Jules I said hello and that I don't appreciate her tactics. I thought she was the nice one out of all of us.

Grayson: I resent that statement. I'm clearly the nice one. And the funny one. And the pretty one.

Levi: Can you come or not?

Grayson: Tell me where to go and I'll be there.

I'm regretting my plan already as I text him where to go. I could have picked up Dahlia and dropped her off at her car, but I didn't want her to worry about it. There's a chance she's still feeling a little raw after everything, too. In which case it wouldn't be good for her to drive.

Not long after our conversation, we go and pick up her car. After a short drive, Grayson parks next to me in Dahlia's parking garage. I shoot her a text saying we're here and she sends one right back that she's heading down. I get out of my truck and stand beside Dahlia's peach Jeep. The vibrant color reminds me so much of her. Even knowing what she told me last night doesn't change how wild and wonderful she is.

"So, what happened last night?" Grayson asks as he leans against the Jeep next to me.

"She needed a ride home," I say, keeping it vague.

Grayson has a tendency to get information out of people with ease, so I've found over the years that it's best to disclose as little as possible. If only to slow down the inevitable.

"Interesting." He doesn't say anything more, which is concerning. A silent Grayson is a plotting Grayson.

Dahlia walks through the door that attaches her building to the parking garage. I have to grip the shreds of my willpower to keep from running in her direction to pull her into my arms. She looks delicate and beautiful in her soft pink pajama set. Her hair is tangled up on her head in some sort of bun, but even so, she looks better than any model or woman I've ever laid eyes on.

"Thank you both for bringing my car back," she says when she gets to us. "I'm sorry I'm such a mess, I just woke up not long ago."

"I guess that rules out inviting you to brunch," Grayson says, making me shoot him a look. "Unless you wanted to get ready real quick and come with us?"

"Oh," she says, a shy smile on her lips. She looks to me, and I don't have time to react–which was definitely the point of Grayson bringing it up so fast–so I just give her an encouraging smile.

"You should come. After last night, you deserve some pancakes," I tell her.

I'd rather it be just us, but maybe it won't be so bad having Grayson there. He's entertaining, to say the least.

"I'd say yes, but I told my sister that I'd get breakfast with her this morning and then go grocery shopping."

"Invite her along," Grayson says with a shrug. "Is she single?" He wags his eyebrows and Dahlia laughs.

"She's seventeen."

Grayson winces, making me laugh too. "Well, you can still bring her. Pancakes are for all ages."

"Okay, I'll ask her." She turns to me. "That is, if it's okay with you? I get the sense Grayson sprung this on you."

I chuckle and shake my head. "He did, but it's okay. I won't turn down more time with you."

Grayson makes a high-pitched *ooo* sound and Dahlia giggles again.

"Okay, I'll go ask Jasmine and text you if she says yes." She rushes across the lot after shooting me one more smile.

"Why are you the way that you are?" I ask Grayson, reaching out to hit him. He dodges my hit with a laugh.

"I just got you a breakfast date with the love of your life *and* you get to meet some of her family. You should be thanking me."

I roll my eyes. "You're ridiculous."

"I'm a genius and you'll be thanking me at your wedding one day."

While I don't think Grayson is a genius per se, I do hope that this wedding day he talks about exists. Even if I don't think I'll be thanking him on it.

Chapter Fifteen

Dahlia Chamberlain

"I knew there was a guy!" Jasmine shouts, pointing her hair straightener at me. "You owe me a latte."

"Why do I owe you coffee just because you think I have a boyfriend?" I ask her as I rifle through the bathroom drawer for a hair clip. My post-night-out hair is atrocious and the only way I'm going to make it remotely presentable is by wrangling it all into a giant claw clip.

"Because you lied, which means you have to pay penance."

I snort and start to twist my hair up. "One, I didn't lie. And two, if we lived by that rule you'd need to get a full time job to cover all the times you told me your homework was done so you could go out with your friends."

She gives me a sheepish smile in the mirror as she finishes straightening the last chunk of her hair. Her dark curls have been transformed into a sleek and shiny curtain. Only Jasmine could pull off both looks equally well.

"Fine," she acquiesces, "but I'm your sister, you should tell me about the men in your life."

"Because you tell me *so* much about the guys you like."

I keep a few strands of hair out of the claw clip to frame my face. I smile at my reflection. Between the claw clip and the concealer I dabbed under my eyes, no one would know I spent last night crying in a parking lot. No one but Levi, that is. My mind takes me back to that moment in his arms outside my door. I was sure he was going to kiss me. I would have let him. Now that the sun is up and my head is clear, I'm glad he didn't.

I have no idea how to feel about him, about us. He made it seem like he'd do anything for me, but I can't imagine why. I'm just a girl he knew once upon a time. Once the sparkle of our reunion fades, will he walk away? He saw a glimpse of my struggles last night, but what happens when they're revealed in their entirety?

"Earth to Dahlia," Jasmine says, waving around her mascara wand.

"Sorry, what did you say?" I ask as I crash back to reality.

"I *said* that I'd tell you about my crush if you tell me about Levi."

That's a deal I can't pass up. Jasmine and I are close, but she keeps her crushes to herself. It's one of those things that changed when I became her guardian.

"Levi and I knew each other a long time ago, before ..." I trail off and watch as her excited expression crumples.

"Before Mom and Dad," she whispers and I nod, drawing her in for a hug.

She takes a fortifying breath then pulls back. "No sad thoughts today. Keep going," she says and turns back to the mirror.

I consider asking her how she's doing, but I don't want to make her upset when she clearly just wants to drop it. If anyone understands holding emotions back until being ready to deal with them, it's me. Sometimes it's better to hold them in until you feel safe to let them out. You just have to do the letting out part before it builds up too much.

"He's a detective at the unit I work for, so we met when I was touring the station. But it's not a good idea for us to date because of my job. So we're *just friends*," I emphasize, but judging by the look on her face, she doesn't believe me.

"I'll be the judge of that," she says and spritzes setting spray on her face before skipping out of the bathroom.

"Hey, what about your crush?" I follow her to the living room.

"I don't have one right now," she says with a faux innocent grin.

"If there weren't people waiting on us I would dump water on your freshly-done hair."

"Thank goodness your boyfriend is downstairs then!"

I grab a pillow off the couch and throw it at her. She dodges it with a laugh.

"I'm *kidding*." She giggles. "Come on, you don't want to keep him waiting."

"Why do I have a feeling that I'm going to regret bringing you?"

"I don't know. I'm an angel," she says with a grin that implies the opposite.

What have I gotten myself into?

It turns out that having Jasmine and Grayson in the same room is a very bad idea. What is it about younger siblings that make them so torturously impish? They spent all of brunch teasing and asking crafted questions to see what kind of answers they could draw out of me and Levi. Now, we're getting coffee–the latte Jasmine claims I owe her–and Jasmine coyly suggested a trip to the neighboring bookstore.

She doesn't care for bookstores, but she knows it will delay us going home. I can't even deny her, because I saw a few books in Sloane's newsletter that I've wanted to see if our local store had.

"Dahlia loves books," Jasmine says as we walk through the door into the warm and cozy space. It smells like cinnamon and old books. If they sold candles that encapsulated this scent, I'd buy a dozen.

"I know," Levi says, "she told me about her favorite author, Sloane Rose."

I smile at him.

"You two should look in your favorite aisle," Jasmine says, pushing me in the direction of the romance section. I stumble a little and Levi grabs my arm to steady me. "Sorry!" Jasmine says. She doesn't sound apologetic in the least.

She mumbles something about the latest Vogue and runs off. Grayson is leaning against the checkout counter nearby, talking to a blushing clerk. How he already found someone to talk to–or rather, flirt with–is beyond me. Even in my wild child days I wasn't as extroverted as him. I bet everywhere he goes he attracts people and he always has time for everyone. No one gets left out.

"I guess it's just us," I say and Levi smiles.

"Looks like it. Is that okay?"

"Yeah, friends can look at books together." Isa and I look at romance books all the time, but I have a feeling that the experience is going to be a *little* different with Levi.

"Then lead the way, Doll." He gestures ahead of him, and I start down the contemporary romance aisle. I feel his eyes on me as I pick up a book and flip it over to read the back. Once I confirm it's what I want, I tuck it in my arms.

Levi holds out a hand. My brow furrows and I tilt my head to the side.

"Let me hold it for you."

"It's just one book," I say and wave him off.

He lifts a brow. "If you're as passionate as you seem about reading, it's not going to be one book for long. Let me carry them for you, it'll give me something to do."

"Fine, if you insist." I hand him the book.

Levi follows me down the different aisles, accepting each addition to the stack without any fanfare or complaints. I'm about to add a historical romance I saw one of my favorite bookstagrammers post about when I look back to see him reading one of the books I picked out. He looks like he stepped right out of a book lover's dream, holding a stack in one muscular arm while reading another with one hand.

"What are you doing?" I ask and he looks up from the page.

"Reading," he says and I roll my eyes.

"*Why* are you reading?" I snatch the book from him and glance down at the page he was on. My face heats when I note the passionate kissing scene.

"The cover intrigued me. I didn't know there was such a thing as romantic suspense. It features a detective." He smirks on the word *detective* and my face gets hotter. I was hoping he'd be nothing more than a shopping cart, ignorant to the books I was placing in his arms. But no, he had to go and read the one I snuck in there that involves a detective.

"Does it? I was unaware," I lie.

"You'd think all your training in body language would make you a better liar." He grins.

I gape at him.

"You are incorrigible," I say and his boyish grin widens.

"Funny, that's exactly what the woman says to the detective in that book right before she–" I smack his arm with the paperback and he laughs.

"No more commentary from you. Hold the books and don't open any of them."

"Only if you grab another copy of the detective one."

"What?" My eyes widen and I look down at the book in my hands.

"I want to know if they catch the guy they're hunting. Put a second copy on top, and I'll be good for the rest of the trip."

I narrow my eyes. "Somehow I don't believe you."

"You shouldn't," he says and I bite my lip, fighting a smile.

I grab another paperback off the shelf and put it on top. "I think I have plenty of books anyway, we can head to check out."

"Are you sure? I can carry more," he says as if he's not already carrying a hefty stack.

My eyes travel down the length of his arms, noting their strength and physique. "I'm sure." My voice comes out a little too breathy to be normal.

When I look up at him, he's smirking like he knows exactly what I was doing. I spin on my heel and walk toward the checkout counter to avoid his eyes. Grayson is nowhere to be found, so he must have moved on from flirting with the clerk.

Levi sets the books on the counter and the woman scans them dutifully, including the extra copy for Levi. He doesn't say a word, and while I don't mind paying for his book, it wasn't something I expected. This stack is already a good chunk of my paycheck.

When it comes time to pay, Levi reaches over me and taps his card on the screen to pay for all of it. I spin around, finding myself caged between him and the counter. The space between us is miniscule and I feel my mouth go dry. If he leaned just a little bit his entire body would be pressed against mine.

"You didn't need to do that," I tell him.

He shrugs. "I know. I wanted to."

He is beyond kissable right now. All I'd have to do is move a touch closer to him and–I mentally shake myself. *Get a grip, woman.*

"You paid for mine and Jasmine's brunch too. This is too much."

Too much like a boyfriend. A really good boyfriend, too. The kind you gush about to your best friends and write his last name next to your first in a notebook.

"Let me be the judge of what's too much."

I bite my lip. "Okay, I'll let you get away with it this time. But you can't keep doing things like this."

I spot Jasmine in my peripheral and slide away from Levi. I don't need anyone thinking we're together, especially her. It just feels so natural to be close to him.

"Do you know where Grayson is?" I ask her when she sidles up to the counter.

"Playing a game of chess with some old guy."

"I'm sorry, what?" I laugh.

"I was looking at the board games and saw him staring intently at the board, sitting across from a guy who looks like Dumbledore."

"I feel for the man, Grayson is a beast at chess," Levi says.

"Okay, I have to see this. Can you hold these books behind the counter?" I ask the clerk and she nods, looking amused at our interaction. "Thank you."

Jasmine leads the way to where Grayson is. When we turn the corner, he shoots up in his seat, arms raised high in victory.

"Check and mate, old man!" he shouts and the elderly man across from him grumbles, but I can see him stifling a smile.

"Bookstores are meant to be quiet places, Grayson," Levi says, turning Grayson's attention to us.

"A victory as hard won as this one cannot be celebrated in silence," Grayson replies before holding his hand out across the table. His opponent shakes his hand.

"Good game, son. It's not often that I'm beat, especially by a youngin."

"Thank you." He beams. "You were a worthy opponent."

I snort, incapable of keeping in my laughter at the way he's speaking.

"We need to get going," Levi says to him. "I've got to get back to work this afternoon."

My heart sinks at the thought of the day being over. Today made the events of last night fade from view, but going home alone will likely bring them back up to the surface. Plus, spending time with Levi has been fun. It's rare that I feel so free and comfortable these days. Isa is the only person that helps bring that side of me out.

We walk back to the counter to collect my books, all the while I'm trying not to overthink how it feels to be with Levi. When he rushes to open the door for me even while carrying my books, it becomes impossible. I spend the whole way home dreaming of what it would be like to say yes to a relationship with him.

Chapter Sixteen

Levi Carter

My plan of showing Dahlia I'm not going anywhere seems to be working. I've gotten to talk to her every day this week. Not just over text either. I've found a reason–and the time–to see her in person too. Getting to see her smile each day has made this week easier to bear. The case I'm working on has been doing a number on me.

It's easy to turn jaded and bitter as a detective. When surrounded by death all day long, it becomes almost mundane. But certain cases hit hard enough to wake you up, and this week we got one in that did just that. Maybe it's because of my niece Maddie, but whenever there's a little girl involved in a case it gets to me. And the victim of this case was twelve years old.

We're on the verge of finding our suspect. It's like I'm standing on the edge of a precipice. Every new lead, new piece of evidence, it adds to the rising tension in my chest. I haven't slept, barely eaten. And I've told no one what's going on. When I get around

Dahlia I put on my best mask. It's not too hard to keep it up during our short interactions over the past few days after the bookstore. I don't want her worrying about me, she already has enough going on dealing with the Chief and taking care of Jasmine. But there's also the niggling thought that if I told her, she'd try to get me in her office as a patient.

I wouldn't mind talking to her as a friend, but I don't want to be her patient–or anyone's patient for that matter. I can't risk getting taken off a case or moved to a 'less stressful' division, not when I'm about to solve this. So I'll just keep pushing. I can rest when we've got this monster behind bars.

"Carter," Captain Woodworth barks, making me look up from my crime scene notes. "Where are we at on the Elizabeth Peters case?"

"I've got an interview with a friend of the victim's family soon, and I'm still reviewing evidence."

"So we're no closer than yesterday?"

I sigh and shake my head, knowing if I try to explain how each step makes a difference, he won't listen. In his eyes, if there's no arrest, then there's no progress.

"The media is having a field day and my superiors are breathing down my neck because of it. We need an arrest, Carter."

I nod and tap the evidence photos on my desk. "I'm doing my best, Captain."

"Your best needs to be better." And with that *encouraging* statement, he leaves my desk and heads back to his office.

I close my eyes and rub my temples. Nothing is ever enough. I could solve every case that walks in these doors single handedly and they'd still want something more from me. If I didn't care so much about what I do, I think this place would have broken me a long time ago.

My phone buzzes on my desk, so I blink my dry eyes open and check it.

Doll: I survived another appointment with Chief Wells. Want to get lunch to celebrate?

I blink a few times, sure that my lack of sleep has me seeing things. When I determine I'm not imagining this message, my heart sinks. Of course the day that Dahlia invites me to lunch I'm too busy to even think about having a lunch at all.

Levi: Congrats! And I wish I could say yes, but I'm swamped.

Doll: I saw your case on the news, I'm sure you're busy. But you have to eat sometime, right?

One would think so, but no. My meals for the past few days have been protein bars and vending machine snacks. The only exception was when one of the detective's wives dropped off dinner for everyone. I just about teared up at the first bite of the lasagna she brought. It honestly could have been disgusting and I wouldn't have minded. The fact that it didn't come out of a machine made it the best thing I've had all week.

An actual meal and it being with Dahlia is too much to resist. I can make time.

Levi: I might be able to spare ten minutes.

Doll: Meet me in my Jeep at 12, I'll bring the food!

Levi: It's a date.

I lock my phone and turn back toward my notes. While having lunch with Dahlia feels like a win, I can't help but wish it was happening at a different time. It's exhausting to pretend that everything is okay. But maybe she won't even ask about the case and I can have ten minutes of reprieve from this darkness.

It's past one when I get out of an interview. The information they gave was slow coming, but valuable. Every time I looked at the clock, a rock of guilt dropped into my stomach. I should have just told Dahlia no to lunch. Now it looks like I bailed on her.

I trudge over to the alcove that houses the vending machines and get a bag of peanuts and an energy drink. My appetite is low right now anyway, so this should do just fine. When I arrive back at my desk I fall into my chair, almost missing the brown paper bag perched on the desk because of how dazed I am.

My brows furrow as I peek inside, noticing what looks to be a wrapped sub sandwich and a small purple sticky note with nothing but a heart on it. *Dahlia*. My chest warms at the thought of her dropping this off even after I missed our lunch date. I pull out my phone to text her.

Levi: Thank you. I'm sorry I missed lunch.

Doll: It's okay, I understand. If you want, we could talk when you get off.

I sigh and type out my response.

Levi: I have no idea when I'm going to get off tonight. It might be late.

Doll: Text me when you get off, I'll wait up and we can talk on the phone.

My lips stretch into a tired smile. A phone call with Dahlia, now that's something a guy can look forward to. The only thing better would be coming home to her. *Baby steps.*

Levi: Okay, will do. Thank you.

Doll: <3

I rake a hand through my hair, letting out an incredulous laugh.

"Is this it?" I mutter as I stare at the large whiteboard I've been scribbling evidence details on for the past hour. "This must be it."

I jog out of the conference room I was holed up in and out into the bullpen. There are still plenty of people here, even though it's past nine at night. I spot Rhodes pouring over photos at his desk.

"Rhodes, come look at this," I call out and he looks up from his desk with wild eyes.

We work together often on cases, and while I've taken over this one, he's been helping too. After our success on the strip mall shooting, I'm hopeful we can pair up and solve another one.

"Did you find something?" he asks and follows me back to the room.

"I think I've got a possible perp. We've been chasing down a person, but I had a thought: chase the gun." I point to the photo of the shell casings. "These belong to a 9mm Glock."

I grab the pile of interviews we've done of friends and family and flip through them.

"I asked each person I interviewed if they knew anyone, or if they themselves had this gun. Most of them answered no, except two people. The interview I did today of the family friend is one. She said she remembered her neighbor Julian Sanders–also the Peters' neighbor–talked about that kind of gun at a neighborhood block party a month ago."

"And the second?" Rhodes asks, studying my evidence board.

I flip through the papers, finding where I highlighted the other instance.

"Abigail, Elizabeth's younger sister, said that she saw Sanders shooting a gun at a target in his backyard not long ago while she was riding her bike." I hand him the interview transcript where I highlighted the words. "I didn't think anything of it at the time because she's so young and it's not uncommon to shoot guns in the South, but–"

He slowly nods, digesting the information. "Now that you have the other interview, there's a thread to pull."

"Exactly."

"This is the first true lead we've had, but you're going to need more than this for a warrant."

"I know. I'm going to look at pawn shops and gun stores in the surrounding area and see if there's any matches to Julian. And we need to interview the family again about Julian specifically, to see if there's any motive there."

"We could search in the woods behind the neighborhood again. If Julian was shooting back there, there's a chance that some shell casings didn't get picked up."

"That's a good idea. We can get some guys out there as soon as the sun is up."

"Okay, I'll handle that if you start on the pawn shops and interviews."

"Yeah, that sounds good."

Rhodes claps me on the shoulder. "Good work, Carter. You should probably go home and sleep. It's only going to get worse from here."

He walks out and leaves me alone in the room once more. Sleep sounds amazing, and I can't get anything more done today. I box up the evidence I was going through and get the conference room mostly cleaned up, then I grab my coat off my desk and head out.

The night air bites at my face, but I welcome the cold wind. It's waking me up for the drive home. I've had so much caffeine today it's a wonder I'm even tired, but I am beyond exhausted. So much so that I almost forgot about Dahlia offering to talk on the phone tonight.

I'm not sure that I'll be a great conversationalist, but I'm craving the sound of her voice too much to text her saying I'm too tired. So I speed home and text her that I arrived.

She calls while I'm changing out of my work clothes. I answer the phone and my muscles immediately relax at the sound of her voice.

"You weren't kidding about a late night," she says and I chuckle.

"I warned you. But it's barely ten. You used to be the one keeping me up."

"Vacation time is totally different," she says with a laugh. "It's not that late, but it is late to just now be getting home. Especially since I know you were up early this morning based on the time you texted me."

I crawl into bed, putting my phone on speaker and laying it beside me. In another life, the woman on the phone would be next to me.

"It's a long day, but worth it. We've got a lead."

"That's amazing! I feel so terrible for the family. I couldn't imagine losing my sister."

I squeeze my eyes shut, taking a deep breath before letting it out.

"Could we talk about something other than the case?" I ask, hating that I even have to. But if she keeps talking about the family I'm going to end up not sleeping because I'll feel guilty for sleeping while they're waiting on justice.

"Of course," she says in a low and sweet voice. "I should have known better. You probably want to decompress. Anything you want to talk about?"

"I don't have a preference, I just love the sound of your voice."

She gets quiet and it occurs to me I maybe shouldn't have said that. I've been trying to walk a line, but that line is looking real blurry now that I'm exhausted and emotionally drained.

"I'll tell you about the book I'm reading, then," she finally says. "That way I can show you how books are the superior form of escapism."

I smile and shut my eyes as she begins to talk about the plot of the book. She describes each character in detail, and even reads passages verbatim. The warmth of my bed and the lilt of her voice lulls me into a blissful sleep. And as I slip from consciousness, it's to the sound of her recounting the love confession of the main characters. I find myself dreaming it's us in the characters' place.

Chapter Seventeen

Dahlia Chamberlain

Chaos. My life–more specifically this morning–is pure chaos.

"Jasmine, we need to *go*," I yell across the house as I hop on one foot to put my shoe on the other.

After talking Friday night, Levi asked if we could again Saturday night ... then I called him Sunday night. It's been nice to have someone to talk to besides Isa and Jasmine. I haven't allowed myself many personal friendships because I was so focused on taking care of Jasmine and not succumbing to the grief that was threatening to consume me. Levi hasn't put any pressure on me, though he also hasn't stopped flirting with me.

So, in the midst of talking to him, I curled up and went to sleep. No big deal, except I forgot to set my alarm. I woke up to sunlight streaming through my bedroom window, which is not usually the case. I jumped out of bed–or rather I tried to, but my legs got tangled in the sheets and I tumbled to the floor. Now, I'm blessed with carpet burn on my arms. I guess that's better than breaking something, but it still hurts.

"I'm *coming*!" The lack of cheer in my sister's voice does not surprise me.

Jasmine did *not* like my abrupt wake up call. Our usual morning routine is rather peaceful. I play a happy playlist over her bedroom speaker to wake her up and we get ready for the day at a nice and easy pace. Not today though. Today we are more hurricanes than women, blowing through the house as we try to get ourselves together.

I rush to the mirror by our door and twist my hair up into a claw clip. There's no way I'm making it to work on time today. I have to drop Jasmine off at school and I just know the traffic is going to be terrible. I hope to save enough to buy a car for her, but until then I'm driving her around. She's offered to get a job plenty of times, but I want her to focus on school and applying for colleges.

"I'm ready, I just need to put on my shoes," Jasmine announces as she enters the living room.

"You have your laptop?" I ask her as I swipe some lipgloss on to give the illusion that I tried today.

"Yes."

"Cheer clothes?"

"Yes."

"Boombox?"

"Ye-what?"

I laugh and pick up my messenger bag. "Kidding. Trying to make you *smile*."

She rolls her eyes, but I can see her lips turning up at the edges. "I don't have time to smile and neither do you, since *someone* decided to sleep in today."

"It was an accident!" I defend myself as we step out the door and speed walk to the parking garage.

"An accident brought on by you staying up all night flirting with Levi," she teases and I whip my head over to look at her smirking face.

"What are you talking about?"

"I got up to get some water last night and heard you giggling like a middle schooler, so I pressed my ear against the door."

"Jasmine Lynn Chamberlain—"

"And I heard a deep manly voice. You forgot to set your alarm because you were up talking to your *boyfriend*."

I yank open my Jeep door and hop inside. "He's not my boyfriend."

"But you were talking to him last night?"

"Well..." I trail off as I start the car, she eyes me expectantly. "Yes, but that's only because he's had a hard few days on this case. Not because we're dating."

"Whatever you have to say to make yourself feel better."

"Shut up," I grumble and she laughs.

Thankfully, she leaves it alone for the rest of the drive to her school. I drop her off, then do my best to get to Sandy Springs PD on time without getting a ticket. It would be painfully ironic if I got a speeding ticket on my way to my job at the *police station*.

Hopefully, the rest of today goes smoother than this morning.

I hum softly as I write down my schedule on the paper calendar I keep on my desk. I have a digital system, but I like seeing everything laid out. Plus, I'm a sucker for colorful pens and this gives me the excuse to use them.

Since I got to work, my day has been relatively relaxed. My appointments have gone well, with the amount of patients that are on-staff being higher than ever, and the blend of lavender and eucalyptus diffusing in my office makes it smell like I'm at a spa.

My desk phone rings and I pick it up, tucking it between my shoulder and ear as I doodle a cute little turkey by Thanksgiving.

"Hello–" I'm cut off before I can go through my professional greeting.

"Dahlia?" a man's voice asks, frantic. He sounds familiar, but I can't place him.

"Yes, who's this?"

"It's Detective Rhodes. There's been an incident."

My pen drops from my fingertips. "What do you mean?"

"Carter and I were out making an arrest. We had to move quick, and SWAT hadn't arrived yet when we went in the house."

My stomach drops and my throat feels tight. I grip the phone and try to take deep breaths to stay calm. *Not another person. I can't lose someone else.*

"The suspect was armed. Levi tried to get the weapon and subdue him, but it went wrong. He–" Rhodes stops and takes an audible breath. "He's been shot."

"Okay," I say, trying with all my might to stay calm. If I panic I can't get details. "Where is he now? Where are you?"

"I'm in the lobby of the hospital. They rushed him here. I think he'll be okay, it hit his bicep. But there was a lot of blood."

Bile rushes up my throat and I worry I'll be sick.

"What hospital?" I choke out.

"Emory. I called our captain first and he said I should call you. We're on the fifth floor."

Captain? Why would he– *Oh*. I'm the department psychologist. I'm being called because it's my job to talk to detectives after traumatic incidents.

"Okay, I'll be there soon." I try to regain a professional tone, even though my mind is spinning. "Has anyone called his family?"

"The captain was handling that."

"Okay, good." I nod even though no one can see me. "Are you okay?" It's the first time I've thought to check on him, which isn't good. I need to get my head right.

"Not going to lie to you doc, I'm a little shaken up. But I'll be all right. Just want him to be okay."

"Me too," I whisper. "I have to go, I'm on my desk phone."

"Okay, see you soon."

We hang up and I grab my purse and jog out of my office and into the parking lot. Someone calls out after me in concern, but I ignore them. Seeing Levi–*alive*–is the only thing I care about right now.

The drive there is agony. Every red light feeds my panic. Tears pool in my eyes when I get stuck in a bout of construction traffic. But finally, *finally* I make it to the hospital.

I have to force myself not to run through the lobby. I can't afford to get stopped by security or a nurse. Once I'm up to the fifth floor though, I jog to Rhodes, who's pacing the hall.

"Any updates? Is his family here? Can I see him?" I blurt out my questions in quick succession.

Rhodes pushes a hand through his hair. "He's in surgery, the bullet damaged some of the muscles and nerves in his arm, but it didn't hit any major arteries." I let out a sigh of relief at his words. "His family is over there waiting on him, he should be ready for visitors in a couple of hours."

I look behind the group of detectives and spot several people I recognize from MJ's house party a while back. "Okay, thank you."

I make my way over to the family and Grayson's eyes find me first. He wraps me in a hug and somehow it triggers the floodgates to open.

"I'm so sorry," I say and sob into his shoulder, my mind flashing back to the phone call about my parents' death. To making funeral arrangements while I felt cold and numb. All of it piles on top of me and I can't get out from under it long enough to get myself together.

Grayson rubs my back and gently shushes me. My throat hurts and my chest aches by the time my crying subsides enough to pull away. I'm grateful for Grayson in this moment. I wish I would have had a brother to hug me while I cried three years ago.

"I'm sorry," I whisper and wipe under my eyes. I feel the heavy gazes of Levi's family on me. There's no hiding that I care for him now, I just have to hope that the people from the department don't notice and think something is amiss.

I glance back, relief washing over me when I see that they're all preoccupied.

"What are you sorry for? You didn't shoot him," Grayson teases, but his usually exuberant smile is dim and weak.

"I'm sorry for soaking your shoulder. I should be taking care of y'all."

"You're one of us," Grayson says in a low voice, giving me a meaningful look.

I take a step back, shake my head and draw in a deep breath. Then I force myself into a more professional mindset. I can't align with the family right now. I'm on the clock.

"Do any of you need anything?" I ask all of them, ignoring the curiosity splashed across their expressions.

"We're okay right now," MJ answers. "Just waiting on results."

I nod and twist my ring, trying to think of what else I should do or say. It's as if Levi getting hurt burned up all the protocol I learned. All I can think about is him lying helpless on a surgery table.

"Dahlia," Grayson says and I look up at him. "Sit with us. That's all we need right now."

I nod and let him lead me to a plastic hospital chair. Everyone remains silent while we wait. Each person is so on edge that every time a nurse or doctor comes near us, our heads snap to the door in unison.

I'm not sure how much time passes before we finally have answers. A doctor comes over but stops at the group of detectives standing nearby. Levi's captain walks over with a grim expression.

"He's out of surgery and doing well," the Captain announces. My shoulders collapse in relief. "We need to ask him some questions about the event that transpired before too much time has passed. Dr. Chamberlain" –he turns to me– "I think it would be beneficial if you were the one who did the interview."

I spring to my feet. "Yes, yes of course."

"He's still waking up from the drugs they used to put him under, but after that we'll have you go back."

"Okay, I'll be right here."

He nods and walks back over to the crowd he was with.

"I'll make sure he knows all of you are here," I say and they all look grateful.

"I'm glad you're here," MJ says and I give her a weak smile.

She's not looking at me like I'm a doctor or someone Levi works with. She's looking at me like I'm exactly what Grayson said earlier–family. And while nothing can scare me more today than Levi being hurt, that thought comes pretty close.

Chapter Eighteen

Levi Carter

"Use your call button if you need anything," my nurse says before leaving the room.

I lean my head back against the bed, closing my eyes against the harsh hospital lighting. The stench of disinfectant fills the air and I wish I was anywhere else right now. Hospitals always make me think of losing my mom.

At the sound of footsteps, I open my eyes. I'm met with a sight that soothes my aches and dulls my pain. *Dahlia*. She clutches a notebook to her chest as she walks toward me. Her oversized royal blue sweater brings out the color of her eyes, but also accentuates how puffy and red they are.

I hold out my good arm, palm up, and she places a soft hand in mine. Her eyes are glassy.

"I'm okay," I tell her and she shakes her head. "I am, they stitched me up. I'll be good as new in a few weeks."

"Your family is out in the waiting room, everyone except Maddie. They left her with Sebastian's mom in case things were really bad. We've been worried sick. They'll be happy to see you up and talking."

She sinks into a chair beside the bed, still holding my hand.

"How are you the first one I'm seeing?" I ask and she keeps her eyes on our joined hands. "Don't get me wrong, I'm glad you're here. But I would have expected one of my siblings, or my dad."

"I'm here on behalf of the department, I need to get your statement."

Her words shouldn't sting, but they do. I thought she was here for personal reasons.

"So you're here as Dr. Chamberlain."

She winces at the title. I'm too exhausted and overwhelmed by the medications I'm on to manage my tone.

"They called me because of my title, yes. But I've been crying my eyes out next to your family in the lobby because I care about you, Levi." She sighs and lets go of my hand, sitting back in her chair.

"I understand," I say and rake a hand through my hair. "I just wasn't expecting you to say that's why you were here."

I was hoping for something more along the lines of: *I begged your family to let me see you first because I'm in love with you.* But that's probably unrealistic.

"I'm sorry, but your captain asked me to get down your report of what happened. I thought if I was the one to do it, you might be a little more comfortable."

"Okay, let's go ahead and get it over with."

She nods and opens up the notebook before clicking her pen and looking at me.

I begin recounting what I can remember about the incident. She asks questions and writes things down. It's not easy going through all of the moments again, especially because of the mistakes that lead to my situation. Rhodes and I probably should have waited on SWAT, but we didn't think it was necessary to take on one guy. We figured they'd get in a minute or two after us. But a lot happened in those two minutes, which led to me getting a bullet in my arm.

"I'll go see if your family can come in now," Dahlia says once we're done.

"Wait," I say as she stands up. "I read the email introducing the new policies when you joined the department. I know there's new procedures around injuries like this. What does that mean for us?"

She gives me a look that confirms the rising fear within me. "It means that I'm your therapist now."

"And?"

"And I think we should talk about this later. You've been through a lot, and your family is waiting."

"I'm fine, I want to talk about it now," I say, but she shakes her head.

"I'm glad you're okay," she says with a soft smile. "I'll send them in."

She rushes out before I can formulate a counter argument as to why she should stay. It's not long before a wave of family members comes crashing into the room. With them comes a cascade of questions and concerns, but my mind is still stuck on Dahlia. What happens now that she's my therapist? Is all of our progress lost?

"I know you got shot this morning, but you look terrible," Grayson says when he comes in with takeout. He's staying the night tonight, even though I told all of my siblings I was fine by myself.

"Thanks."

I take the foil-wrapped burger from his hand. He knows better than to try and unwrap it for me. I might be hurt, but I'm not a child.

"I just meant that you look like there's something on your mind. I'm no therapist, but you can talk to me about it."

He plops down in a chair and starts unwrapping a giant cheeseburger. Grayson's always had the biggest appetite. I thought it would slow down as he got older, but nope. I think it's because he works out so much.

"My therapist is the problem," I grumble before taking a bite of my dinner. It's significantly better than hospital food, and for that much I'm grateful Grayson is here. Even if I hate being coddled.

"What did the doctor do? From the way she was crying on my shoulder this morning, I figured you two had tied the knot without telling anyone."

I give him a look, but he just shrugs and says, "I wouldn't put it past any of you to do that. MJ basically did with her destination wedding. I'm convinced the only reason Adrian and Juliette aren't married already is because she wants a fairytale wedding."

"We're not married, we're not even dating." I take a sip of my drink. "She's been hesitant to date because of her position in the department, and now that I'm required to be in therapy, she's going to close herself off completely."

"You won't be in therapy forever though, so just wait it out. You've waited five years, what's a few more weeks?" he asks before shoving a handful of fries in his mouth.

"I'm worried at the end of this she'll have distanced herself again. I don't think I can afford to wait it out, and there's a chance after this she'll see me as just a patient. But this therapy stuff is protocol now."

"You never know, it could bring you closer. Contrary to Dad's belief, talking about your feelings doesn't weaken your relationships, it strengthens them."

I think as I take another bite of my burger. Grayson has a good point, but I'm not sure if it works in this situation. If I told Dahlia what really goes on inside my head, I don't think it would bring us closer together. It would probably scare her to no end. I've been dealing with death on a daily basis for years now. Even if I haven't wanted to get help, it doesn't mean I'm not aware of the fact that this job takes a toll on my mind.

"We'll see, I guess."

"I'm telling you, she cares about you. It could be friendship, but I think it's a lot more. I wouldn't give up if I was you."

"Who said I was giving up?"

"You're sitting here looking like Eeyore with a rain cloud over your head."

"I got *shot* today, cut me some slack," I say with a laugh.

"It was just your arm, no big deal. Talk to me when you puncture a lung or hit a major artery."

"So you'll only feel sorry for me when I can't breathe or I'm bleeding out?"

He shrugs. "Only major things could make me shed a tear over you. Carters are too tough to be taken down by a bullet to the arm."

He says all of this as if I can't see how red his eyes are. I'm sure he shed a tear or two today. That alone makes me hate the mistakes I made. If I would have waited a little longer on SWAT, maybe my family wouldn't be so worried. They've already hinted at me going in a safer direction with my career. But somebody has to do this job. If everyone went for the safe career, there would be no one to risk their lives on behalf of others.

"We are pretty tough," I agree with him.

"On a real note." Grayson clears his throat, keeping his eyes on the food in his lap. "I'm glad you're all right. It was hard not knowing if you were going to be okay."

I know it's bad if Grayson is being serious. Guilt makes a bed in my heart right next to regret. "I'm sorry I worried y'all. I'll do my best to be safe in the future."

Grayson nods and looks up, opening his mouth like he's going to say something and then closing it again.

"Please don't ask me if I want to come and work with you and Adrian," I say and he quickly puts on a smile.

"I wasn't going to ask that."

"Oh, really?" I raise a brow. "Then what were you going to say?"

"I–"

He's cut off by the sound of my phone buzzing on the side table. Dahlia's name–or rather, her nickname–lights up my screen. I immediately grab it and answer.

"Hey, Doll."

Grayson stays grinning at me until I point at the door and mouth *leave*. He rolls his eyes but complies.

"Hey, I hope it's okay that I'm calling. I just wanted to check on you."

"Of course it's okay, I'm glad you did."

"I know we left things in a weird way earlier, but I do care about you and I want you to know that I want to stay friends throughout this process."

"Friends," I echo in a hollow tone.

"Yes. Normally I wouldn't even allow myself to be that much with a patient, but since we have a friendship already, I'll just be careful with the rest of my boundaries. For both our sakes."

"I don't know if I can do that."

"What do you mean?" Her voice gets small. "Did you not want to be friends at all anymore?"

"I want more than that, I think I've made that clear."

Her sigh speaks volumes. "Levi, I've told you I can't. This job is too important to me. My sister relies on me."

"I know there has to be a way around this, you just have to be willing to find it with me."

"I don't know that I can. My life is so different than it used to be." She sounds far away, as far away as she feels. "Why can't we just be friends?"

"You and I both know we've never been good at just friends, Doll."

Memories of our first kiss come flooding back. I wish I could go back to that moment and know what I do now. Maybe things would be different. Maybe Dahlia would feel differently than she does now.

"We're going to have to try to learn."

Words like that almost make me lose hope. *Almost.*

Flashback

Levi Carter

Summer, Five Years Ago

"I don't think we should kiss."

I choke on my smoothie, coughing and sputtering for a moment while Dahlia looks at me with wide eyes.

"*What*?" I wipe my face with a napkin. "Where is this thought coming from?"

"Last night at the bar, you looked like you wanted to kiss me."

Because I did. I most *definitely* did. Just like I want to right now, even though she's saying we shouldn't. Maybe even *more* now that she's said we shouldn't.

"And this led you to conclude that we shouldn't kiss?" I ask and she has the audacity to bite her lip.

"Quit it!" she scolds and I look up from her mouth.

"What?"

"Don't look at my mouth after I said we shouldn't kiss."

"Don't bite your lip after reminding me of a time I wanted to kiss you."

Her sun-kissed face deepens a shade. She swirls her straw around the foam cup containing her mango smoothie. She takes another sip now and I stifle a groan. It's not fair that everything she does makes me want her more. All she has to do is *exist* and I want to kiss her senseless.

"I think this would end up too messy if we kissed. I'm headed back home and so are you. So, no last names, no kisses, just friendship."

"Does the no kissing rule end the same day as the no last name one?" I ask, attempting to sound nonchalant. Her blue eyes dance in the early morning sun.

"Are you already looking for loopholes? Do you want to kiss me that bad?" She leans toward me, and because I love torturing myself, I mimic her movement so we're practically nose to nose, sitting under a palm tree.

"Why are you asking, is it because you want to kiss me just as bad?" I challenge and she smirks.

"I bet you try to kiss me before the day is up, that's how *bad* you want to," she teases, and I chuckle.

"Try within the hour, Doll." Her smirk falls away as her stunning coastal eyes dip down to my mouth.

"Friends don't kiss friends," she murmurs.

"I never said I wanted to be friends."

Chapter Nineteen

Dahlia Chamberlain

"Isa, don't look at me like that," I tell my best friend as I shovel another spoonful of apple pie in my mouth.

It's officially too cold outside for ice cream to be my comfort food, so pie was my choice when I stumbled into the grocery store late last night. I ate a slice of it then, but now that Isa is here to push me into talking, I'm eating more. All while fully aware that eating instead of addressing my emotions is not healthy. You don't even have to be a therapist to know that.

"You're eating pie straight out of the pan and the only man you've ever cared about enough to mention to me got shot yesterday. I'm entitled to a worried glance or two."

"Fine," I say around a mouthful of pie. "Look all you want, it won't change anything."

"Honey, you've got to talk about all of this sometime. You of all people should know not to hold things in."

"Hey." I point my fork at her. "Therapists are allowed to make bad choices too. I can hold in all my trauma and emotions if I want to."

"You *can*, but is that what you really want?"

I sigh and drop my fork into the lukewarm pie tin. "No, it's not."

"Then tell me what's going on, besides the fact that a terrifying event happened yesterday."

"Why do you think it's more than that?" I mumble, picking up my fork again to stab at my pie instead of meeting her gaze.

"Because you're acting like you just broke up with your boyfriend."

I scrunch up my nose at her words. She's—unfortunately—telling the truth. On some level it feels like Levi and I have broken up, even though we were never in a real relationship to begin with. Everything had been going so well recently. Now there's yet another roadblock.

"Levi is going to be my patient now."

"Which means?"

"I can't date a patient. Being friends is a bit of a gray area, but even then it's not very ethical. *Dating* my patient would get me in so much trouble. I could lose more than this job. I could lose my credibility altogether."

"Okay, so have Levi see someone else."

"What?" My forehead crinkles. "No, I'm the department therapist."

"So? He can see someone out of house. All he has to do is say he'd be more comfortable with a different therapist."

"He's one of the top detectives, Isa. If he doesn't want to see me, then that will give Chief Wells another mark against me. He's still set on proving my methods wrong. I just started this job. If someone as important as Levi goes somewhere else, it would ruin the progress I've made."

"Well, Levi could say that he can't see you because you're dating."

"No, absolutely not." I shake my head. "It makes me look unprofessional to have just started this job and to already be dating one of the detectives."

I stab at a piece of crust, poking at it until it crumbles into what resembles sand.

"I think that disclosing your relationship early on wouldn't make you look that bad, but that doesn't really matter right now."

I look up, meeting her knowing gaze.

"You, Dahlia Elizabeth Chamberlain, are scared."

"Of course I'm scared! I don't want to lose my job."

"Nope, you're scared of losing your heart."

"I—"

She cuts me off. "Sorry, facts aren't up for debate." I scowl at her. "You're scared, which is understandable. You've been through a lot. But if you don't take risks anymore, you're going to be lonely, D."

"I have Jaz, and you," I defend, and her eyes soften.

"You'll *always* have me, but I want you to have more than that. Even if it's not Levi, you haven't opened yourself up to anyone, not even other friends."

I look down at my pie—which resembles more of a gooey blob now. I know she's right. Isa was the only risk I took after my parents died. And I only did that because she basically didn't give me a choice. She saw Jasmine and I were hurting and did everything she could to wiggle her way into our little bubble. Now I feel like I can't live without her. Which is a real problem because, well, *people die*.

The smaller the list of the people I care about, the less hurt I'll be if something happens to them. Crying my eyes out about Levi yesterday just proves that point. There's just no way I can date a man who puts himself in harm's way on a regular basis. I need someone safe, like an accountant or a manager of a grocery store. Someone who's low risk both for my job and in general.

"I just don't know if I can take a risk on *him*, Isa." My voice cracks with emotion.

She reaches over and squeezes my hand. "You don't have to figure it all out right now."

I want to believe her, but I don't know if she's right. What if I take too long and then he moves on, leaving me heartbroken anyway? It's all too much to deal with.

Not for the first time in the past three years, I wish I could just curl up and have all my issues go away.

Silver glints in the sunlight streaming in through my office window as I twist my ring round and round. It's the only thing keeping my hands from shaking. I haven't spoken to Levi in over a week. I've spent each of those days pretending it doesn't bother me.

The first day he didn't call or text, I chalked it up to recovery. The next day, the same. I mean, the man had a *bullet* in him. That could make someone stay off their phone. But then Rhodes told me when he came in two days ago that he had talked to Levi *every day* to check on him. I spent the entirety of Rhodes' appointment forcing away thoughts of Levi. And then the days after it drafting messages to him before deleting them.

Was my request for friendship so reprehensible? He wasn't deterred by it before. I was just as clear about wanting a boundary as he was about wanting to burn said boundary. So it can't have surprised him all that much when I wanted to maintain my position.

I pinch my lips together as tears threaten to escape for the millionth time since Levi got hurt. Everything is so complicated. I already care for him far too much, but I can't risk any more than I already have. It doesn't make it hurt any less when another day goes by without hearing from him. I shouldn't be allowed to feel upset when this is what I want. But if humans had complete control of their feelings, my job wouldn't exist.

A knock sounds at the door and my heart leaps into my throat. Time for Levi's appointment. I snatch a tissue from the holder on my desk and dab under my eyes before throwing it into the trash.

"Come in," I say, proud of the way my voice doesn't waiver. I can do this. I can face him.

The door opens and Levi enters the room. I spin my ring faster as he sits down across from my desk without a word. His hazel eyes are rimmed in darkness, like he hasn't slept. One of his arms is in a sling, and when he adjusts in the chair, the bottom of his shirt sleeve rides up, exposing a sliver of black ink. The design almost looks like flower petals. I remember him telling me about sunflowers being his mom's favorite, maybe that's what it is.

"You have a tattoo," I blurt instead of greeting him like a normal person.

He stiffens a little, then glances at the exposed skin before tugging his sleeve back down. "I do."

I'm probably going to get a rash from how much I'm twisting my ring. We sit in silence before I can't take it anymore, bursting out of my seat and turning away from him. My hands press to my stomach as I watch brown leaves get blown about by the wind. I feel like a leaf myself, getting blown around by life. What I wouldn't give to be a tree, rooted deep without fear of the wind's strength.

"Dahlia." A shiver dances down my spine at the sound of my name on his lips.

It must be a good sign that he didn't call me Dr. Chamberlain. He didn't call me Doll, but that's okay.

"I'm sorry," I say on a shaky breath. "I just need a moment. You can sit on the couch if you prefer. It's probably more comfortable. I know couches are associated with stereotypes though, so some people prefer chairs. When I bought the furniture for the office I considered getting a daybed, but then I worried that people would find that too weird–"

My words stutter to a stop when Levi steps between me and the window. He lifts my chin up to meet his eyes, the swirling hazel depths capturing my attention and pausing my rambling.

"Take a breath," he murmurs and–as if under a spell–I draw in his smokey sweet scent. It's stronger than usual and when I notice his damp hair I'm worried I won't be able to hold myself up much longer. Resisting Levi is hard enough, but a *freshly-showered* Levi? If I survive I deserve a medal. If I don't, I still deserve one for making it as far as I have.

"We haven't talked since you got hurt," I say once my thoughts have gone from a boil to a simmer.

He closes his eyes for a moment as pain mars his expression. I want to comfort him, but fear keeps me rooted in place. "I thought you wanted space."

"I said I wanted to be friends, not strangers."

It's not fair, what you're doing isn't fair. The voice of truth in my head carves through me, hollowing me out. Is it so terrible of me to ask for friendship with a man who wants more? He said he'd be a doormat, being friends is definitely an upgrade from that. But that voice continues to pour guilt like salt in a wound.

"The last time you said you wanted to be friends, we kissed for the first time." His eyes dip to my mouth, making me warm all over. "You'll have to forgive me if the word *friend* confuses me when it comes to you."

My breath quickens as our eyes lock. Emerald and gold flecks sparkle in his irises, a mesmerizing combination of colors that never fails to captivate me. Quite suddenly, I'm overcome with a desire to kiss him. The feeling is so urgent, like getting caught up in a riptide. I almost give in to the craving, but the force of it shocks me so much that I take a step back, bumping into my desk behind me. The sting wakes me up and I move to the side to get around him.

"I'll make an effort to be more clear," I say, my voice coming out shaky. "But first I need to say that if it's harmful to be friends, I can be professional and keep more of a distance."

"I meant what I said outside of the pub. Name it, and I'll be it, Doll." He sighs and goes to sit on the couch. "You just have to tell me exactly what you want. And if it changes, tell me so I don't make any mistakes."

I sit in an oversized chair across from him, tucking my leg under me. "I want to be friends. I–" *Deep breaths, Dahlia.* "I don't have many friends."

His expression is soft and open. I'm worried I might cry again, so I turn my attention to my lap. "Okay, we can be friends. What does that mean to you?"

I pick at a hangnail as I consider his question. "We can talk on the phone, but we probably shouldn't stay up too late."

"You've never stayed up late talking to a friend?" he asks and I glance up at him.

"Are you going to find a loophole for everything I say?"

He shrugs, clearly trying to hold back a smile.

I laugh and shake my head at him.

"I've spent the last five years waiting on you, Doll." My heart skips at his words. "I'm not going to give up until it's really over."

"How do you know it isn't?" I ask him, hating how breathless I sound. He has an effect on me without even trying.

He shrugs one shoulder. "I just know."

"I feel like you're not telling me the whole truth."

"If I did, it might be over for real. But I'll play by your rules, beautiful. Keep 'em coming."

"We're supposed to be having your first appointment," I say with a pointed look.

"I'll be back next week for the real thing. You know you won't be able to focus if we don't iron this out."

"Okay, fine." I walk over to my desk and get my notebook and a pen. "Let's do this."

Chapter Twenty

Levi Carter

"Okay, rule number one: keep a foot of distance between each other at all times."

"Do I need to carry around a ruler?" I ask and she rolls her eyes.

"Whatever you *think* a foot looks like, add a little extra to be safe. Basically, no physical contact."

I bite the inside of my cheek to avoid showing the disappointment on my face. "None whatsoever?"

She just looks at me.

I hold my good arm up in a surrender pose. "Friends high-five each other, even hug sometimes. I just wanted to be sure you took that into account."

She rolls her eyes. "We can high-five, but definitely no hugging."

"Okay." I sigh. "I'll agree with that."

"These are *my* rules, Detective. They don't require your approval," she sasses, making me grin.

If she's being sassy, it means we're getting closer to our normal. And after the past few days, I *need* normal. Just getting to sit here messing with her is the best time I've had since I was in the hospital. The recovery has been harder than I expected. Not the physical side, though. Sure, it doesn't feel great to have my muscles shredded by a bullet and be stuck in a sling. But that's manageable when compared to reliving the moment each time I lay down at night.

I should probably be talking to Dahlia about all of this, but I just want to feel like myself again. And when I'm with her, I do.

"Just give me the next one," I say with a smile.

"Number two: no talking or texting after midnight."

My brows push together. "Why not?"

I was really enjoying falling asleep together on the phone the few nights we did. I think it might help alleviate some of my problems with sleep lately, too. But I'm not going to bring that up to Dahlia. I won't guilt her into doing something she doesn't want to do.

"Because nothing good happens after midnight."

I smirk at her implication. "Depends on your definition of good."

"If you weren't injured, I'd throw something at you," she says, but still smiles. My heart kicks up at the sight. She's the most beautiful woman I've ever laid eyes on. I could spend the rest of my life watching her smile and it would never get old.

"You have the prettiest smile," I tell her and she points her pen at me.

"Nope, no compliments. That's rule number three: no complimenting physical appearances."

That's going to make flirting with her a little more difficult, but I'm sure I can manage. There's so much more to Dahlia than her looks anyway.

"Okay, continue." I nod to her and she eyes me, probably expecting me to argue more. I know how to choose my battles though.

"Number four: no date-like activities without a third-party present."

"First of all, is this a real contract? Who says third-party in a casual conversation?" I laugh and she crosses her arms. "And second of all, what classifies as a *date-like activity*?"

"I'm using this wording to be clear. And a date-like activity is anything a couple would do."

"So we can't go to the movies, or get breakfast, or even go to the park because a couple does it?"

She hums, thinking it over. "We can't go to the movies by ourselves, it's too dark and intimate. We could get breakfast, but you can't pay for me. And we can go to the park but no picnics."

I frown. "Picnics are too romantic for friends to have?"

"For us, yes. You'd turn it into–" she cuts herself off, blushing. "It doesn't matter. No picnics. I reserve the right to veto any activity that seems too romantic."

I want to push her so she'll tell me what she thinks I'd do during a picnic that's bad enough to make her blush, but I refrain. I don't want her to make extra rules based on what I say.

"Okay. Anything else?"

"No, that's all."

"I'll do my best to abide by these rules."

Her phone buzzes on her desk. "See that you do," she says with a cute nod before she gets up out of her chair. She sets her notebook down and picks up her phone.

"I'd like to make a few requests."

"Hm?" She keeps her attention on her phone, paying me no mind.

I stand and walk toward her. "First, let's have the rules start when I leave the room."

"Sure." Her tone shows just how distracted she is.

I close the space between us, pressing against her back. What I wouldn't give to be able to wrap both my arms around her in this moment, but judging by the way she's frozen in place, this will have the desired effect regardless.

"Levi," she breathes out and heat pools deep within me. "What are you doing?"

"I have a rule of my own," I say, tracing a line down her arm with my fingertips.

She doesn't move or say another word. What I'm doing could be a huge mistake, but I think I know her well enough to see how close I can get to the fire without getting burned.

"If you break a rule, I get to break one," I say and she lets out a shaky breath.

"I won't break any rules." She huffs a laugh and says, "I made them."

"Then you won't have to worry about anything."

"Okay, I can agree to that."

"Good. Anything you want to do before the rules start?"

She turns around, and we're so close it hurts to hold back from her.

"Yes," she whispers and my breath gets caught in my lungs.

Before I can process her response, she tucks herself into my side, wrapping me up in a hug. Of all the things she could have done, her wanting to hug me hits my heart the hardest. I wrap an arm around her and kiss the crown of her head.

"I've been worried about you," she says into my shirt and I sigh.

"I'm okay, much better now that I've gotten to see you."

She pulls back, eyes shining with tears. I reach up to cup her cheek, but she moves away.

"You need to make another appointment." She sniffles, and then walks around her desk to her computer. "We didn't talk about anything that happened."

My stomach turns. That's the last thing I want to do, especially with Dahlia. But I can tell she needs to get back in her professional mode. It's where she feels safe.

"Put me down for next week. I'm on light duty anyway, so I don't have as much going on."

Her brunette waves fall into her face as she bends over to type on her computer.

"Oh," she says, straightening her back. "Next week is Thanksgiving. I forgot that I took the week off unless there's an emergency. I can come in for you, though."

"Don't worry about it, we can do the week after."

She nods and starts fidgeting with things on her desk. It dawns on me why she's even more uncomfortable now. She likely doesn't have any family to celebrate with except for Jasmine.

"Dahlia, do you have a place to go for Thanksgiving?"

She continues moving around trinkets and pens. "Jasmine and I have plans."

"That didn't answer my question."

She turns her tissue box 180 degrees, then turns it again. It's now the exact same as it was before. "We're going to have dinner at our apartment. My best friend Isa invited us to her parents' place, but Jasmine didn't love it the last time we went since we only really know Isa."

"Come to my dad's house."

She shakes her head. "No, Levi, I couldn't do that. It's too much. We're not dating."

"You just said Isa invited you to her family's, and you're friends with her," I point out. Her expression turns conflicted.

"Jasmine got along with me and Grayson the last time we hung out. And you've met the rest of my family already. It wouldn't be awkward."

She sighs. "I'll think about it and talk to Jasmine."

"Okay, good. Text me to let me know," I say before heading toward the door. Even while being on light duty, I've still got work I should get done. "But not after midnight, unless you want to break a rule," I say, making her crack a smile.

"Okay, I'll text you."

"Are you sure you don't want to change any of the rules? Or break one while you have the chance? Once I walk out they begin, you know. So if you want to steal a last minute kiss..."

"*Get out.*" She laughs and it lights up my soul. The sound of her laughter and the sight of her smile makes everything warm and bright. It chases away the dark clouds that have been hanging over me since the incident.

"See you later, Doll."

I walk out the door, but instead of feeling the weight of the rules we just put in place, I feel light and excited.

These rules may make things difficult, but I've always loved a challenge. And what better reward than winning Dahlia's heart?

Chapter Twenty-One

Dahlia Chamberlain

"Is this too much?" I ask Jasmine, standing in the bathroom doorway as she does her makeup. "Does it look like I'm trying too hard? Maybe I should just wear an oversized sweater and leggings. These pants are a lot."

I take a step back, but Jasmine snags my arm.

"You're being ridiculous. You look gorgeous. And those pants are perfect and very you. If you wore leggings and a sweater I'd be disappointed."

I look down at my white-and-brown tartan print pants. They are *really* cute. Especially with the chocolate-brown sweater vest and white turtleneck undershirt. It feels like the kind of outfit I'd take a million photos in and post on Instagram with a caption that would make Jasmine cringe like *thankful, grateful, blessed* or *oh my gourd I love this outfit.*

"You're wearing leggings and a sweater," I point out as she turns her attention back to her plum lip liner.

She's sporting an oversized cream sweater, brown leggings, and her platform Ugg slippers. Somehow she makes what's essentially loungewear look chic.

"Because this fits my aesthetic. But it isn't yours, so you're not allowed to change who you are because you're worried about your boyfriend's family judging you."

"First of all, he's not my boyfriend. And second of all, since when did you become the older sister who gives advice?"

"Since you decided to start overthinking everything when it comes to Levi?" she spouts off sassily and I'm tempted to bump into her while she's applying her lipstick. "You'd wear the pants if we were going to Isa's."

She's got a point. After I decided to take Levi up on his offer, I started spiraling. I used to make sweet potato souffle every year, but I wondered if I should make something fancier. And then I thought maybe I shouldn't make anything at all and just bring drinks or ice so that I didn't have to worry about people liking my dish. Jasmine and Isa have been tag-teaming calming me down.

"Okay, I'll keep the pants. But no more talk about Levi in a romantic way. We're just friends. I don't need you telling his family something different."

"I won't have to," she says in a low voice, but I still hear her.

"I'm going take a candid photo of you eating and tag you in it so everyone will see if you keep it up," I warn her and her eyes get big in the mirror.

"My lips are sealed!"

"Good. Now hurry up, I don't want to be late."

Grayson's smile is as wide as an alligator's when he opens the front door to greet us.

"My two favorite sisters!" he cheers and I laugh.

"Shouldn't your actual sister be your favorite?"

"Yes, but she's at the bottom of the pyramid this week because she hid Maverick's pecan bars from me."

"She hid them because you would have eaten them all." Levi's voice makes my stomach flip-flop.

When he appears next to Grayson, I'm not prepared for how handsome he looks. I almost drop the souffle I'm carrying. His scruff is back in full force and the green shirt he's wearing brings out the color in his eyes. Even with the sling, he looks like he stepped right out of one of my romance novels. A scenario of him getting hurt and me being the one to take care of him flashes through my mind, making me blush. Thankfully I'm wearing makeup, so hopefully the only blush he sees is the powder one I swept onto my cheeks this morning.

"C'mon Jasmine, I'll introduce you to my niece Maddie. She's younger than you, but I think you'd still get along." Grayson winks at me as he guides Jasmine inside.

"Does he ever stop scheming?" I ask and Levi chuckles.

"Only when he's asleep, and even then I'm convinced he's still concocting master plans."

I smile and shake my head.

"I really wish you'd break a rule right about now."

My forehead scrunches in confusion. "What? Why?"

"Because not complimenting you right now is killing me."

Once again adding makeup to my gratitude list. It's embarrassing how warm my face is even in the late November weather.

"That's almost a compliment," I tell him as we walk inside.

"But it wasn't one, so I haven't broken any rules."

"Why do I get the feeling that you're going to bend a lot of rules today?"

"Because you're a very intelligent woman," he says with a wink.

"That's a compliment!" I point at him accusingly but he shakes his head.

"The rules say no *physical* compliments. So I can talk about your beautiful mind and sexy wit all I want."

I bite the inside of my cheek to keep from smiling as we walk into the living room. The room is full, and I recognize most everyone from the hospital lobby. There's a couple with an adorable toddler that I don't recognize, but they're the only ones I can't name. It's comforting to know most everyone here. At Isa's, I only knew her and Marcus. She tried to introduce me to everyone, but it felt forced, like we were puzzle pieces that didn't fit.

We only went to Isa's the first Thanksgiving after our parents died. In the years after, we'd make a small but special dinner together and then watch *How the Grinch Stole Christmas* because that's what we did growing up, taking silly photos in our Christmas pajamas. It never made seeing everyone else's family photos on social media any easier, but it felt like a new tradition for the two of us. Something to hold on to when the holidays felt empty.

"Where should I put this?" I ask Levi instead of acknowledging his cheeky comment.

"The kitchen, it's over here." He shows me to a beautiful kitchen. It's not as large as MJ's, but it's still lovely in its own right. The counters are butcherblock and the cabinets are white. There's an array of food on the counters and cooking on the stove. Everything is warm and bright.

"Dahlia, it's nice to see you again," MJ says as I walk in the kitchen. "Here, I'll take that. Have you had a chance to talk to Juliette?" She takes the dish from my hands and tips her head toward a petite blonde woman in the most gorgeous cream sweater dress I've ever seen. I remember seeing her a few times, and each time she looks like a Pinterest model.

"You're Adrian's fiancée right?" I ask and she beams.

"Yes, that's me. I still can't believe we're getting married next year." She sighs, placing a hand with a beautiful diamond ring on her chest.

"None of us can." Levi chuckles, making her dreamy expression fall away. "It's a mystery how you two work."

"We complement each other," she says. "Like MJ and Sebastian."

"Naming another couple that doesn't make sense doesn't prove your case," he says, but I can tell by his smile he's teasing her.

"Oh go watch football and leave us girls alone. You're ruining my engagement bliss." Juliette shoos him out of the kitchen. He winks at me on his way out.

"I think you and Adrian are so sweet together," I tell Juliette once Levi is gone. "Same for you and Sebastian, MJ. I mean, the way you look at each other ... it's the stuff people write romance novels about."

MJ wears a reserved smile as she arranges vegetables on a serving tray. Juliette resumes her dreamy expression while stirring something on the stove.

"I think you have what we have too," MJ says and my eyes widen.

"Oh no I don't think so," I say in a rush while MJ gives me a knowing look.

"My brother is infatuated with you. And I saw you when he got hurt. I don't know what's going on between you two, but it's not nothing."

Before I can respond, a flurry of blonde curls and pep rushes into the room. I recognize her as Maddie, MJ's daughter. She's got on a rust-colored turtleneck with tan corduroy bellbottoms. If I saw her on the cover of a magazine, I wouldn't even question it. When did thirteen-year-olds start dressing so ... chic?

"Mom, what time–" Maddie cuts off, her eyes widening when she sees me. "Ohmygoodness your outfit is *amazing*!" She squeals and grabs my hands. "Can I take your photo?"

"Maddie sweetheart, personal space," MJ chides, but doesn't lose her smile.

In my short time interacting with MJ, it seems like she's rather reserved and can be blunt, but when it comes to Maddie and Sebastian? She's soft for them.

Maddie gives me a shy smile and drops my hands. "Sorry, you just look so pretty."

My heart melts at her words. "You're too sweet. I'm no model, but I'm happy to pose for photos."

"Yay!" she cheers, then turns to MJ. "I was coming to ask what time dinner will be ready because I wanted to take photos outside."

"You have time for a few photos. I'll come get you whenever it's time to come inside."

"Thanks Mom," she says and hugs her. I can see the glow of love on MJ's face.

A stab of jealousy hits my heart as I watch them embrace. When Sebastian enters the kitchen, the pain increases. His easygoing smile widens when he sees MJ and Maddie.

"My favorite girls." He wraps his large arms around both of them. "Can't believe you were leaving me out of a hug." He squeezes them tight, lifting them up off the ground a little.

Maddie squeals and MJ laughs and my heart cracks. Oh how I wish I had something like that. The love between them is practically palpable. Juliette regards them with a quiet kind of happiness where you can tell she's imagining Adrian and her in the future. But I don't have anyone to imagine in their place. Not anyone I *should* be imagining, anyway.

"I should check on Jasmine," I say and take a step back. "Let me know when you want to take those photos," I tell Maddie and she nods, still wrapped up in her little cocoon of happiness.

I can feel the observant eyes of the adults in the room on me as I leave. Who knows what they think of me, but I just can't stand there watching them have exactly what I want any longer.

I find Jasmine in the living room, sitting on the floor across from Grayson. In between them is a coffee table with a chess board on it.

"Now this is a knight, and it moves in an L shape," Grayson says, holding up one of the pieces. Jasmine nods, her brow furrowed as she listens to him.

I watch him explain different pieces to her and find myself overcome by it. Grayson doesn't know us, none of these people do. And yet here they are, taking us in on a holiday like it's no big deal. And they aren't just making space for us at the table, but they're going out of their way to make us feel included.

If I was with Levi, would this be our life? I cross my arms, hugging my midsection. A vision of us here for every holiday flashes in my mind. Except I'd be wrapped up in Levi's arms the way MJ was in Sebastian's. A deep ache flares within me and I hate myself for even allowing my imagination to go there.

"Hey, Doll," Levi says as he comes in from outside. Behind him I see a few of the guys playing cornhole. "You okay?"

"Yeah." I smile, willing my tears not to fall. The last thing I want is to draw attention to myself by crying over a game of chess. "I was just checking on Jaz."

"I'm turning her into a prodigy," Grayson says from the floor and I laugh, the tightness in my chest beginning to dissipate.

Jasmine groans. "I think I'm forgetting everything as you're saying it."

"She doesn't sound like a prodigy," I tease.

"I'm not one," Jasmine states plain as day and I snort.

"Not with that attitude you're not. Now, focus up, I'll make a challenger out of you yet." Grayson points to the board.

Jasmine sighs but listens to him. The kid can't even watch a movie without checking her phone a hundred times, but here she is playing chess instead of being glued to TikTok, all because of Grayson.

"I think he could convince someone to bungee jump without a cord," I say in awe and Levi laughs.

"I've only known one person who could convince me to do something like that," he says, voice laced with meaning.

"We had a cord," I say and he smiles.

"I'd have jumped without one as long as I still got to hold you that close."

I press my lips together and shake my head. Thinking of being pressed up against Levi is the last thing I need right now. Unfortunately, the image can't be shaken from my mind's eyes once he brings it up. I can feel the rush of the air as we jumped, hear our screams dissolve into laughter. And I swear I can still taste the kiss we shared at the end of it all. When I meet Levi's gaze, I'm convinced we're thinking of the same thing.

"Are you ready for your close up?" Maddie suddenly appears in front of me, making me jump.

"Yes," I quickly say. "Let's go outside."

New plan:

Stay as far from Levi as possible.

Chapter Twenty-Two

Levi Carter

This is one of the best Thanksgivings I've ever had, probably the best since my mom died. Dahlia and Jasmine fit into our wild family like they've been here for years. They tease and laugh like we do, and there wasn't a single lull in conversation at the dinner table.

Now we're around the firepit for some s'mores, the perfect end to a perfect evening. The only thing that could make it better is if Dahlia broke all of the rules we set in place last week. Watching her now, smiling and laughing in the glow of the firelight, I'm wishing we could be one of the couples cuddled up together.

"Uncle Levi!" Maddie skips up to me, curls bouncing around her face.

She's spent a lot of time with Dahlia today, and it means a lot seeing them get along. Maddie became the center of the Carter family as soon as we got to meet her, so if someone came in and didn't embrace that it wouldn't go over well.

"What's up, Mad Dog?" I ask and ruffle her curls.

She swats my hand away, giving me a look that showcases her disapproval. And even though she doesn't have any Carter blood in her, the look she shares is the spitting image of MJ's glare.

"If you knew how long I spent on my curly hair routine you wouldn't do that," she says, making me laugh.

"My sincerest apologies," I reply, earning myself an eyeroll to pair with her glare. "What did you come over here to ask me? Or did you come over here because you wanted to spend time with your favorite uncle?"

Maverick chuckles from his chair next to me. "If anyone is her favorite, it's Grayson," he says.

I turn to Maddie, but she just shrugs.

"Grayson is everyone's favorite," I say.

One look across the fire proves my point. He's currently playing with Drew and Kayla's son, making the little toddler laugh and laugh. Drew is Maverick's closest friend and has been since childhood. They occasionally spend their family events here because Drew's family situation is tense, and Kayla's family lives far away.

"*Anyway*, I came to tell you that I was talking to Jasmine and she said that her and Dahlia usually watch *How the Grinch Stole Christmas* on Thanksgiving night," Maddie says.

"So?" I ask and she blesses me with another eyeroll.

"*So* we should watch it here. It will mean a lot to both of them and then Dahlia will fall in love with you."

I shake my head at her words. "Maddie, you shouldn't meddle in adult relationships."

"It worked for Mom and Dad," she points out. "You can't tell me it's not a good idea."

Maddie meddled in MJ and Sebastian's relationship when they first met, tricking MJ into going to where Sebastian was coaching. It obviously worked out in the end, and it seems as though Maddie wants to try her hand at matchmaking again.

"Go ask Gramps if we can stay longer to watch the movie," I say, because I'm terrible at telling her no and ... her idea is pretty great.

Maddie runs over to my dad, who's nursing a glass of whiskey while sitting in silence by the fire. He's not the most talkative man, but he loves Maddie the same as all of us, if not more. He'd do anything she asked, which is why she gives me a thumbs up from a few feet away, indicating that he approved of the idea.

"You must be really desperate if you're letting a thirteen-year-old help you," Mav says and I sigh, sitting down in my chair. The warmth of the fire bathes my face.

Dahlia is talking with Juliette on a picnic blanket, her hands are waving around as she tells a story I can't hear, one that results in both of them laughing. Adrian looks away from his conversation with Sebastian to smile down at them from the chair he's in. Juliette, as if she could sense his attention, tilts her head back to look at him. Adrian bends down to kiss her, and I turn my attention back to Maverick in an effort to not watch my brother kiss his fiancée.

"I'm not desperate, but it was a nice idea."

Maverick chuckles. "The way you've followed her around all day shows how desperate you are. How are things going?"

"It's not going bad, just ... slow."

Maverick nods, then takes a drink from a travel mug filled with hot cocoa. I don't know how MJ manages to make dairy-free hot cocoa with no refined sugar taste *good*, but she does. I guess after living with her restrictions for so long, she found the right recipes.

"Sometimes slow is good. Better than rushing and making a mistake."

"Speaking of rushing, how is Evie?"

He tenses at my question, and I direct my attention to Evie's brother Drew and his family. They've been a part of our family since we were all kids, but Maverick is definitely closest with them. When Evie eloped last month, Maverick didn't seem too happy about it.

"She's pregnant," Maverick grits out and my eyes widen in shock.

"That was fast."

"Yeah, Drew found out yesterday. Over text."

I frown. "That doesn't sound like Evie."

"I don't think it is her. I called her the day after her elopement to congratulate her and she didn't answer. So I texted her. I haven't heard back from her once. It's been a *month*, Levi."

"She could have seen your text at a bad time and then forgot to respond. I know she's got a busy job."

"Does that sound like Evie to you?"

I raise my eyebrows at what he's insinuating.

"What are you saying?"

"I'm saying I think her *husband*" –he chokes the word out– "is a controlling jerk who is keeping her from her friends and family."

"She's married now, Mav. She might not be texting guy friends one-on-one because of that. So, besides not answering you, what makes you think that of her husband?"

It's no small thing to accuse someone of that level of manipulation.

"She used to call Drew once a week, but now she barely talks to him."

"You know Drew has always been overprotective of her. Maybe she's just busy or wants to feel like her own person."

Maverick shakes his head, running a hand over his short beard. "Something isn't right here. I've got a gut feeling."

"Well, let me know if that gut feeling turns into more concrete evidence. I love Evie too; I'll go up to New York to get her and make sure the guy regrets his choices."

"Thanks, hopefully I'm wrong."

"Hopefully," I agree.

Maddie waves me over to where she's standing by the back door. I pat Maverick on the shoulder on my way back to the house. My left arm is starting to ache in the sling. If we weren't going to do something special for Dahlia, I'd probably be heading home now to take some pain meds and try to sleep. But her happiness is worth the pain.

"I got the movie set up," she whispers to me. "I'll distract Dahlia by getting her to do a TikTok with me. You get everyone inside."

"What about Jasmine?" I ask.

"She knows about the plan."

"Okay, I'll take care of it. Thanks, Mad Dog."

She grins up at me. "Being flower girl at your wedding will be thanks enough."

I shake my head, laughing at her. "You're hanging out with Grayson too much."

She just shrugs with a faux innocent expression before going over to Dahlia and getting her to face away from the house for a video.

While she's distracted, I go around and explain what we're doing to everyone. They all seem happy to participate, and even Adrian gives a small smile when I tell him and Juliette.

We all get inside, gathering up the leftover desserts to put on the coffee table in case anyone wants them. I set a Sprite on the table because I remember seeing Dahlia drink it a few times.

"Hey, Levi," Jasmine says, making me look up from the table.

"Hey Jaz, are you excited for the movie?" I ask and she smiles.

"Yeah, I wanted to say thank you."

"Oh, this was Maddie's idea, I'm just helping with the execution," I explain, but she shakes her head.

"I meant everything you've done for my sister. The bookstore and talking to her at night and inviting us here. She probably won't admit it, but this is the best she's been in a long time. I haven't seen her happy like this since our parents died."

Her words sink into my heart and fill it with warmth. "I'm glad she's happy. That's all I want for her. And you're *both* welcome at our family events anytime."

"Thank you," she says and hugs me.

The back door opens, so Jasmine pulls away and rushes to take a seat on the pallet MJ set up on the floor. Dahlia's expression is confused when she walks in behind Maddie, until her eyes land on the TV with the movie title on it.

She stops in her tracks, covering her mouth with one hand. Her eyes shine with tears and my throat feels tight with emotion watching her reaction.

"Surprise!" Maddie exclaims, splaying her hands toward everyone. "Jasmine said this was your tradition, so we thought we could join you this year."

"Oh wow," Dahlia says, her voice barely audible. "This is–"

I cut her off. "Don't say too much. It's just a movie, you deserve even more than that."

If they didn't before, everyone in my family knows how I feel now.

Dahlia gives me a watery smile, laughing a little. "Okay, I won't say it. But this is really sweet of y'all, thank you."

She hugs Maddie as I take a seat on the couch. There's a spot next to me open, but there's plenty of space on the pallet and my dad went to bed early so his recliner is available too. So when Dahlia comes around to choose a spot, it surprises me in the best way when she sits down next to me.

Her leg presses against mine and I grin before leaning down to whisper in her ear.

"You're breaking a rule, Doll."

"There's nowhere else to sit," she lies, dabbing under her eyes with her shirt sleeve to dry her tears. "Now, be quiet so I can hear the movie."

I chuckle before slinging my arm over her and drawing her into my side. "Whatever you say, Doll."

Chapter Twenty-Three

Dahlia Chamberlain

I take a sip of my pumpkin spice latte, relishing in the warmth emanating from the paper cup. Levi had this and a slice of pumpkin bread sent to my office this morning. When I told him he shouldn't do that, he said it wasn't against the rules and that friends can buy friends coffee. His logic was sound, and I can't turn down a pumpkin spice latte, so I'm enjoying it before my first client, Audrey, comes in.

While the department is absent of fall decorations and isn't the coziest place, I've been able to make my office quite autumnal. Cinnamon and vanilla essential oils diffuse on a shelf nearby, my throw pillows are in shades of rust and brown. I've even got a few faux pumpkins scattered throughout the room. To top it off, my office window showcases a beautiful tree that has been changing colors and raining leaves since the day I moved in.

I'm gazing out that window now, enjoying this quiet moment before the day begins and basking in the glow of last week. Thanksgiving filled my emotional cup in a way I didn't know I needed. I've been in survival mode for so long I forgot what it was like to thrive. It's funny how often I tell clients to take care of themselves, slow down, take each moment as it comes, and yet I've barely done any of that. Last week was the first time in a long time I felt completely relaxed and at peace.

The emotions surrounding a holiday without my parents were actually bearable. Usually, I end up crying myself to sleep because I felt like I failed Jasmine as her guardian. But with the help of everyone there, I felt like she had the best holiday she could have without our parents alive.

My only dilemma was the hope steadily climbing within me that this won't be our first *and* last holiday happy. I know Levi wants it to be the first of many, but my heart is still teetering in that area. I can't just hope that his feelings fade over time or that he meets someone else. What if I'm only hurting him by insisting on friendship when he wants more? What if he meets someone and she doesn't like our relationship? Then, Jasmine and I are out on the street without a family again unless Levi chooses us over her.

It's all so complicated, and the client I'm seeing in a moment is a reminder of that. Chief Wells' wife Audrey has been doing incredible. Her progress is amazing and she's said how much better she's felt since coming to see me. If I started dating Levi and it became an issue, the Chief would have reason to fire me. Then all the people I've been helping would have to find someone else. I know how hard it was for each of them to reach out in the first place. If I get fired, they may not open up to another counselor again for a long time, or ever.

A knock sounds at the door, forcing me to turn to face it and hop off that train of thought. I need to focus on work. There's too much at stake for me not to.

"Come in," I say and the door opens.

Audrey walks in ... with Chief Wells right behind her. My eyebrows pop up and I attempt to school my expression before it becomes noticeable.

"Good morning, Dahlia," Audrey says with a gentle smile. I usually insist on my clients calling me by my first name.

"Good morning, Audrey. I see you brought a guest today." I nod to her husband. "Chief Wells." He nods back.

"Yes, I was speaking with Charles about our sessions and felt like it would be beneficial if we had a couples session. I know that I'm springing this on you though, he just had time this morning so I thought I could bring him and see."

I've spoken with Audrey in the past about the benefits of couples therapy, but I thought we were a long way off from the Chief agreeing to one.

"We can do that today," I say. "I think it would be a great idea."

"Of course you do," the Chief grumbles.

"Charles, you said you would give this a try. That means being cordial."

He sighs. "I'm sorry, I will make an effort. All of this mushy junk isn't what I'm used to."

I laugh a little at his words and gesture for them to sit on the couch. When they do, the Chief immediately grabs Audrey's hand

and squeezes it. She smiles at him and it warms my heart. No matter his gruff exterior, it's clear he cares for his wife.

"It's okay, I understand your reservations, Chief Wells. Therapy is a foreign concept to many people and it can seem scary at first."

"Call me Charles," he says. "And I'm not scared, I just don't understand the point of it all."

I've tried to explain the point over our last two sessions together, but maybe with Audrey here it will sink in better.

"It's good to get out our emotions in a healthy way, and after that discuss ways to cope with those day to day. In couples therapy, I also tend to talk about ways to reconcile after arguments and understand how to walk through difficult times as a team instead of enemies."

He nods in understanding, but doesn't say anything more.

"So, Audrey" –I turn and face her– "what made you want to bring Charles in today?"

"I think we need to learn better communication skills," she answers.

Charles straightens up at this, giving her an incredulous look. "We communicate. You've told me since we were dating that I'm a great listener."

"You *listen* just fine, but you don't *talk* very much at all."

He frowns, gesturing a hand to me. "And you brought me here to change me into someone else? I say what needs to be said and that's it."

"What I'm hearing," I interject, "is that Audrey wants to have a healthy balance of communication in your marriage. She doesn't want to change you, just to grow together."

Audrey nods emphatically and Charles sits back once more, brow furrowed in contemplation.

"Okay, that makes sense."

I release a breath, happy he's settled down. Working with an antagonistic client is much more difficult than a willing one. Maybe we'll make some progress after all. And maybe, just maybe, he won't hate me as much after this.

Levi: What are you doing for lunch?

My stomach growls as I read the message.

Dahlia: Haven't had time to think about plans, but I'm starving.

Levi: Want to eat lunch in my truck? I can pick up food for us.

I smile at his offer, but it falls when I remember the rules I set.

Dahlia: You can't pay for me, especially after you got me coffee today. I'll place a mobile order and you can pick it up.

Levi: Fine, but let the record show I'm not happy about this rule of yours.

Dahlia: You can pay for me if you invite Grayson to sit with us.

I laugh when his reply comes in.

Levi: NOPE. I'm good. Being in an enclosed space with that much energy might result in an injury.

Dahlia: Like you hitting him?

Levi: Yes, exactly. You get me, Doll.

We iron out the details of where to order from and times to meet, I put in my mobile order, then I get back to responding to emails and updating my calendar with appointments. I put down Charles and Audrey for next week with a smile. Couples therapy seemed to go well. Charles managed to be not so antagonistic and I sent them home with an exercise that would help them learn how to communicate more and better. I'm hoping next week will bring good reports and progress from both of them.

As I'm writing down appointments in December, I notice the doodle of a birthday present I drew over my birthdate. Each birthday since my parents died has felt strange. My mom would always call and sing happy birthday off-key while my dad laughed in the background. So, missing that makes the day feel emptier. But Isa and Jasmine both try to make it special for me even without that.

I turn my focus back to writing down appointments so that I don't get too sad. Maybe my birthday will feel more like Thanksgiving did. Bittersweet, but the sweet part outweighs the bitter instead of the other way around. Unfortunately, comparing those days makes me think of Levi and wonder what he would do to celebrate my birthday. He doesn't know it's coming up, but if he did I'm sure he'd try to make it special.

My phone buzzes on my desk, breaking my reverie.

Levi: I'm parked outside when you're ready.

Dahlia: On my way!

I lock my computer, then slide on my heeled booties that I took off earlier to be more comfortable at my desk. After adjusting my bellbottom jeans so that they hang properly over my boots, I grab my phone and head out through the lobby into the parking lot.

Levi's truck is parked around the side of the building, likely so he can be discreet. Most people park in the front parking lot, or in the back if their offices are on that side. I open his passenger door and climb in, the smell of warm, delicious philly cheesesteaks filling my senses.

"I did not realize how hungry I was until you texted me. Thanks for picking it up."

He smiles and passes over a bag with my sandwich in it. "Of course. I figured I needed to eat too, and being on light duty gives me more time to actually do that."

I give him a sympathetic smile, noticing how he's unrolling his sandwich wrapper with one hand. Or rather, attempting to.

"Let me help," I say and reach over to get it situated for him.

"I was figuring it out," he defends and I shake my head.

"You don't have to do everything yourself."

"Have you said that in front of a mirror lately?"

I set his sandwich on the console and give him a look. "I let people help me all the time."

"Wow, you manage to look beautiful even when you're lying," he says, making it sound like he's in awe.

I throw a napkin at him and he laughs. I don't. "I let you pick up lunch, that's something."

"Sure, we'll pretend that you texted to ask for my help instead of the truth, which is that you were going to work through lunch until I texted."

I roll my eyes at him and take a bite of my sandwich.

"You can't talk about working through lunch. I know for a fact when you get on a big case that you barely eat," I say after I finish chewing.

"I didn't say I was good at it, just that you should be." He grins and I shake my head.

"How is light duty going, by the way? You haven't made your next appointment."

He takes a bite of his sandwich and shrugs one shoulder. "It's fine, like normal work just no field time. And I'm sorry about the appointment, I just haven't had time between work and my other doctors' appointments."

"Don't worry about it," I say with a smile. "Just make one as soon as you can. I have to be the one to sign off on you going back full time."

He nods in acknowledgement while eating. "I will. Now, can we talk about something other than work? Like maybe ..." he trails off, a wicked grin taking over his face. "That detective book?"

His question surprises me. I know he got the book, but I didn't think he'd actually read it.

"I haven't read it yet, so I can't exactly talk about it."

Lies. All lies. It was the first one I read from the stack Levi bought for me and I loved it so much I read it for a second time. I might also be waiting for my library app to send me the audiobook version of it.

"I've already told you that you're a terrible liar, Doll." He smirks and heat creeps up my neck. "You loved it, didn't you?"

"Fine, it was amazing and I can't wait for the next one about the guy's partner!" I blurt out and he laughs.

"Same here. The partner reminds me–"

"Of Rhodes," I say at the same time as him.

"And a little bit of Grayson," he adds, to which I nod in agreement.

"I hope he gets paired with a no-nonsense girl who will make him work for her attention."

"That would make for a fun read," he agrees.

We spend the rest of my lunch break talking about different scenes in the book, and thankfully Levi only teases about the kiss scenes one time. It feels like the perfect start to the week, and something I'd love to do every day.

I need to make a decision about Levi soon, or else one or both of us is going to get really hurt.

Chapter Twenty-Four

Levi Carter

Another sleepless night, another morning spent guzzling caffeine and prying my eyes open. It's probably not good to drink energy drinks with the medication the doctor has me on, but the medication makes me tired and when I sleep I have nightmares. Sometimes they're reliving the moment I got shot, sometimes they're reliving other moments in my career where I had a brush with death–there's no shortage for my subconscious to choose from.

Logically I know I can't avoid sleep forever, but I've found that if I exhaust my body enough it quiets my mind. I just have to find the perfect balance of postponing sleep and giving in. I tried not taking the medication, but then it felt like my arm was being ripped off, so I'm back to fighting exhaustion with drinks that taste like sour candy.

I walk out my front door to head to physical therapy–energy drink in tow–and run straight into Grayson. A groan falls from my lips as the pain of hitting my arm against his torso radiates through me.

"Are you okay?" Grayson asks, and instead of answering I use my good arm to shove him backward.

"What is wrong with you? Why are you on my porch?" I grind out and he rubs the back of his neck.

"I'm sorry, I was about to knock when you came through the door."

I sigh, my anger dissolving with the pain. "It's fine, what are you doing here?"

I've been avoiding my family this past week, because I know they'll see through me. They're too observant not to. The longer I spend around them, the greater the risk that I make them worry. And the last thing I need is more guilt about what happened the day I got shot.

"I came to check on you. All you've sent in the group chat is one-word messages."

"I'm fine, just busy and resting from my injury. I'm headed to physical therapy right now," I say, hoping that will get him off my case.

Grayson and Adrian own their security company, so Grayson can make his own hours and spend all day here if he wants to.

"Want me to drive you?" he asks.

"Nah, I'm fine. I just need to go before I'm late."

He studies me and I pull from all my energy reserves to look normal.

"You look tired," he finally says.

I walk around him and head toward my truck, setting my drink on the hood before opening the car door. I'm hoping that I'll be able to get out of my sling soon. Doing everything one handed is getting on my nerves. It adds to the pity factor, too. Which is why when Grayson grabs my drink for me I snatch it from his hands.

"I can do things for myself," I snap.

Grayson holds his hands up in surrender. "No one said you couldn't."

I set the drink in the cup holder then turn back to Grayson. "I'm really fine, I didn't get much sleep last night, but that's no big deal."

Lying to my brother isn't good, but neither is carrying the weight of him wishing I would quit my high-stress job as if he didn't work in a stressful career for his whole adult life until recently.

"Okay, if you say so."

"I do. Now, I need to go to my appointment."

"All right, let me know if you need anything."

He steps back from the truck and I get in. I back out of the driveway, looking behind me, glad for an excuse to not look at Grayson. I know he's probably watching me with worry lining his features. I just don't want to see it.

A soft bell rings as I walk into The Secret Door. The scent of cinnamon and coffee greets me upon entering. It's darker in here, the lights a warm yellow that should make everything look dingy, but instead gives the shelves a touch of character.

I head toward the romance section, on a mission to find Sloane Rose's latest series. Dahlia's birthday is coming up–I know because Jasmine informed me at Thanksgiving–and I wanted to read her favorite books and annotate them as a present. I saw the idea while scrolling through TikTok late last night when I couldn't sleep, and I immediately knew she would love it.

So, since I have a limited amount of time, I need to get started right away. Hopefully they're as intriguing as the detective book I read, because if not I'm in danger of falling asleep while reading.

I'm trying to get the books into a stack I can carry with one arm, when I hear my name. I turn around to find a woman I don't recognize, with a baby in a sling across her chest.

"Yes?" I ask cautiously.

Sometimes the families of victims remember me when I don't remember them. It's one of the more uncomfortable parts about being a detective. I deal with so many cases, it can be hard to remember every single one.

"I'm Isabella, Dahlia's friend. I recognized you from a photo."

I wonder where she saw the photo? I know I have photos of me on social media, so that's one possibility. But another is that Dahlia showed her photos of me...

"Oh, uh, it's nice to meet you. Dahlia has said a lot about you."

"She's said a lot about you too," she replies with a mysterious smile.

I nod slowly and she looks to the stack I was forming on top of the bookshelf. Her eyebrows raise. "Are you a big Sloane Rose fan?"

"Oh, no." I chuckle. "These are for Dahlia. I'm going to annotate them as a birthday gift to her."

As soon as I say the words, I worry that I made a mistake. Don't best friends tell each other everything? I wanted this to be a surprise for Dahlia. Isa's eyes are wide, as is her smile.

"But please don't tell her," I add. "It's a surprise."

"My lips are sealed! She's going to love it," she gushes.

The baby in her arms stirs at the outburst, so she starts to sway back and forth.

"Good, I'm glad my instincts were right."

"I wish she'd just get over her issues already." She sighs. "I keep trying to tell her that she should take the risk, but I think she's still scared after what happened to her parents. Everyone dies at some point though, she shouldn't hold it against you that you're in a line of work where it happens more often."

My brow furrows. I thought Dahlia's reservations had to do with *her* job, not mine.

"What are you talking about? Is my job what's keeping Dahlia from taking a chance on me?"

Isabella looks as though she regrets her words. "Oh, I need to go! Fletcher here needs to be fed or else he's going to start screaming soon. I'll see you around."

She hurries off before I can say another word. I'd follow her if I wasn't a grown man. I'm sure I'd get more than a few looks for chasing down a woman with a baby in her arms.

I heave out a sigh, then grab the stack of books and lug them over to the checkout counter. The woman gives me an odd look as I'm checking out, and I'm not sure if it's because of how tired I must look or because she's one of those women who thinks men don't read romance books.

Isabella's words are bouncing around my skull, beating down my strength. It's not like I wanted to tell Dahlia about everything I've been going through, but now I know I can't. If she hears everything that's happened to me, it'll push her further away. Our relationship is in a precarious state as is.

As the cold air whips against my face on the way to my truck, I wonder if I should still try to be with Dahlia if she's so afraid of my career choice. Are we doomed to a terrible life together because I'm a detective? You'd think she'd be more understanding since she's the department therapist, but maybe hearing all of the stories she does has made her more fearful instead of less. Maybe it would be better for her for me to bow out and let her find a guy who loves her and is safer.

But then I remember the look on her face when she saw *How the Grinch Stole Christmas* on my dad's TV screen. She was so happy and she fit right in with my family. They all loved her and Jasmine, and the feeling seemed to be returned. I don't want to lose her, but even more than that I don't want her to lose that family time. Her needs will always come before my own.

I climb into my truck, feeling resolute in my decision to keep pursuing her. I'll avoid her appointments until I can get myself together, then she'll see what's true–it's just a job, like every other one. I might be struggling right now, but that's just because of the medication. I'm sure once I'm out of my sling and back to normal that the nightmares will leave and I'll be able to take care of her the way she needs. If I just stay steady and a constant in her life, she'll choose me in time.

As I drive home with heavy eyes and limbs, I hope that I can manage to put up a front long enough for me to recover for real.

Flashback

Dahlia Chamberlain

Fall, Three Years Ago

My parents are dead. My parents are dead and the only person who understands my pain is my sister, who needs me to be strong for her, to take care of her. She's asleep in her room after our awkward Thanksgiving dinner at Isa's and a movie night just us. We watched *How the Grinch Stole Christmas* together and I made jokes so maybe we wouldn't cry. I think I managed to make her smile twice. She used to smile all the time.

Every day I wake up and it's like finding out it happened all over again. It's the cruelest kind of torture. At night I lay awake crying, like I am now, because everything I thought my life was going to be is suddenly different. I didn't get the chance to prepare myself. One day they were laughing on FaceTime, telling me how they're going to take the boat without Jasmine, a date to keep the romance alive.

The next I'm flying to Florida to pick up my little sister because there was an accident and now they're gone.

Now there's no more holidays spent sneaking food from the kitchen, no more FaceTime dates every Sunday detailing what went on that week, no dad to walk me down the aisle, no mom to button up my wedding dress. I'm going to spend the rest of my life without my parents.

It's a pain that knows no bounds. Grief doesn't care that I have to take care of my sister now. In fact, it just reminds me that Jasmine looks just like my mom. Some mornings I see her sitting on the couch and for a moment I feel as though I stepped off the last stair but expected there to be another. My stomach jumps to my throat and I have to count backwards from a hundred to keep from spiraling.

I place a hand tight over my mouth to conceal my sobs. Jasmine doesn't need to hear me crying, it will only make things harder on her. Tears stream down my face until my eyes are swollen and I'm too tired to cry anymore.

When I close my eyes I hear the words of the woman who called to tell me my parents died, see my sister sobbing at the cemetery. I clutch the blankets tight and force a happy memory into my brain. My mind conjures up Levi. His strong arms around me, the warmth of his kiss, the heartfelt words he shared under a canopy of stars.

Somehow I know he'd understand. He lost his mom, he'd know my pain. It's been over two years since I've seen his face, but I wish he was with me. I wish I could go back in time and be braver. Then maybe I wouldn't be so alone now.

I fall asleep while thinking of him, hopeful that a day will come where I can feel safe to love someone again. And maybe that some-one will be him, if I'm lucky.

Chapter Twenty-Five

Dahlia Chamberlain

"Hey stranger, it's been a while," I say to Levi, who's standing outside my apartment door.

We haven't seen each other since our lunch Monday, and it's Friday now. He's been more absent than usual lately, and most of our interactions have been over the phone–either texting or calling. Every time I've tried to make an appointment for him or even just make plans as friends, he's claimed to be busy. It's rather unusual for him, but I know he has a lot going on with work and physical therapy. I wouldn't put it past the department to be giving him more work than he should have.

"It has been a while. Did you miss me?" He winks and I roll my eyes.

"Come in, Jaz is in the living room waiting."

Jasmine is taking a communications class and was given an assignment to interview someone local about their career. She chose Levi, and he agreed to make time for the interview tonight. Based on the sly looks Jasmine has had, I think she chose Levi just so I'd have to invite him over. But I can't prove it, so here he is, taking up my tiny apartment with his gorgeous, muscular frame.

"Something smells amazing," he comments as he walks inside.

"I made coffee cake muffins for us to have while Jasmine does the interview."

"That's nice of you, you didn't have to do that for me."

"Who said it was for you?" I joke and he chuckles.

We get into the living room and it occurs to me that he hasn't been inside here before, only to the door. I watch as he takes it in, unable to tell exactly what he's thinking.

"Hey Levi, thanks for agreeing to do this," Jasmine says from her spot on the couch.

Even if her choosing Levi was for my sake, she's still taking the assignment seriously. She's loved this class and her current set up reflects her passion for it. She's got notes, her laptop, and her phone with a recording app on it at the ready.

"Of course, I don't mind at all," he says, taking a seat on the couch.

"I'll go get the muffins while you get started," I tell them and then head to the kitchen.

I arrange the muffins on a plate, then set them on a mirrored serving tray that I took from my mom's dining ware collection. She loved to host and always got in little spats with my dad about buying dishes they didn't need.

Grief–unexpected as usual–comes rising up as I begin pouring coffee into mugs. It's a little late in the evening, but never too late for coffee. Another thing my mom would have agreed with me on.

She'd love seeing me bringing a tray of goodies to a man like Levi. She was always pushing me to find love. I used to resent it, but now that she's gone, I realize she just wanted for me what she had herself, a loving husband and children.

I set a small bowl of sugar and pitcher of hazelnut creamer on the tray, then take a deep breath as I ride the swell of this grief wave. It's not as tumultuous as it used to be, but it still takes a minute for me to catch my breath. Once I do, I carry the tray out to the living room and set it on the coffee table.

Jasmine's eyes snag on the tray for a moment mid-question. She stumbles over her words but manages to stay focused on asking Levi why he became a detective.

I scoop a teaspoon of sugar into my cup while he answers.

"Well, I first became a detective because I liked the idea of helping people and catching the bad guy." He laughs a little. "But then I realized I could catch things that other people didn't, and I saw patterns that helped discover leads faster. So that lead me to the homicide unit, where those skills are imperative."

I stir creamer into my drink, then settle into a chair that's perpendicular to the couch, propping my feet up on the little footstool in front of it. Levi starts to fix his coffee as well, while Jasmine continues to ask questions.

"What's it like dealing with such gruesome crimes on a daily basis?" Jasmine asks and Levi freezes.

The spoon he was holding clatters against the rim of his mug. He recovers quickly, resuming stirring, but the action is concerning.

"Is everything okay?" I ask him in a low voice. He looks to me with a smile, but I can see the tightness around his eyes.

"Yeah, I'm all good. Her question caught me off guard is all." He lets out a nervous laugh and takes a sip of his coffee with one hand. "I should have expected it though, it's a pretty common question."

I look to Jasmine, who seems to share my concern.

"You don't have to answer it if you don't want to," she says. "I have plenty of other questions."

"No, it's fine," Levi assures her. "It's definitely not easy, which is why the department hired your sister." He shoots me a smile.

I return it, feeling marginally better about his reaction. It's odd that he was caught off guard by the question considering the nature of the interview, but I know he has a lot going on. I'm beginning to wonder if something more is going on.

Jasmine continues asking questions, but I can tell she's purposefully choosing ones that aren't difficult or too personal. I know she has a lot more on her list. By the time she's finished, Levi looks ready to fall asleep right there on the couch.

"Are you okay to drive home?" I ask him once Jasmine leaves to go put away her notes and laptop.

"I'm fine, though I wouldn't turn down the notion of a sleepover," he says with a playful grin.

If he's flirting, maybe he's not in so bad of a state. Plus, it's not like he can stay here. It wouldn't be good for either of us, and Jasmine doesn't need to see him here either. I can tell she wants him around in a more permanent way, which is difficult enough already. She'd meddle even more if she thought there was a real chance for us being more than friends.

"No sleepovers, Detective. I am worried about you though," I say, trying to study him.

He looks tired, and he's clearly avoiding meeting my eyes. "There's nothing to be worried about, Doll. I'm fine, it's just been a long day."

"Okay, well I'd feel better if you made an appointment with me so we can talk about things."

I watch him wince as he pushes up off the couch.

"Let me look at my schedule when I get back in the office and I'll make one."

I stand up as well and follow him to the door. Why does it feel like he's hurrying to leave? The Levi I know would flirt and stay planted on my couch until I kicked him out. Is he *that* tired?

"Okay, that sounds good. Be safe going home. Text me when you get there so I know you didn't fall asleep at the wheel," I say with a pointed look.

"It's sweet how much you care about me. I'll text you, don't worry."

He leaves and I get the distinct feeling something is wrong, but I don't have any concrete proof to back up what I'm sensing.

I gasp, shooting up in bed. My palms go to my chest, pressing against my pounding heart. Tears wet my face and I wipe them away with the edge of my comforter while taking cleansing breaths.

I haven't had a nightmare in months, but tonight broke that streak. And in an intense way at that. I dreamt of the day Levi was shot, except the ending was much different. The pain of losing him was so vivid and raw that I'm shaking as I reach for my phone. I need to hear his voice. I don't care that it's three in the morning, well past midnight. I don't think I can have any semblance of rest without knowing that he's okay.

Fear isn't rational, so even though I know that my nightmare wasn't real, I press call on his contact anyway, and curl up in bed with the phone on speaker nearby.

"Dahlia?" His voice comes through the phone after one ring. The sound of it breaks free another round of sobs. "What's wrong? Do you need me to come over? I'm getting up right now."

"No," I choke out. "I'm okay, I just had a nightmare. I needed to hear your voice."

I don't tell him that it was about him. I can't bring myself to.

"I'm sorry." He sounds both relieved and sad for me. "Are you sure you don't want me to come over? I swear I wouldn't try anything, I care about you too much to take advantage–"

I cut him off. "Levi, it's okay. I know you wouldn't do that, but I'm all right. Could you just stay on the phone with me?" I ask weakly.

He lets out a breath. "Of course I will. Do you want to talk about the nightmare?"

"No, I don't really want to think about it," I whisper.

"Okay, that's all right. What if I read to you for a little while?"

"That would be nice."

He starts to read, and I recognize it as a scene after the couple gets together in the detective book we both read. It's a sweet scene, where the hero buys the heroine a journal to write their story in, because she talked about wanting to be a writer. Levi is the perfect narrator, his voice low and gentle. He doesn't shy away from the mushy words the couple shares. In fact, it could just be how tired I am, but it seems like he says their confessions of love with more fervor than any other line. It's beautiful and heartwarming.

"Do you think you could write a book?" Levi asks after the chapter ends.

My eyes are heavy with sleep, and I'm no longer shaking or panicked. It occurs to me that just his voice did that for me. If he was here, I'm sure I'd feel even safer.

"I don't know," I murmur. "Maybe, if I had a good enough idea. What about you?"

"I don't think so. I'm probably not talented enough for that."

"I think anyone can write a book if they care enough about what they're writing."

"And if they hire a good editor to make sure it's not terrible," he adds, making me laugh.

"Yeah, that too."

"How are you feeling? I can read more. I know you like the wedding scene at the end."

Tears prick at my eyes. I'm tired of crying, but I don't know that I could stop if I tried. He's so wonderful, and yet I'm terrified of giving my heart over to him. How can I deny a man who's this good to me? I've dreamt for my whole life of finding a man who would care about me in actions and words. He does all of that and more. Plus, he's incredibly attractive. And I know just how well he can kiss. I've imagined it several times since the day I left him behind in Florida. I can't make decisions while half-asleep like this, but I'm tempted to tell him I don't want to be just friends anymore.

"I'm feeling better. I do love the wedding scene, but I think I'm close to falling asleep."

"I can read until you fall asleep, if you'd like," he gently offers.

"No, that's okay." I pause, wiping away my tears. "Could you just stay on the line though?"

"Sure, and if you need anything, I'll be here."

"Thank you."

We settle into a comfortable silence. The safety I feel just from him being on the phone is astounding.

"Hey, Levi?"

"Hm?"

I smile at his sleepy response. "I broke a rule by calling you so late."

"We don't have to count it. You're more important than a rule, Doll."

Warmth spreads through my chest. "I know, but I want to count it."

My small admission hangs in the air, and I suddenly regret saying it. Did I go too far? Am I going to regret this when I wake up in a few hours?

"If I was there, I'd pull you into my arms," he says, his gravelly voice sending a tingle down my spine. "But since I'm not ... do you remember the scene where the detective sees the main character for the first time?"

I nod, then remember he can't see me. "Yes, I remember."

"He said her beauty was so mesmerizing, so all-encompassing that he could barely breathe when he looked at her. And when she smiled it was like basking in the sunshine after a lifelong rainstorm." He pauses. I hold my breath. "That's how I feel when I look at you."

I don't know what to say. All my words have left me. No one has ever said anything so beautiful to me. I've never felt more cherished in my life. I thought he would say some cheeky comment about my looks to make me laugh, not confess something so heartfelt.

"I don't know what to say," I whisper.

"You don't have to say anything, just get some rest. I'll be here when you wake up."

I fall asleep, and this time instead of a nightmare, I dream about a future with Levi. One where we're in love and spend our days reading and laughing. It's a perfect picture, but I'm not sure if I'll ever allow it to be more than a dream.

Chapter Twenty-Six

Dahlia Chamberlain

"Dahlia, are you up?" Jasmine shouts through my door, making me groan.

"I am now," I grumble.

"Some guy dropped off a bag and a drink carrier at our door, but I didn't order anything and you always say not to open the door without you there."

I sigh. "I'll be right there."

"It's from me." Levi's voice makes me jump. I forgot we stayed on the phone all night.

"You scared me," I breathe out, then take the phone off speaker and put it to my ear. "What did you have delivered?"

"Pastries and lattes from The Sweet Bean. I figured you could use a pick me up after last night."

"Levi, that's so sweet of you. I should be the one sending you breakfast though after keeping you up," I say as I get out of bed.

"It's no big deal."

I slip my feet into my fuzzy yellow slippers and leave my room. Jasmine is on the sofa, watching an old episode of *Dance Moms*. She's been binging it since Thanksgiving. Maddie and–surprisingly–Grayson got her hooked on it. He's apparently a big fan of reality TV.

I open the front door, tuck my phone in between my shoulder and ear, and then pick up the carrier and bag. Once inside, I set them on the kitchen counter.

"It's a huge deal. You don't know how much it meant to me," I tell him in a low voice before tilting the phone away from my mouth to yell to Jasmine. "Jaz, Levi sent over breakfast, come get what you want."

Jasmine comes into the kitchen and grabs the iced coffee with a giant smile on her face.

"He remembered I like iced coffee best." She looks at the sticker indicating the kind. "*And* it's a cinnamuch, my favorite." The cinnamuch latte is one that has what a non-cinnamon lover would say is *too much* cinnamon. I've seen Jasmine ask for extra before, so she would never say it's too much.

"I think you might have made her whole weekend," I tell Levi.

"She's a good kid," he says, making me smile.

Jasmine looks to the phone in my hand. "Can I talk to him?"

I blink in surprise. "Jaz wants to talk to you, is that okay?"

"Of course."

I hand off the phone and Jasmine immediately thanks him for the coffee, then she walks into the living room while talking about how she thinks that the article based on his interview is going to get an A.

I grab my chai latte with extra cinnamon and a chocolate croissant from the bag, then follow after her.

When I get in there, she's asking him if he'll come watch her cheer this Friday night for their big rivalry game. I sit down on the couch, trying to mask my shock. I knew Jasmine liked Levi, but not enough to talk to him like this. My heart can't take seeing her so animated and happy. I always wanted the guy I marry to have a good relationship with my little sister. That way she'd always feel comfortable coming to stay with us or calling one of us for help.

Now, here's Levi, buying her favorite iced coffee and listening to her talk about cheerleading. I press my lips together as emotions swirl within me. Jaz hasn't had a father figure in her life the last three years, and as I watch her light up, I know that's what Levi is becoming to her. The thought creates a war within me. One side is fighting for the notion that Levi is already so much more than a friend, while the other is coming in with fear at the ready, telling me I'm bound to lose him and my job too.

The thing is, sitting here in the morning light, the darkness of fear seems less powerful than before. It makes me think maybe there's a chance for healing after all.

"Have a great day, I'll see you in two weeks," I tell Victoria, a captain's wife who has been seeing me for a few weeks now as she walks out of my office.

"Thank you, you too!"

Today has been a great day so far. All of my sessions have gone better than anticipated, and it looks like I should have time for a nice lunch break today. Maybe if I text Levi, we can have lunch in his truck again.

He's been a little off the grid this week, but he still texts me each day and he even preordered paperbacks of the next book in the detective series we love. He hasn't made an appointment with me, which is a little concerning, but it could just be that he's nervous to talk to me now that we're getting closer. If he can swing lunch today, I have plans on telling him there's no reason to be anxious and that I'm still able to be professional with him so that he has the help he needs to be cleared for duty.

I pull out my phone to text him, but before I can press send it starts to ring. Grayson's name pops up on my screen. He gave me his number in case me or Jasmine needed anything and Levi wasn't able to come help. He's also started reading Sloane Rose's books based on my enthusiastic recommendation, so he occasionally sends me a book title, chapter number, and GIF reaction.

He's never called before though, which is what makes this strange.

"Hello?" I answer.

"Dahlia, are you busy? Can you talk?" Dread settles into my gut at the panicked sound of his voice.

"What's wrong? Is Levi okay?"

Flashbacks of him in the hospital plague my mind, making it hard to take in a full breath.

"Well, he wasn't shot or anything. Wouldn't it be crazy if that happened twice? It's the kind of thing you'd say if I had a nickel for every time Levi got shot I would have *two* nickels, which isn't much but it's weird that it happened twice."

It's clear that Grayson uses humor and rambling to cope. Which is fine, but not in a moment where I'm in need of information.

"Grayson, are you really quoting *Phineas and Ferb* right now?" I pinch the bridge of my nose.

"You know that reference? I knew I liked you, Doc."

"I'm glad you like me. Now let's get back to Levi. He's okay?"

"Right. Sorry." I hear him take a deep breath in and then let it out. "The whole family is really worried about him. He's been dodging our calls and barely responding to our texts. Maverick went to his house earlier to check on him because he said he was getting his sling off today. He found Levi *asleep* parked in front of his house with the truck still running."

"Oh my gosh," I breathe out.

Now I feel even worse for keeping him up late with my nightmare. This whole time he's been struggling and I didn't see it.

"Maverick woke him up and tried to talk to him, but he said he was fine then went inside his house and locked the door. He won't answer the phone or the door for me either. I told Adrian and MJ not to go because it might make him more upset. I thought maybe you could go, especially since you're his therapist on top of being so close to him."

"He told you he's been coming to therapy?" I ask and the line goes silent for a moment.

"He hasn't come to see you, has he?"

"No, he's been avoiding me too. I just thought he was actually busy. I was going to talk to him today at lunch. But I can go now. Can you send me his address?"

I lean over my desk and quickly cancel my appointments for the day, putting illness as my reason.

"I'll text it right now. Can you let me know if you get to talk to him?"

"Yes, of course."

"Thanks, Dahlia."

We hang up and I rush out to my car. The drive to Levi's house is mercifully short. His small suburban neighborhood is lined with what looks to be two-bedroom garden homes. I count each one as I pass as a way to calm my nerves.

I park behind his truck, shuddering when I think of what could have happened if he hadn't parked before falling asleep.

The doorbell is too quiet for the level of panic I have right now, so after hearing the soft chimes within, I knock on the door too. No answer.

"Levi, it's me, Dahlia," I call out before knocking on the door again.

The door opens mid-knock. My hand falls to my side as I take Levi in. His scruff is on the verge of becoming a beard, his usually styled hair is mussed and the bags under his eyes are so dark it looks like he has two black eyes. His sling is gone too, his arm hanging by his side.

"Hey, what are you doing here?" he asks, trying to mask his exhaustion but failing.

He's likely out of the energy required to fake it, which just might be perfect timing for an intervention.

"I'm here because you fell asleep in your *truck* this morning, Levi. And you've been lying to your family about coming to therapy while avoiding me."

I push past him so he can't keep me out.

"I've just been a little tired because of the medication. It's not a big deal."

I follow the hallway to where I see his living room at the end.

"What if the car wouldn't have been in park? You could have had a serious accident."

"It was in park though, so nothing happened."

I turn to face him, but his head is down. "We need to talk about what's going on. You can't keep going like this. Your family is worried about you. I'm worried about you."

He looks up at this, eyes shining. "As my therapist or something more?"

"I think we both know I'm much more than your therapist."

He sinks into the couch, dropping his head into his hands. I sit down next to him and rub his back.

"I don't know where to start," he says into his hands. "The only time I opened up about things like this is with you on the beach."

"Then just pretend we're there again. Start with whatever comes to mind first."

"I've been having nightmares about the day I got shot," he begins with words that pain my heart. "It makes me not want to sleep, but my medicine makes me drowsy. So I've been counteracting the meds with caffeine until I crash. If I'm tired enough, I won't dream."

I dig my fingernails into my palm to stay grounded and not give into the tears that are trying to push their way out. He needs someone to lean on right now.

"I thought I had it under control, but it's been harder to keep the balance of the caffeine highs and crashes."

"Why didn't you come to me?" I ask in a soft voice. "I could have helped."

"I wanted to handle it on my own. My family always gets so worried about me that they make me feel guilty for being in this field in the first place."

"I wouldn't have done that," I tell him and he lifts his head.

"I ran into Isabella at the bookstore," he says, making me draw my brows together. "She let it slip that you're scared of losing someone like you lost your parents. I've been afraid that if I told you everything, I'd scare you away. My job isn't safe, I'm in danger a lot of the time. I thought if I just got over this then we could work on getting over your fear."

My chest tightens at his words. He did all of this so he wouldn't scare me.

"Levi, that's not healthy. You can't protect me that way. I work with detectives every day, I know what goes on."

And I've been falling for you in spite of it. I don't say my thoughts aloud. I don't know if I can, or if now is the best time.

"I know." He sighs. "Things have been going so well though. I wanted you to forget this stupid injury even happened."

He yanks up his sleeve to show where his scar is, and exposes dark swirls of ink as well. I gasp and as if he's just now realizing what I'm seeing, he pushes the sleeve back down. But I reach out and gingerly push it back up.

"Dahlias," I whisper, staring at the garden of blooms on his upper arm. "And sunflowers, too."

I can't hold in my tears any longer. They stream down my face and blur the image before me. A beautiful array of flowers marred by a white scar from his surgery.

"When?" I ask in a quiet voice.

"The winter after we met. It was around my mom's birthday and I kept hearing your voice telling me she'd want me to live, not just survive." He keeps his eyes on his feet, his jaw tight. "So I did something I thought I'd never do–got a tattoo. But I wanted to commemorate you and what you taught me too, so I got your flower."

I trace my fingertips over the petals. My heart and mind are racing. It's been five years, and he's held onto that memory all this time. Held onto *me* all this time. I've been so afraid of opening up my heart again, all the while he's been patiently waiting on me. He could have showed me this tattoo the first day at the office. But instead he sacrificed his emotions for my own, biding his time while treating me like I've always dreamt of being treated.

Instead of embracing him, I kept him at a distance because of fear. I've kept everyone at a distance. Five years ago, I told him to *live*, but when I lost my parents, I gave up my own motto. I shut myself off to both friendship and romance. And yet, he's been a constant, someone steady for me even while his own world was in a tailspin.

Before my parents died, they showed me that true love is sacrifice. Laying down one's life for another. And Levi has been doing that, all without knowing if I'd ever return his sacrifice in my own way. My realization of his feelings overwhelms me to the point of breaking.

"You love me," I whisper and he nods his head.

"More than anything. I'd sooner stop breathing than stop loving you."

He seems like he's going to say something more, but I cut him off by grabbing his chin and turning him toward me. I crash my lips against his in a searing kiss. He reaches over and pulls me into his lap. He's warm and strong and *perfect*. I sink my hands into his hair and a low noise rises from the back of his throat in response.

His hands squeeze my hips as I deepen the kiss. The taste of him transports me back to the kisses we shared years ago. It's as if we're hovering between then and now, a beautiful moment suspended in time and space just for us. Memories collide into the present, crashing through any defenses left between us. A tidal wave of love and adoration overwhelms me and our sweet kiss turns salty from my tears.

He pulls away to blaze a trail of heat down my jaw to my ear. When he nips at my earlobe my stomach swoops. He knows me so intimately and remembers everything. He knows that kissing below my ear takes my breath away, that when he places a soft kiss against the corner of my mouth I can't help but smile.

"You're so beautiful," he murmurs against my skin, trailing kisses down the other side of my neck now. I run my fingers through his hair again, trying to catch my breath.

The joy of being seen and loved is one I thought would elude me. That very joy is now bubbling up within me so much so that my cup is overflowing. He knows my deepest fear and loves me just the same.

I take his face in my hands and stare into his hazel eyes. Green flecks dot the brown depths, like sprouts pushing up from the ground on the first day of spring.

"I love you," I breathe out the confession. "I loved you then, and I love you now. I don't know if I ever truly stopped."

He smiles bigger than I've ever seen and pulls me in for another kiss. This one is warm and languid, as if he knows we have forever to spend. And now that I've opened my heart to this love, I hope that we get the forever this kiss feels like.

Chapter Twenty-Seven

Levi Carter

I thought today was one of the worst days I've ever had, and now it's by far the best. With Dahlia here in my arms, I can take on anything. Which is good, because I'm going to need that strength for what's to come.

She traces a fingertip down the bridge of my nose, still sitting in my lap. I'd happily stay in this spot for a long, long time, gazing at the soft smile on her pink lips, listening to her happy sighs. The only issue is that the comfort and warmth of her being with me is making me even more drowsy than before. My eyelids are heavy, falling shut when she runs her nails softly over my scalp.

"You need to sleep," she says in a gentle voice, but I tense up at the idea just the same.

"I just want to stay in this moment with you." I hate how weak my voice sounds, but the fear of experiencing another flashback saps my strength.

"I'll stay with you," she says, brushing her lips over mine. "I took the day off, and I can have Isa get Jasmine from school. I'll be here as long as you need."

"Are you sure?"

"I'm more than sure. Why wouldn't I want to cuddle up with my hot boyfriend?" She giggles, which makes me smile.

I don't even question her calling me her boyfriend. I'd be so much more if I thought I wouldn't overwhelm her by asking right now. And if I had a ring.

"Then I'd really love it if you stayed."

"Could I borrow some of your clothes to sleep in? These aren't very comfortable."

She looks down at her burgundy corduroy skirt, which is currently riding up her legs, exposing more of the black tights beneath. I clear my throat and look back up at the same time as she does, our gazes catching. A blush tints the apples of her cheeks.

"Sure, you can choose what you want from my dresser." My voice is hoarse.

She bites her lip and moves off my lap to stand. "Thank you."

I take her back to my room without saying anything more, because seeing her blushing and innocent just makes me want to drag her back into my lap. Not that leading her to my *bedroom* is any better, but knowing that I'm going to have face my fear of sleep dampens the mood some.

"The second drawer has t-shirts and the third has sweatpants and shorts," I tell her, then sit on the bed and watch her open them.

When I pictured Dahlia coming to my house, and my room, it looked a lot different than this. I didn't expect to be aching and exhausted. Nonetheless, I'm grateful for this, and for her.

She closes the drawers and I gesture to the door that leads to my master bathroom.

"I'll be right back," she says and then disappears behind the door.

I lie down, putting an arm behind my head and focusing on the blades of my ceiling fan spinning round and round. Just being in bed is revealing how tired I truly am. It's a marrow deep sort of tired that has me close to sleep by the time Dahlia exits my bathroom.

She pads over to the bed barefoot. The white t-shirt and gray shorts she took are so big on her that they're swallowing her up, but she still manages to look more beautiful than any other woman I've ever seen.

"I'm totally stealing these clothes by the way," she says as she climbs into bed and pushes under the covers. "They're so soft it should be a *crime*."

I groan. "You did *not* just make a detective joke."

She tucks herself into my side, pulling the covers up to her chin with a smile. "I did, and there's many more where that came from."

"You're lucky I'm in love with you," I say and she hums.

"I know."

I kiss her forehead and she traces shapeless patterns on my chest over my shirt.

"I'm so tired but I really don't want to go to asleep," I admit before I convince myself out of sharing. "The flashbacks are always so intense."

"I know, but I'll be here the whole time. We can work through it together. Putting yourself through the wringer like you have been only increases your stress and chances of them happening."

I nod and close my eyes, focusing on the gentle movement of her fingertips.

"I love you," I say and feel her lips brush against my jaw.

"I love you too."

I blink open my eyes to find myself in a dark room, the only light coming from a phone screen. It takes me a moment to realize where I am and who's curled up next to me, her back pressed to my chest.

Dahlia is in my bed. Not only that, but she's mine now. I pull her closer and nuzzle into her neck, breathing in her sweet scent.

"Good morning, or I guess I should say evening," she says with a soft laugh. "How did you sleep?"

I kiss the place where her neck meets her shoulder.

"Amazing, the best sleep I've had in months."

"Good," she says, setting down the phone in her hands. "I'll have to make a note that this method works for future clients." Her tone is teasing.

"Is that so?" I ask then pepper her neck with kisses. She squeals and tries to wiggle away.

"I'm kidding, I'm kidding." She laughs and I relent.

"That's what I thought." She settles back against me. I smile in contentment. "What time is it?"

I haven't had much of an appetite with the medicine I'm taking, but I don't want her to be starving because she's taking care of me.

"It's almost seven."

"Oh wow, I slept forever. Do you want to order in dinner? Or if you have to go, I'll send something over to your apartment for you and Jaz."

She turns over in my arms to face me. "Jaz is okay, she ate with Isa. *But* I was texting Grayson and he offered to bring over food. Actually, your brothers and sister all wanted to come over and check on you. I told him I'd ask. It's okay if it's too much."

I sigh. "No, I know they're probably really worried about me. I guess if I'm going to spill my guts I might as well get it over with all at once."

"Okay, I'll be right by your side through all of it. And I can kick them out if it gets to be too much."

I chuckle at the idea of her taking on all of the Carter siblings. I don't doubt her abilities though, she's always had a fire to her, even if its dimmed lately while she's been grieving.

"Hopefully it doesn't come to that, but thank you."

She texts Grayson and then changes back into her clothes before joining me in the living room. I leave the door unlocked and enjoy the peace of having Dahlia by my side, just us. We don't have to wait long for my family to come barging in, with Grayson at the head of the charge.

"If you think you can just ignore us while you tear yourself apart you–" Grayson cuts off, his eyes falling to where I'm holding Dahlia's hand. "Are you two together?"

"Yes," Dahlia says on a laugh. "We are."

Grayson drops the bags he was holding on the coffee table. "Why wasn't I informed of this?"

"Because it just happened today," Dahlia replies.

"And because it's none of your business," I add.

Grayson spears me with a look. "You don't get to talk about sharing things versus hiding them. We've all been worried sick about you."

I run a hand over my face.

"I know I'm one to talk, but you really can't shut us out like this," Adrian says next. "Especially not after what happened."

Maverick and MJ nod in agreement.

"This is why I keep telling you to come work with us–" Grayson starts, but I stop him.

"That's the reason I don't tell you about when things are wrong," I say and his face falls. "You make me feel guilty for having this job. I know you mean well, but I'm not ready to leave. I may *never* leave the department, and I need y'all to be okay with that. This is the career I chose. It's hard and messy and dangerous, but it's also important and rewarding and I'm good at it."

Dahlia squeezes my hand and I smile down at her. A weight lifts off my chest at being able to say all of this out loud.

"I'm sorry, I've been a terrible brother," Grayson says and launches himself at me, wrapping me up in an incredibly awkward hug. I let go of Dahlia's hand to pat him on the back.

"It's okay, you didn't know."

"I should have known. But I'm going to do better. Whatever you need, I've got your back."

"Same here, but in a much less dramatic way," MJ says, making me chuckle.

Grayson pulls back then wraps Dahlia into a hug next. "Thank you for coming here. And welcome to the family."

I swat his side and give him a warning look. While I love where his head is at, I don't need him scaring Dahlia.

"Thanks, Grayson." Dahlia laughs and he pulls back.

"How about we hang out and eat? All of this emotional stuff is kind of depressing. It's a good day," I say and pull Dahlia into my side.

"As long as you promise to tell us if you need to talk or something is wrong," Maverick says.

Being the oldest, I'm usually the one that takes care of everyone, but Maverick tends to take over at times and this is one time I'm glad for it. It's nice to have everyone looking out for me, now that they know how I really feel.

"I promise," I say and he nods.

MJ starts to pull out food containers, while Grayson asks a million questions about how Dahlia and I ended up together. I dodge most of his questions and manage to actually eat a full meal for the first time in days.

Sitting with my family around me and Dahlia by my side has me feeling normal again. It's been so long since I've felt any semblance of normalcy and it's amazing to finally have it after struggling. I know I've got a long way to go with recovery, but I can finally see the light at the end of it all. And now that I'm with Dahlia, maybe the journey through this won't be so hard.

Chapter Twenty-Eight

Dahlia Chamberlain

I breathe in the chilly night air as Levi and I walk hand in hand through the crowd of high school football fans. After some much-needed rest, Levi felt well enough to come tonight to support Jasmine, and once word of her important halftime performance got out, all of the Carter siblings decided to come.

"I've never been to a football game just to watch the cheerleaders," Levi says and I laugh.

"Not even when you were in high school?" I tease.

"Well, when I was in high school I was too busy on the field to watch the cheerleaders."

"I didn't know you played football."

I'm suddenly imagining him in a football uniform and it's a *wonderful* image...

"I did, but I preferred baseball. I ended up playing just baseball my junior and senior year."

Scratch the football fantasy. *Baseball pants?* It's freezing out but I might need a fan.

"What are you thinking about over there, Doll?" he asks with a smirk.

"What? Nothing, I'm just listening, learning more about my boyfriend." I try for an innocent smile.

"With how much you're blushing, I'm inclined to believe your mind is somewhere else."

I shake my head. "Nope, my mind is *very* in the present." We pass a concession stand. "Ooo let's get hot chocolate!"

I start toward the stand, but he pulls me back against him, his mouth next to my ear.

"You were imagining me in uniform, weren't you?" His breath is hot on my neck, making a shiver run down my spine.

I bite my lip. "I do love a man in uniform."

He spins me around and wraps his arms around me. My breath catches at the heat burning in his eyes. "Love, huh?"

I nod, at a loss for words with how he's looking at me. He dips his head to press a kiss to my lips. It's the kind of kiss that promises more, one that hovers on the edge of passion in a way that has me clutching the collar of his flannel to stay standing.

"You know there are *children* around, right?" Grayson's voice pops our blissful bubble.

I press my face into Levi's neck to hide my fire-hot blush.

"Aren't you supposed to be saving everyone's seats?" Levi asks.

"I've got it covered, don't you worry your lovestruck head."

I pull back to look at him. He's wearing a purple hoodie, which is the main team color, and gray joggers, which is the secondary color. He even bought a team beanie that his dark hair is poking out of. It looks as if he goes to every game even though I know he's never been to one.

"Nice to see you this evening, Doctor." Grayson grins. "You're looking ... red."

"Shut up," I mumble and he just laughs.

"I can't say I wouldn't be the same if I had a beautiful woman to shower affection on."

"You'd be worse," Levi says and I giggle. "I'm genuinely afraid of the amount of PDA I'll have to suffer through when you fall in love."

"You should be afraid," Grayson says with a wicked grin. "Now, who's craving hot chocolate? I came up here because I saw someone walk past with a cup."

"I for sure want some. I'm pretty sure it's just powder and hot water, but it's the best," I say with a smile.

We end up with two carriers full of hot chocolates, a bag filled to the brim with candy–Grayson's idea–and a couple of overpriced water bottles. After securing the goods, we follow Grayson up the center of the bleachers to our seats.

I burst into laughter when I see how he's secured them. He roped off the seats, and there's a sign hanging on the ropes saying reserved for special guests. Not only that, but the entire section is covered in thermal blankets, so we don't have to sit on the cold metal bleachers.

"You never do anything halfway, do you?" I ask him as he lifts the rope for us to walk through.

"What's the point in halfway? It's so much more fun to go all out."

"Fair point."

I settle in next to Levi, with a perfect view of the center of the field. The cheerleaders will spend most of the game to the left of us, but come halftime this is the spot to be. Grayson chose the spot well, not that I expected anything less.

MJ, Sebastian, and Maddie arrive next. Maddie sits down next to me after taking a hot cocoa from Grayson and my heart warms at the thought of her wanting to be next to me. Almost immediately after they arrive, Juliette and Adrian come up the stairs. They both look overdressed for a football game, but I've realized over the course of our encounters that they tend to dress like a Pinterest board all of the time.

Maverick is the last to arrive, the leather jacket layered over his flannel making me think he rode his motorcycle here. It still baffles me that a man so *burly* bakes bread and pastries for a living. Talk about not judging a book by its cover.

The game kicks off and I quickly realize that watching football with the Carters–and Holts–is not for the faint of heart. We're the loudest section on both sides of the stadium by far. I thought MJ and Adrian were quiet, but as soon as that whistle blew, they were on their feet. Even Maddie is standing in her seat, yelling at the referee to make better calls. Juliette is the only one who's more reserved, though she is waving a purple-and-gray pompom in the air.

I look over at Levi with wide eyes during a timeout and he grins. "You didn't expect this, did you?"

"Definitely not." I laugh. "You don't know any of these people or care about this team. Why are you yelling?"

He throws an arm around my shoulders and squeezes. "Competition is in our *blood*. Doesn't matter the sport or the people playing. If we're at a game, we're invested."

The next play starts and steals his attention. I watch him clap and yell at the team as if he were the one coaching, all with a smile on my face. Even though I don't understand it, Levi being so passionate is fun to see because it's more I get to know about *him*. Five years ago I left thinking I'd never get to discover more about who he is, but now I'm here by his side, getting to see a part of him that only makes me fall even more.

"She was amazing," Juliette says with a smile as we push our way through the crowd.

The game is over–Jasmine's school won–and her halftime performance was perfect. I've seen her practice the dance a million times in our living room, but seeing it on the field was even better. Now everyone is headed home, once we can make it through the throng of people.

"I'll tell her you said so," I shout over the crowd. "I know she loved seeing y'all in the audience."

When Jasmine's eyes found us in the bleachers her smile was dialed up to a hundred. I think having a whole family of people there to support her made her perform even better than if it would have been just me. I teared up seeing her joy, and Levi let me use the hem of his flannel to dab under my eyes.

I think if Jasmine wasn't so excited about the party I told her she could go to, she'd be here with us, soaking up the love of everyone.

"We had fun," Sebastian adds, his arm around MJ. "I love seeing my wife get fired up about football. Makes me want to–"

"Do not finish that sentence," Grayson says with a gag. "I love you guys, but save it for the bedroom."

"Agreed," Maddie says with a shudder.

I'm laughing at their exchange when I spot a familiar stern face a few feet away.

"Oh no, it's the Chief," I say and squeeze Levi's hand.

We haven't revealed our relationship yet, and I don't think him finding out this way would be good. I can't lose my job. All this joy from seeing her performing will fade away if I lose the ability to provide for her.

"We'll catch y'all later," Levi says then turns us so we're headed away from the Chief, before pulling me underneath the bleachers.

He cages me against a fence, blocking me from view. Anyone passing by would see a couple, but shouldn't be able to recognize us. I peek one eye around Levi's arm to see the Chief walk past, not even a glance in our direction.

"That was close," I breathe out.

My heart is racing from the thought of being found out before we're ready to share. It could have been so bad.

"Yeah, it was," Levi says and I look up at him.

The heat from earlier is back in his eyes, making me warm all over in spite of the cold metal I'm leaning against.

"I think we're safe now," I murmur.

"Probably, but maybe we should stay a little while longer for good measure."

I nod once and he tucks my hair behind my ear with one hand, the other above my head on the fence.

"You have the softest lips," he says in a low voice, his thumb brushing over them. "I'd cross an ocean in a rowboat if someone told me a kiss from you was waiting on the other side."

"Is that a line from a book?" I ask, breathless as I attempt to keep my wits about me. It's futile, though. I'm putty in his hands.

A soft smile stretches his lips as he presses his forehead to mine. "No, it's just what comes to mind when I look into your tropical blue eyes."

My eyes flutter shut. His breath fans my face, warm and sweet from our shared hot cocoa. The memory of his lips touching the same spot mine did makes my stomach do a little flip.

"I think you should write a book," I whisper.

"I don't think anyone wants to read hundreds of pages about how in love with you I am, but if it'll make you smile, I'll write ten."

He presses a kiss to the corner of my mouth.

"Ten?" I question, clutching his shirt when he brushes his lips down my jaw. "Do you really think you could write that much?"

"I could write about just this, beautiful." He tastes the skin beneath my ear, making me gasp. "That little noise is enough material for a whole book." His lips against my skin makes desire pool in my stomach.

I pull him by his collar to my mouth, unable to wait anymore. Our lips mold together and I melt into him like a toasted marshmallow on chocolate. His hand pushes into my hair, pulling gently to the side to guide me into a deeper kiss. My knees are weak beneath me, but he wraps his other arm around my waist, holding me up against the fence.

The world around us is a blur. Here in the shadows it's just us, and the noise of the crowd has faded away. My only thoughts consist of wanting *more*. Levi doesn't hold back, kissing me with the kind of reckless abandon that's more thrilling than any bungee jump or parasail ride.

When he finally slows the kiss and pulls away, his pupils are dilated and his lips are swollen. Warm satisfaction rains down on me at the knowledge that he's this way from *my* kiss. It's *me* that he'd cross an ocean for, no one else.

"I love you," I say and he holds my face, pressing a smiling kiss to my lips.

"I love you more."

"Good morning, Charles and Audrey," I say as the couple walks through my office door.

My smile is tight and my palms are damp. Sitting across from the Chief for this session while knowing that I'm hiding my relationship from him is going to be rough. I hate the thought of lying, but I guess I'm not *lying*, just ... postponing the truth.

Levi and I decided to wait until next week to tell the Chief. He has a meeting to discuss returning back to work, so it just makes sense to wait until then and not raise any concern. I'm hopeful that the two meetings I'll have with Charles and Audrey before then will help soften him. Maybe I won't get fired. A girl can hope.

"Good morning," Audrey says in her kind voice. Charles nods to me as per usual, but he's not scowling, which feels like a win.

"How did the communication exercises go?" I ask after we all sit down.

"Great," Audrey replies with a smile. "I feel like we've talked more than we have in years."

Charles says nothing, so I direct my attention to him, raising a brow. He seems to respond more to me being sassy and pushy than relaxed and gentle. "It's been good, I'm glad she's happy."

"You aren't happy?" Audrey asks, concern lining her face.

"It's just that talking isn't my thing, it's yours. I'm happy to do it, but it takes a lot out of me."

I tilt my head to the side, considering what he's saying.

"Talking doesn't fill up your emotional tank," I state and he nods.

"That's a weird way of putting it, but yeah, it doesn't."

I stand up and walk over to my bookshelf, pulling a book off of it. "I think you both would benefit from reading this book about the different love languages."

Audrey looks intrigued, while Charles looks like he'd rather walk barefoot over Legos.

"It will reveal how each of you prefer to receive love, so that this journey isn't so one-sided. I can email you a quiz as well that helps determine your love language. Next week we can talk about the results and what to do with them."

"That sounds amazing," Audrey says, while Charles just nods.

"Is there anything else you'd like to talk about?"

Audrey starts to describe an issue with one of their children that she wants advice on how to handle in a healthy way. I'm able to relax more, even with the Chief here. He's benefitting from what I'm doing, and so is his wife. It gives me hope that he'll recall these moments when Levi tells him about our relationship. This job is so important and rewarding to me, I don't want to have to leave the people I've come to know and care about because of who I'm dating. I'll just have to do the best I can to convince him to keep me on.

Chapter Twenty-Nine

Levi Carter

I pinch the bridge of my nose after opening up my sibling group text. Why is my family like this? All I'm trying to do is pull off a small surprise birthday party for Dahlia. It's not that difficult, just make sure the food arrives at MJ's house and wait there. But of course, everyone has decided to make my life difficult. And by everyone, I mean Grayson.

Grayson: MJ, your rich people neighborhood doesn't have anything against fireworks, does it?

MJ: I don't live in a neighborhood. There are just houses in the vicinity of ours. And why are you asking about fireworks???

Grayson: No neighborhood means no rules, great!

Adrian: I told him not to do it, but he didn't listen.

Maverick: Just dropped Dahlia's cake at MJ's. I decided to do three tiers instead of two, because Grayson always invites extra people.

Grayson: I can't help it that people love hanging out with me. If you had my charisma you'd have more people as guests too.

Maverick: It's impolite to invite people to someone else's party.

MJ: I'm sorry, are we ignoring the fact that Grayson mentioned FIREWORKS? Someone please tell me what's going on.

Grayson: Levi said he wanted the party to be special, what's more special than explosions of color and light?

Adrian: Let the record show I did my best to stop him.

Grayson: Let the record show he failed. Because I am the more powerful twin.

I sigh and type out a response to the chaos.

Levi: All I asked was for there to be food, a cake, and everyone to get there before Dahlia and I do.

Grayson: And I decided to make your plan better like a good brother. You're welcome.

MJ: Were you going to ask before setting things on fire in my backyard?

Grayson: Already asked Sebastian. He said it was good with him.

MJ: Of course he did.

I sigh and slide my phone back in my pocket. I don't have time to worry about fireworks. Dahlia is waiting on me to pick her up for what she thinks is an afternoon and evening spending time together just us. This morning I had flowers and breakfast sent to her apartment while I finished up some paperwork at the department. Then I paid for her, Jasmine, and Isabella to all go get manicures and pedicures.

According to her near constant texts illustrating her gratitude, all of these things have made her birthday amazing. But I want it to be *perfect*. I step down out of my truck and walk to her apartment building. My knock on her door is answered almost immediately. Dahlia throws herself into my arms, and I spin her around with the momentum.

"Hello to you too," I say with a laugh as I set her down.

"Today has been perfect," she says, smiling up at me in my arms.

"It's not even over yet."

"You're spoiling me."

I lean down and kiss her softly. "I just want your day to be special."

"Thank you," she says in a soft voice. "I feel loved."

"Good, because you are." I press another kiss to her lips. "Are you ready to go?"

"As long as my outfit works for wherever we're going, I'm ready," she says, taking a step back and gesturing to her clothes.

I make a show of taking in her appearance. She looks the perfect mixture of gorgeous and adorable in her long jean overalls with a fuchsia sweater layered underneath.

"Can you spin around for me?" I ask, trying to sound serious.

She takes a step like she's going to turn, then realizes I'm messing with her.

"You're terrible," she says, hitting me while I laugh.

"You're beautiful."

She rolls her eyes, but she's smiling. "Let me get my bag and tell Jaz I'll see her later."

I watch her grab a brown purse off a hook and then she yells, "I'll be back later tonight, love you!"

"Have a great time, love you too!" Jasmine yells back, as if Isabella isn't going to drive her to MJ's house in a couple hours.

Dahlia locks the door behind her, then slides her key into her bag. "So, where are we headed?"

"You'll see, it won't take long to get there."

"I wish you would just tell me, I hate surprises."

"You love surprises."

She crosses her arms with a huff. "Fine, I do love surprises. But I still want to know."

"Then it wouldn't be a surprise."

"Stop making sense. It's my birthday, you're supposed to feed into my delusions."

"Apologies, I'll try to do better the rest of the evening."

I open the passenger side door for her. She climbs in.

"See that you do."

I chuckle and close the door for her. She tries to get me to tell her where we're going the entire drive, only relenting when I park in front of The Secret Door.

"You're the best boyfriend ever," she says with a wide smile.

"You don't even know why we're here."

"All I need to know is we're at a *bookstore*. Even if we just look around and don't buy anything it'll be a great birthday."

"You've got to raise your standards, Doll."

She shrugs and we get out at the same time. I take her hand and lead her toward the bookcase that opens up into a secret room. I have to stop her from changing our course to look at various books several times, but we eventually make it to the room.

I let her pull on the book lever to open the door. Inside, there's an arrangement of balloons attached to one of the tables and a tray of pastries and tea sandwiches to hold us over until the surprise party. The employees were happy to help me set up the surprise. They know Dahlia well from how often she comes, and they loved the idea. There's also her present from me, the stack of Sloane Rose books I read and annotated. While I prefer romantic suspense over regular romance, it was fun to read knowing how much Dahlia loves the books.

"Levi," she breathes out my name, standing in the doorway.

"Come on," I say with a smile and tug her into the room, closing the bookshelf door behind us.

"Sloane Rose books?" she asks, her brows furrowed.

"Open them."

She opens the first one and gasps, tears filling her eyes when she sees the note I made on the title page.

"You read all of them?"

"All of this series, yes. I wrote notes in the margins. I hope you're not one of those people who hates that sort of thing."

She lets out a disbelieving laugh, her fingertips shaking as she covers her mouth. "This is the sweetest and most romantic thing anyone has ever done for me. I can't believe you took the time to do this."

"You said you loved them, and I wanted to share in that love."

"I'm so glad I put on waterproof mascara," she says, her voice slightly high-pitched as she fans away tears.

"I'm glad you like it, I was a little worried you wouldn't."

"Like it? I love it." She sets the book down and throws her arms around me. "I love *you*. Thank you."

"I love you too." I wrap her up in my arms and squeeze her tight.

Making her smile and feel loved brightens my whole world. I hope I get to do it every day for the rest of our lives.

"SURPRISE!" everyone shouts and I rip away the blindfold I made Dahlia wear on the way here. Dahlia jumps in surprise, but smiles big when she sees everyone standing in a huge semicircle, balloons and streamers everywhere.

"I don't even know what to say. This is all so much." She looks to me and I grab her hand to squeeze it.

"Don't say anything, just enjoy it."

"Happy birthday!" Grayson cheers, running up to wrap Dahlia in a hug and spin her around. I have to step back so I don't get hit by her flying legs. "Here's your birthday sash," he says, removing the gold glitter sash from around him. "And crown." He takes off the paper crown and places it on her head.

"Thank you," Dahlia says on a laugh.

Grayson approaching starts a line for everyone else to come to wish her a happy birthday and hug her. Maddie uses her camera to take photos of everyone, then MJ yells out that it's time to eat.

I asked MJ's best friend Sophie to cater the event, and she thankfully had time to. She's by far the best chef in Atlanta, and I wanted only the best for Dahlia.

After eating, Maverick brings out the three-tier cake decorated with real dahlia blooms. I had to order them from a special greenhouse since they were out of season, but the look on her face was worth the extra trouble.

We're about to start singing, when Jasmine steps forward and starts to speak with tears in her eyes.

"I've been going through old home videos," she begins and the room instantly quiets. "I know you haven't been ready to look back, and honestly neither was I but I wanted to for you. Every year, Mom would sing "Happy Birthday" in her own special way to us. For the past three years, you haven't gotten to hear that."

Jasmine pulls out her phone, scrolling for a second before taking a deep breath and looking to Dahlia again, who's frozen in place, watching her.

"She may not be here in person, but I see her in you every day." Jasmine's voice cracks. "I wanted you to hear her voice again for your birthday and to thank you for everything you've done for me."

Jasmine presses play and Dahlia hugs her tight as a woman's voice begins to sing "Happy Birthday" to her. I'm wiping tears away watching them embrace and cry together. I don't think there's a dry eye in the room though, so I don't mind anyone seeing me cry.

The video stops playing and it's silent for a moment, before Grayson breaks the tension like only he can.

"Let's cut the cake so I can eat my feelings," he says, making everyone laugh, including Dahlia and Jasmine.

My throat is tight watching the two sisters cut the cake together and laugh at their hands shaking. They've spent the past three years swimming in grief all alone, and yet here they are smiling bright and celebrating life. It's inspiring and makes me grateful for my big family that I had to lean on when our mom died. It wasn't easy, but we got through it together, and we still work through the pain to this day.

Dahlia looks up, her tearful eyes meeting mine. In them I see a whirlpool of emotions, but I also see the woman who taught me to live life to the fullest five years ago. The one whose namesake I had branded on me because it was already branded on my heart from the moment we met.

If I didn't already know it, I know for sure now, I'm going to marry her. I'm going to marry her and give her the best life I can. And that starts with making sure the meeting with the Chief goes well this week. I'll fight tooth and nail to make sure she gets to live out her dream.

Chapter Thirty

Dahlia Chamberlain

"Don't say everything is going to work out, because you don't know that it will," I say into my phone.

"I can say that, because it will. Everything always does," Isa replies in a calm voice.

I twist my ring as I stare out the window, hoping that my nerves will lessen before my meeting with the Chief. Levi suggested we go in together, even though the Chief is expecting just him. I stayed up all night preparing a speech on why I shouldn't be fired. The lack of sleep is severely affecting my capacity for optimism.

"I think that's just something people say to make themselves feel better."

"Dahlia, it really is going to be okay. No matter what happens, you'll pivot and adapt. You've done it time and time again, this is no exception. I just want you to walk into that office with the confidence you should have."

"I could get fired, Isa. I don't know what confidence I should be possessing." My throat is tight with worry, making my voice come out high-pitched.

"You walked into a department where therapy was a curse word and turned it into a blessing. That's no easy feat, but you did it. If you can do that, then you can face one grumpy old man."

"That grumpy old man is the Chief of Police."

"And you're *you*."

"You have too much confidence in me," I say with a sigh.

"I've seen you walk through some terribly dark things, Dahlia Chamberlain. This meeting is not going to take you down. You've got more fire than he's got water to put it out with."

Her words start to sink in, boosting my spirits.

"You're right, I have walked through much harder things than this."

The sound of my door opening makes me turn around. Levi stands in the doorway, looking unbelievably attractive in his fitted long sleeve shirt and jeans. His badge hangs on a chain around his neck. He usually dresses more formal, but he's become more relaxed while on light duty. It reminds me of the detective in the book we both read. He's just missing a leather jacket and the bad boy detective image would be complete.

He leans against the doorframe and I stifle a lovestruck sigh.

"Levi just walked in, didn't he?" Isa asks and I realize we're still on the phone. My pause must have given it away.

"Yeah, he did. I should probably go."

"You've got this."

"Thanks, Isa."

We hang up and Levi closes the door to my office before crossing the room. He wraps me up in his arms and I breathe in his smokey sweet scent. I press my face into his neck, soaking up the comfort of him.

"Isa says everything is going to be all right," I tell him and he squeezes me tight.

"She's right, it will be. I'm not going to let him fire you."

I pull back and place a hand on his jaw. "You can't risk your job trying to save mine."

"He won't fire me. He might suspend me, but he won't fire me."

"Just be careful." I push up on my tiptoes to press a soft kiss to his lips.

"Don't do that, or else we'll be late," he says against my lips, making me smile.

"Come on then, detective. We've got plenty of kissing in our future."

I pull out of his arms and he grins down at me.

"We definitely do."

After leaving my office, we walk side by side to the Chief's office. I want more than anything to be able to hold his hand or lean into him, but we need to talk to the Chief first.

Levi knocks on the office door and a familiar gruff voice calls for us to come in. Chief Wells sits behind his desk, arms crossed over his chest, eying us as we enter.

"What are you doing here?" he asks me, and my confidence begins to quickly fade.

"We have something we need to talk to you about," Levi says and the Chief raises a brow.

"Proceed."

We both sit down in the pair of chairs opposite his desk.

"Dr. Chamberlain and I are dating."

My eyes widen. I didn't expect him to start out so strong. I thought we'd ease into the water, not jump headfirst into the deep end.

"We knew each other before she arrived here," Levi continues. "But we didn't start dating until recently. I'm prepared to fulfill my requirement for post-injury therapy outside of the department so that there aren't any ethics violations."

"How do I know there hasn't already been a violation?" the Chief asks and I tense up.

"There has," I say and Levi looks at me, concern in his hazel eyes. "I had feelings for Levi for a long time, but I tried to avoid them because of my position. It was unavoidable though, and I crossed boundaries I shouldn't have even though we weren't technically dating at the time."

Chief Wells nods, but stays silent. I take his silence as an opportunity to present my case.

"I know you could fire me for this. I'd understand if you did, but you should know how much I care about this precinct. My main goal in coming here was to lighten the heavy burden placed on the detectives and their families. I believe I've done that. All I want is to be able to keep doing that."

He remains silent. I look down at my lap, defeat creeping its way into my mind. Levi reaches over and takes my hand, running his thumb over the back of it.

Maybe the Chief will have enough kindness in his heart to let me resign so that I can go work somewhere else as a therapist. I've been saving for Jasmine's car, but we can use that to live off of while I find a job.

"I'm not going to fire you." My head pops up at his words. "You have done good work here. You saved my marriage, and I didn't even realize it was in trouble."

I have to bite the inside of my cheek to keep my mouth from falling open in shock.

He looks at Levi. "You will need to go somewhere else for therapy, and you'll need to be approved for work before I'll let you off light duty."

"Yes sir, thank you," Levi says and I nod.

"Thank you, Chief Wells."

"You can call me Charles," he says with the faintest of smiles. "Keep up the good work, and you should be fine. Just don't date any other detectives."

I look at Levi with a smile. "I don't think that will be a problem."

"I can't believe you've never decorated for Christmas here," I say as I hang a gold ornament on the tree we just bought.

I thought Levi hadn't decorated because of his injury, but then he revealed that he hasn't decorated for Christmas since he moved out. He always just celebrated with his family and decorated his dad's house with his siblings. So, after we were both off work, we went and scrounged up what we could find.

Most of the decorations were picked over, since it's already mid-December, but we manage to find a tree, ornaments, and a few trinkets to make the place festive.

"It felt weird decorating for just myself. No one comes over to my house. Everyone always goes to Grayson's or Dad's, and now MJ's."

"I understand that. I guess I didn't decorate as much when I lived on my own, but I still put a tree up to get in the spirit." I hang another ornament on one side of the tree while Levi works on the other. "I'm glad your first time decorating is with me though."

He looks around the tree and gives me a heart melting smile. "Me too."

"And what better way to celebrate not losing my job than with cookies and decorating?"

A crash comes from the kitchen, followed by the sound of hysterical laughter.

"We might not get any cookies with those three in charge," Levi says.

Grayson picked up Maddie to come bake cookies. I brought Jasmine to help too. They disappeared into the kitchen a while ago and all we've heard is giggles and concerning noises since.

"We haven't checked on them in a while ... should we be worried?"

"Grayson is with them, that's reason enough to be worried. Let's go see what they're up to."

We walk into the kitchen and the scene we find should be surprising, but isn't. Every surface is covered in flour and sprinkles. Grayson's usually dark hair looks grey with how much flour is in it. Jasmine is doubled over laughing as Grayson tries to scoop up what looks to be an entire bottle of edible glitter. Maddie is giggling as she films the entire ordeal.

"What is going on?" Levi asks and Grayson freezes.

"The cap on the glitter bottle broke," Grayson says with a sheepish smile. "Don't worry though, I'll clean it up."

"I thought I specifically said *no* glitter."

"I thought you were talking about the decorations, not the cookies."

Grayson tries to funnel the glitter back into the bottle, but his hand slips and it goes all over him and the floor. I look at Levi with wide eyes. He does not look happy. One thing I've learned about Levi is he keeps his house *very* clean. Like *eat off the floor* clean. So the fact that there's glitter everywhere is not going to go over well with him.

"I can't believe–"

I cut Levi off, placing a hand over his mouth. "It's not a big deal. You guys just finish up the cookies then clean up as best as you can."

Levi narrows his eyes at Grayson, who's smiling nervously by the stove. Even without words, he's communicating his feelings on the matter.

I pull Levi out of the room and back into the living room.

"I'm going to have glitter in my house forever. When I sell the house, the new owners are going to inherit the glitter because it will still be there."

"It gives the house character," I say on a laugh and he shoots me a look. "It's just a little sparkle, no big deal."

He sighs. "You're right, it's not a big deal. Hopefully Maddie got it on video so the whole world can tease him about it."

"There's the Christmas spirit," I joke and he shakes his head, smiling at me.

"But..." He draws the word out and eyes me in a way that makes me feel like I'm in trouble. "None of this would have happened if you wouldn't have invited him over." He takes a step toward me.

"What are you doing?" I ask and he smirks before lunging at me and picking me up.

I squeal as he throws me on the couch and starts to tickle me. I try to fight him off, but it's no use. I'm basically just flailing my arms and legs hoping to make contact.

"S-stop!" I sputter around my laughter.

He keeps going for a moment longer, before finally relenting.

"You're evil," I say, out of breath.

"And yet you love me. What does that say about you?"

He hovers over me on the couch, his hands on either side of my head.

"That I have poor judgment?"

He laughs and dips his head down to kiss my forehead. "I love you, Dahlia Chamberlain."

The laughter in his eyes dims to something more serious. Passion and love swirl in his irises.

"I love you, Levi Carter."

I reach up and toy with the button of his Henley. Being with him has been so easy. I never have to question if he loves me, because he tells me constantly and shows it even more. But sometimes, I get overwhelmed by the feeling of being loved so fully. During those times, I tend to focus anywhere but his gorgeous hazel eyes. Because each time I look into them, my breath is stolen away.

"If I asked you to marry me, would you say yes?"

My hand falls away from the button and I look up at him, met with the full force of his love.

"Is this you proposing?" I whisper my question.

"That would be a pretty underwhelming proposal." He smiles and gives me a soft kiss. "No, I'm not proposing, just asking if I did–*soon*–would you say yes?"

"I think that's cheating. I don't think you're supposed to ask me. You can't pre-propose."

"I just want to make sure I'm not moving too fast for you."

Warmth flows from my chest through my whole body. He's so considerate and caring. I can't believe he wants to marry me. "I'd say yes. If you got down on one knee right here and now, I'd say yes."

His smile widens into a boyish grin. He brushes my hair away from my face with one hand. "You don't know how happy I am to hear that. But I'm not proposing now. I want it to be perfect."

"As long as you're the one asking, it's perfect."

"Hey, the cookies are–" Jasmine's voice comes from behind the couch. "Oh, ew, gross. Get a room!"

My face heats, but Levi just laughs.

"This is a room," Levi replies.

"Ugh, you two are insufferable. If you'd care to take a break from being all *in love*, the cookies are ready."

Levi pushes up off of me and helps me up.

"I don't think we can take a break from being in love. That's not really how it works," I say as I comb my fingers through my hair. I'm sure the waves are all wild after being thrown onto the couch.

"You know what I meant. Being all mushy and kissing. You're my sister, it's too much."

I laugh and take Levi's outstretched hand as we walk to the kitchen. "Fine, we'll try not to be so *mushy* around you."

"Thank you," she says as if we're the most exasperating people in the world.

We get into the kitchen–which looks slightly cleaner than before–and Grayson presents a tray of red-and-green cookies covered in sprinkles and glitter.

"Merry Christmas!" Grayson sings out.

"Are there any cookies on this tray or just icing and sprinkles?" Levi asks, making me laugh.

Grayson glares at him and sets the tray on the kitchen island. "This is the thanks I get for creating a masterpiece for you?"

"Hey, what about us? We helped too," Maddie says.

"*You* filmed me the entire time while *Jasmine* laughed and ate raw cookie dough from the bowl. Y'all were the opposite of help."

I smile as they bicker back and forth. Levi takes a bite of a cookie and crinkles up his nose at the amount of sugar. This prompts Grayson to eat one of his creations and the look on his face is priceless. We all dissolve into laughter when his mouth turns green from the icing. My sides hurt and I can't catch my breath, but it's one of the best days I've ever had.

When I look around the kitchen I see a family. A silly, messy, family that loves big and walks through hard things together. I can't help but tear up once my laughter fades, because three years ago I thought I'd never experience joy like this again, and two years before that I thought I missed out on the love of my life because I was afraid.

Now, standing in Levi's kitchen, I'm overwhelmingly glad that I was wrong. Grief and fear tried to keep me from living, but I pushed through and now I have the kind of love my parents had.

Epilogue

One Month Later

Levi Carter

"What are you doing?" I ask Grayson as he looks around his backyard. He picks up one of his lawn chairs and looks underneath it.

"I'm looking for your brain because it must have fallen out of your head."

I smack him on the stomach with the back of my hand. He doesn't even react to the hit.

"What are you talking about? All I said is that I wanted your help to propose to Dahlia on Valentine's Day."

"Yes, which is why your brain must be missing. You don't propose to a woman on a holiday, Levi."

"Why not? Valentine's Day is the most romantic holiday there is. It's perfect for a proposal."

"*Because* then she'll have to celebrate her anniversary on the same day as a holiday."

"Who celebrates an engagement anniversary?"

He gives me a look that says he's still questioning the location of my brain.

"Does Dahlia like getting presents?" he asks instead of answering me.

"Yes, of course she does."

"Then why would you make it to where she only gets *one* present on Valentine's Day instead of a present for that *and* your engagement anniversary?"

"I don't think she would mind, but I guess you have a point. I just thought if I planned something on a regular day that she would guess."

"She's going to know when you're proposing to her. You're not doing grand gestures every single week, so she'll see it coming. Even if it was on Valentine's Day."

"How do you know my proposal was going to be some grand thing? Maybe I was going to put the ring at the bottom of her champagne glass at dinner and propose that way."

"I'd like to think you have more sense than that," he says in a dry tone. "Plus, you came to me, which means you want extravagance."

"You don't do anything less," I say and he grins.

"No, no I don't." He walks to his back door. "I've got just the thing to help us."

"If you come back with fireworks I'm leaving," I yell after him.

He returns rolling a giant whiteboard in front of him. I help him get it out the back door. If his fireplace and space heaters weren't out here, I'd tell him to keep the whiteboard inside. But it actually feels nice out here with the blazing warmth of the fire.

"Why do you have this?" I ask.

"There are many situations one could need a whiteboard for."

"Name one." I cut him off before he can reply. "*Besides* this one."

"My fantasy football draft, playing Pictionary, explaining fan theories for *The Office*." He rattles them off as if they're all things he's used the board for.

"What fan theories require an entire whiteboard?"

"Good ones."

He pulls a marker out of his pocket and writes *Bookstore Scavenger Hunt* at the top of the board. I tilt my head to the side, impressed with his idea already.

"Okay, I'm intrigued."

"Of course you are, my ideas are amazing."

"Shut up and give me a marker."

Dahlia Chamberlain, Two Months Later

Levi is proposing today. Isa and Jasmine brought me to the nail salon even though I wasn't planning on getting mine done for a few more days. If he wanted to fool me, he should have had just Isa ask me to go. Jasmine wouldn't ever ask to join us. But I'm grateful they're both here anyway. Having my best friend and little sister help pick out my engagement nail design will be an amazing memory to hold on to.

"What do you say we head to the bookstore?" Isa asks and Jasmine gives a nonchalant shrug.

"I'm down."

"I don't know," I say, eying them as we walk out of the nail salon. "I'm feeling kind of tired. I was thinking of going home."

I shouldn't give them a hard time, but they're so terrible at this that I can't help it. They've both been sharing little looks the entire time we've been out. Even now they share a panicked one. It's like they think I can't see them.

"I'm sure a chai and some book browsing will perk you right up!" Isa says and links her arm in mine. "Don't make me go by myself. It's way more fun when you're there."

Okay, maybe they're a little better at this than I thought.

"Okay, I'll go with you." I turn to Jasmine. "But Jaz, I know you're not a huge fan of the bookstore. I can drop you off back home on the way."

"Oh, um, that's okay. I saw this book on TikTok that I want to check out."

I raise my eyebrows. "What book?"

She flounders, earning a glare from Isa.

I burst into laughter. "I know he's proposing. You don't have to keep pretending."

"Ugh, I knew you'd guess," Isa groans. "Levi said you'd guess, but I wanted to try and pull one over on you."

"So, he's proposing at a bookstore?" I ask, bouncing a little on my toes. "He knows me so well."

"You'd only have to talk to you for five minutes to know that a bookstore proposal would go well," Jasmine drolls and I laugh.

"Fair point, but it's still so sweet of him."

"Just wait, you're going to be a puddle of tears when you see what he has planned," Isa says with a smile.

"I can't believe I'm getting engaged," I say as we pile into Isa's SUV.

"I'm so happy for you," Isa squeals.

We drive to the bookstore blaring love songs and screaming the lyrics. I can't help but tear up a few times on the way. Jasmine teases me for being so weepy, but I catch her swiping away a couple of tears too.

Once we're there, I see Levi standing outside the door. He smiles at me as I walk up to him. Isa and Jasmine follow behind me at a distance.

"Fancy seeing you here," I say and he bends down to give me a quick kiss.

"When did you know what was happening?"

"As soon as they asked me to go to the salon," I reply and he chuckles.

"Well then, are you ready?"

"I was ready in December, and I'm ready now."

He kisses me again, as if he's unable to resist. And if we didn't have anything to do–like get engaged–I'd pull him into a dim corner of the bookstore and kiss until we got kicked out.

"Since you're ready, here's your first clue," he says and hands me a notecard with his handwriting on it.

You didn't think you would like this genre, but this book changed your mind.

"Wait, is this a scavenger hunt?"

He nods and I squeal in excitement.

"I love you," I say.

"I love you too, now get started, you've got a lot of clues."

He opens the door for me and I rush straight to the romantic fantasy section. I didn't think I would like it, but last month MJ loaned me one she loves and I binged the whole series. I find the book on the shelf and pull it off, opening the cover to reveal another clue.

Your favorite author's favorite book.

"How do you know Sloane Rose's favorite book?" I ask him and he just smiles.

"I pay attention to your bookish rambles more than you think." He pauses. "And Grayson is subscribed to her newsletter."

I laugh and head to the book the clue corresponds with. I'm led all over the bookstore, laughing at some clues, tearing up at others. Eventually, I find what Levi tells me is the last clue.

The next book in our favorite series.

My brows draw together. "The next book in the detective series isn't out for another month."

"I wouldn't be so sure about that."

He takes my hand and leads me to the aisle where we first stumbled upon the book we've both read multiple times now. The aisle is lined with flowers and LED candles. I'm already starting to cry and Levi hasn't even said a word. I find our favorite book and right beside it is a copy of the next one, even though I know it hasn't come out yet.

"Open it," Levi says in a low voice.

I do as he says and gasp when I see it's signed by the author and made out to both Levi and me.

To Dahlia and Levi, I hope you'll have a love as fierce as Detective Colt and Evangeline. Always remember to cherish the little things and live in the now.

On the other side is a note that almost makes me drop the book.

Dahlia Marie Chamberlain, will you marry me?

When I look up from the book, Levi is in front of me on one knee. With shaking hands, I set the book on a nearby shelf.

"Dahlia, I have loved you since the moment I saw you. I know that's not practical or logical, but it's true. And I've only fallen more in love with you since then. Please let me continue to love you more every day for the rest of our lives. Will you be my wife?"

"Yes," I whisper as tears flow down my face. "Nothing would make me happier."

His smile is brighter than all the stars in the galaxy combined. He slides a ring on my finger.

"Oh, it's beautiful," I murmur, staring at the way the oval cut diamond glints beneath the lights.

Levi rises to stand and wraps me up in his arms. He kisses me and it feels as though I'm the safest I've ever been, yet on the edge of the greatest adventure I'll ever go on.

When our family pops into the aisle to yell congratulations, I'm overwhelmed by all the love surrounding me. Not long ago I was crying myself to sleep, worried about doing it all on my own. Now I have a future husband and huge family that has embraced me as their own.

Today feels like opening the first page of a book I've waited my whole life to start reading. I'm filled with anticipation for what's to come, but I also want to savor every page, every word, because I don't want it to ever end.

Keep reading for a glimpse into the next brother, Grayson's, story!

One Month Later

Grayson Carter

"I'm so sore," Dahlia whines when Jasmine and I walk up to her.

"What are you sore from?" Jasmine asks. "You walked on the treadmill for ten minutes then came and sat at the smoothie counter reading for the rest of the time."

"The stool at the counter wasn't very comfortable," Dahlia grumbles.

"That's probably because you aren't supposed to sit on one for an hour. The gym is for *working out*, and you get a smoothie to-go *post*-workout."

"Hey, I brought you here to see if it's worth the *exorbitant* monthly fee. You can keep going to our dingy apartment gym if you'd like."

I brought Dahlia and Jasmine here while Levi was at work because Jasmine mentioned wanting a better place to do strength training. Apparently, cheering at the college level–which she hopes to do–requires a lot more muscle mass and endurance.

"Ah, sisterly banter," I say with a sigh. "Like brotherly banter, but less punching."

"If she keeps being sassy, punching might become a real possibility," Dahlia says and Jasmine rolls her eyes.

"We do have an excellent boxing ring. My only request is that I get to film the fight to show at future family events."

Both of the sisters crack a smile at my joke, successfully dissolving the tension between them.

"Did you like the gym?" Dahlia asks and Jasmine nods enthusiastically.

"I can train *way* better here than at the apartment gym. And a personal trainer comes with your membership fee."

"It should for the price," Dahlia mumbles.

"I asked the front desk, and I can add Jasmine to my account. So you won't have to worry about the money, except for the amount she's going to spend on smoothies. I'm pretty sure they put something in them to make them addictive."

"It won't cost you extra to add her?"

I wave her question off. It *will* cost me extra, but she doesn't need to know that. Family takes care of family. Dahlia has been taking care of Jasmine on her own the past three years, and while I know Levi would help, I want to do something nice for them. If I can play my cards right, I'll take care of this without them knowing.

"They said it wouldn't be any hassle. All she has to do is fill out some liability paperwork."

"That's awesome, thanks Grayson!" Jasmine gives me a hug and I smile as I squeeze her back.

"Yes, thank you Grayson. This is a huge help."

Dahlia hugs me too, but suddenly gasps and pulls away.

"What's wrong? I didn't think I was that sweaty." I laugh.

"*Oh my gosh that's Sloane Rose!*" Dahlia whisper-shouts.

I turn around to find a petite brunette headed toward the exit. She's wearing a sage green workout set, with a cream gym bag over her shoulder. She walks with an air of grace about her that reminds me of a ballerina. But that could be because of the ballet-style bun she's wearing on top of her head. It's sleek, somehow not a hair out of place even though she's leaving the gym instead of entering it.

"That's not how I pictured her," I say.

Dahlia gives me a funny look. "You don't follow her on Instagram?"

"No, that seemed weird. I'm sure she doesn't have many avid male readers."

"Oh, yeah, you're probably right." Dahlia lets out a little laugh. "Well, that's definitely her. She's even prettier in person too."

The brunette–who I suppose is Sloane–pushes out the gym doors.

"You should go talk to her," I say and Dahlia shakes her head.

"No, I don't want her to think I'm creepy for following her out."

"It would be creepy if *I* followed her out, but not you. You couldn't hurt a butterfly."

Dahlia gives me a dry look, while Jasmine laughs.

"Are you really going to miss out on meeting your favorite author because you might seem a little weird?" I ask her and she looks to the door, then back at me.

"Will you go with me? You love her books too."

It's true. The woman can write. I've read everything she's written, including bonus scenes and novellas. I *might* have made a fake email to sign up for her newsletter and send in my five-star reviews. It's not that I'm embarrassed about reading romance. I'm vocal about what I love and don't care what anyone thinks. But I don't want her to think my reviews are disingenous because I'm a man. Now that I've seen her, I'm sure she has no shortage of guys bothering her on social media and in person. There's a chance she gets plenty of book-focused emails from men, but I still don't want her to be uncomfortable.

"Sure." I shrug. "We can go together."

"We need to hurry before she's gone," Jasmine says.

We rush outside, just in time to see her pulling out of the parking lot, in a *beautiful* sports car, I might add. She's gorgeous, a talented author, *and* has great taste in cars. I'm tempted to chase her car down just to get her number.

"Ugh, that stinks." Dahlia huffs.

"Maybe we'll see her around at the gym, she obviously has a membership," Jasmine says in an encouraging voice.

"She could just be stopping in at this branch, your membership works all over the country," I say, not wanting Dahlia to get her hopes up too much.

"Her author bio says she lives in Atlanta though," Dahlia says. "Hopefully that means this is where she works out and you can tell her I'd love to meet her."

"I hope it is so you can meet her."

I'd love to meet her, too. Not even because she's Sloane Rose, but because she's *stunning*. So gorgeous that I spend the rest of the day trying–and failing–to get her out of my head.

Preorder *But He's My Fake Fiancé* to see what happens when a shy romance author and an extroverted security executive end up (fake) engaged!

And sign up for my newsletter to get a FREE BONUS SCENE set in Levi + Dahlia's future!

Also By Annah

Sweet Peach Series

The Love Audit

One More Song

Out of Office (FREE)

The First Taste

One Last Play

But He's a Carter Brother Series

But He's My Grumpy Neighbor

But He's My One Regret

But He's My Fake Fiancé (04/04/24)

Author's Note

Hello lovely reader,

Thank you for reading my book! This book has been a roller coaster. Which is ironic, because one of the songs on my book playlist is Roller Coaster by Luke Bryan. Levi and Dahlia's story was going to be very different. In fact, up until a month before my editing deadline, it *was* a different book.

But something just wasn't right. So, I scrapped most of it. Everyone around me was quite concerned with the predicament I put myself in, but we made it! And hopefully it doesn't read like a book that was written in a month (really more like two weeks if you count all the procrastinating I did...).

I'm so happy I took the risk though. I truly believe this was the story that was meant to be told. These two needed a story with pain and depth but also laughter and heat.

As for the pain part, I know that writing about the trauma and difficulties of being a homicide detective isn't *conventional* in sweet romantic comedies, but some characters just end up with a story that has to happen. That was how it was for Levi. I wanted a guy who was funny and loving, but who dealt with atrocities and death on a daily basis.

When it came about that he was going to be a homicide detective, I immediately reached out to my uncle, who has worked in that area of law enforcement. He's solved several homicides himself. We got on the phone and he told me about how detectives become jaded, they work long hours, they don't see their families, and all of this often goes unnoticed by the public.

We also discussed the stigma around mental health and how little help there is for many detectives. And sometimes when that help is given, they choose to lie in order to keep their positions. It was a subject I knew I wanted to touch. And the way I chose to do that, was to have Dahlia's character become a therapist passionate about helping them and their families.

I know this doesn't represent every single detective, department, or Chief. But I knew it was Levi's story. And maybe it's someone else's too.

I'd say the same about the thread of grief that connects each Carter brother, and this time Dahlia, too. We all walk through this at some point, and my prayer is that if you have or do, that you'll remember grief isn't linear. And it's okay if you need help. Don't be so afraid of the pain of grieving that you miss out on the healing.

Happy reading,

Annah

Acknowledgements

All praise, honor, and glory to Jesus Christ, Lord of my life. Thank you for bringing beauty out of the ashes of my pain and for loving me enough to be so kind and patient as I learn to trust you more.

To my husband, Ryan, thank you for letting me be my weird self when it comes to writing. When I came to you late at night saying I was going to scrap this book and start over, you didn't even blink. You just supported me and helped me through the process. You are what book boyfriends are made of! I can't believe I get to be your wife. I love you to the moon and back!

To my lovely critique partners, Dulcie and Amanda, thank you for talking out the plot, and sometimes talking me off the edge of a cliff haha. Also for reading this when I was writing so fast to catch up! You two are the best author friends a girl could ask for.

To my Uncle Shawn, thanks for answering all my questions, even the weird ones. Your insight into this world was invaluable. All credit to you for comparing interrogation to a bad date, and for the 'chase the gun' method of solving a case.

To my parents, thank you for supporting my work and sharing it with all your friends! And specifically to my Momma, thank you for reading all of my books and asking right after when the next one is going to be out, LOL.

To my editor, Caitlin, thank you for loving my books and characters. The author business can be tough, so having an editor who actually cares is such a blessing.

To my cover designer, Stephanie, thanks for creating covers that people covet. You're so talented!

To my proofreader, Charity, thank you for catching what I miss. You're amazing and so kind!

To my assistant, Beth, thank you for everything that you do. You are amazing and a wonderful asset to my team.

To my best friends, Baylie, Kathryn, and Beth (again), thank you for lifting me up when I get down. And for supporting my books like no other. You are true sisters.

Lastly, thank you to my ARC team who reads and reviews these books. And to my readers, who do the same after release day. You're all so terrific. I could write a book about how much I adore your messages and mood boards and review posts.

About the Author

Annah Conwell is a sweet romcom author who loves witty banter, sassy heroines, and swoony heroes. She has a passion for writing books that make you LOL one minute and melt into a puddle of 'aw' the next. You can find her living out her days in a small town in Sweet Home Alabama (roll tide roll!) with the love of her life (aka her husband), Ryan, and her two goofball pups, Prince and Ella. Most of the time she's snuggled up under her favorite blanket on the couch, reading way too many books to call it anything other than an addiction, or writing her little hopeless romantic heart out.

Find out more on her website: annahconwell.com

Made in United States
Troutdale, OR
11/24/2024